Rowena and the Viking Warlord

To Chris —
One of my favourite
Students & Star-to-be!

Melodie

Melodie Campbell

ROWENA AND THE VIKING WARLORD
Book 3 in the Land's End series

http://www.melodiecampbell.com

FIRST EDITION Trade Paperback

Imajin Books - www.imajinbooks.com

July 2, 2014

ISBN: 978-1-927792-77-3

Cover designed by Ryan Doan - www.ryandoan.com

For the boys of Powderkeg BBS: Karl, Malcolm, Wil and Murray.
In memory of Camelot.

Acknowledgements

One special person influenced me in the creation of Rowena's adventures.

Most readers don't know that the name Huel is a family name, and that the castle in Land's End was once a real stone castle that stood in Shropshire on the site of what is now Hawkstone Park.

Many thanks to my late cousin Tony, Viscount Clegg-Hill of Shropshire and Shrewsbury. Bless you for those wonderful tales you told me of the ancient family castle of Huel. The seeds of Rowena's adventures were sewn during those many hours in the west of England, when you regaled me with family history. You would have loved these books, I know. How I wish you were still here.

Thanks also to my beta readers, Cathy Astolfo, Jeannette Harrison, Nancy O'Neil, Mark Alldis and Cheryl Freedman, for their suggestions and cherished enthusiasm.

The team at Imajin books, including editor Todd Barselow, cover artist Ryan Doan and publisher Cheryl Tardif, have done a stellar job bringing this tale to book form, as usual.

Finally, readers from distant lands whom I have come to know through this series: Inga Kupp-Silberg, Janet Hsieh, Larry Pearson, Shirley Ewing, Brandi Gillilan and Rosanna Leo, to name just a few; thank you for coming on this wild and wacky journey with me.

Will we all go back to Land's End after *Rowena and the Viking Warlord*? Readers will make that final decision.

Praise for Rowena and the Viking Warlord

"*Rowena and the Viking Warlord* is a collective of sorts; fantasy, thriller, adventure and mystery, laced (pun intended) with historical accuracy, the electrically charged dynamics between the sexes and a startling climax that gives a sharp new edge to fantasy writing...the polished style of an award winning writer. Author, Campbell's off-the-wall humour has an added feature...she builds the wall first with the zesty timing of a great one liner...*Rowena and the Viking Warlord* is an intriguing story told with the passion of a fine writer." —Don Graves, *Canadian Mystery Reviews*

"A heart-pounding thrill-ride full of adventure, lust and magic. Once again, Campbell has spun words into gold." —Brenda Dyer, award-winning author of *Love's Prophecy*

"Edgy, sexy and fast. Leaves you breathless with laughter and craving more." —Sheri Fredricks, award-winning author of *Remedy Maker*

"Magic, mayhem and a healthy dose of sensuality make Melodie Campbell's Rowena books winners. This series will live on my favorites shelf for a long time." —Rosanna Leo, author of *Predator's Kiss*

"Magic and mayhem, demons, a dragon and a Viking who has eyes on more than just Land's End. Another winner in the *Rowena Through the Wall* series." —Mark Alldis, former editor *Distant Suns Fantasy Magazine*

"Campbell is a writer who can deliver delicious punch lines. She creates a fantastic world with a pregnant heroine who loves her freedom as much as her lusty suitors. Magic." —Garry Ryan, award-winning author of *Blackbirds*

Dear Reader,

Welcome back to the magical, medieval world of Land's End...

In *Rowena and the Dark Lord*, book 2 of this series, Rowena returns to Land's End. There, she learns more about the ancient world through the wall from which her mother escaped to Arizona, long ago.

Things are not well in Land's End. Due to a witch's curse, no females have been born there in more than fifty years. Rowena's Grandfather is ailing, and Cedric, her distant cousin and feared husband, now rules Huel.

Cedric is a master mage, a follower of the dark arts. Through his teaching, Rowena discovers her own powers of magic. But she is still in her infancy as a witch and makes mistakes. First, she conjures a Roman Legion out of time. Then, she turns back time to save the lives of those she loves, including Thane.

But at what cost?

When we left *Rowena and the Dark Lord*, time had shifted, and the true cost of Rowena's spell had not been reckoned.

Now, the price must be paid.

War has come to Land's End, and even Rowena can't avoid it now.

Come with me back to Land's End, and meet the man who threatens to conquer everything in Huel, including Rowena's heart.

Her enemy and her lover...the Viking Warlord.

~Melodie

The Houses of Land's End

House of Sargon
(Colors purple and silver)
Brothers:
Sargon (killed by Cedric)
Thane (the new King)
Rhys
Cousin:
Logan

House of Huel
(Colors green and gold)
Rowland, the old Earl (dying)
Brothers:
Cedric (the new Earl)
Ivan (killed by Cedric)
Cousins:
Jon
Rowena
Richard
Kendra (adopted, from Arizona)

House of Norland
(Colors blue and white)
Brothers:
Gareth (Earl)
Janus
Cousins:
Roderick
Collin
Val

House of Gredane
Lars (prince from overseas)
Brothers:
Soren
Nial
Cousins:
Jory
Sven

PART 1

Chapter 1

My name is Rowena Revel and I am the last hereditary witch of Land's End.

Unfortunately, I'm not a very good one.

The trouble is, I have a magic bracelet but no idea how to use it. My mother died before she could teach me. And it won't come off. Spells are a matter of trial and error, so the outcomes are rather sketchy.

I honestly didn't mean to conjure up that Roman Legion in mid-battle.

And apparently I screwed things up by moving back time.

Val, my wizard friend, told me there would be a price to pay for messing with dark magic. But I had to stop the pending war. Thane and Cedric were about to kill each other. Things were so desperate I couldn't wait to find out the penalty.

So I went ahead and used dark magic to turn back time. Now I was finding out how steep that price would be.

If I could use only one word to describe Land's End, it would be 'luscious.' The colors are deeper and richer than home, the scents more intoxicating. And emotions are heightened...

I stood on a hill overlooking the dark green grass below. The sun was a brilliant ball of orange in the sky. The river below sparkled deep blue and teemed with life.

It was gorgeous, absolutely gorgeous. But it was different from home. And I was different from home while in Land's End.

How can I explain the change to my desires, in this, my ancient homeland? My inhibitions were like a filter on a camera, suddenly removed. Life was more sensual, intense, and dangerous because of that.

At times, it scared the bejesus out of me.

I turned away from it all to travel back through the portal to Arizona.

But only for a little while.

I smiled at this adventure, so excited was I to escape from the constant guard.

My lover Thane, the king of Land's End, was engaged with his troops to the north. Kendra had promised to cover for me back at Sargon, Thane's castle. No one would know I had slipped away for just a few hours.

I had a chance to go home through the wall to Arizona. Thane wouldn't approve of this trip, of course. He refused to consider anything that might jeopardize my safety or that of my unborn baby. This had the effect of ruining paradise for me. Yes, I loved the man, but I felt trapped.

This feeling had been coming on for days. It haunted me now. Was I the kind of woman who could spend her entire life within the walls of a medieval castle?

It had only been a month, and already I was desperate to get free.

A trip back home might be just what I needed. It had been weeks since I had seen my Dad, and I just needed to hear his voice on the phone.

Val said he would help me by opening the portal. I would have exactly one hour…

Earlier this morning, Kendra had helped me to dress for the occasion.

"Wear the white linen. It won't look so out of place in Scottsdale. Luckily it's summer so dresses are everywhere," she said.

"Thanks for shortening it." I gave her a big hug.

"Enjoy yourself," she said. Her big brown eyes twinkled. "Next time it's my turn. Oh, and don't forget to buy chocolate."

I had traveled by horseback to the clearing in the forest. Now the split oak was directly in front of me. I put my hand through the air to the side of it to test for the opening. My hand disappeared from view.

The portal was open between our worlds.

With a deep breath, I walked forward.

The forest disappeared. All around me, the air shook and shimmered. One foot, then the other hit hard floor, and I wavered slightly.

The classroom was empty, as I knew it would be at this time on a weekend.

Pure yellow sunlight streamed in through the windows. The sizzling hot Arizona sun...I was home at last.

I walked to the window and just gazed out over the college grounds for a moment. The Palo Verde trees were a soft powdery green. Agave and teddy-bear cacti rose from the pebbled gardens between the parking lanes. Pure bliss.

First I would phone Dad. Then I would get a large coffee across the street at Starbucks. I would bring one back for Kendra, of course. She wouldn't be expecting that. It would be cold by the time I got it back to her, but we could heat it up in the castle kitchen. I smiled thinking of her reaction.

There was a *whoosh* behind me, and then some vulgar cursing.

I spun around.

A man stood on this side of the wall. He was tall, with wide shoulders and massively muscled arms. Red-gold hair streamed down his back. He wore a dark green tunic with leather belt and dagger, but no armor.

He was absolutely magnificent, and I knew him well.

Cedric.

"What the hell?"

He laughed, a throaty, good-natured bellow. "By the gods, what a ride!"

I stared, mouth gaping. Cedric on this side of the wall? In Arizona?

"How did you get here?" I blurted.

"The same way you did. I followed you through the portal."

His head whipped from side to side. One hand was on his dagger hilt. I could see he was assessing the place for danger. Instinct, of course.

Crap. Crapity crap. Cedric was here in Arizona. And Thane was way the hell up north in some blasted field, a whole wide world away.

Thank God there was no one around. How the heck would I ever explain a medieval warrior-knight in my classroom in Scottsdale, Arizona?

Think, Rowena. Think!

"What is this room?"

My mind was whirling, but I tried to keep cool. I leaned back against the window sill for support. "This is my classroom. I told you I was a teacher."

He nodded and moved forward. One hand went to touch the back of the chair nearest him, which was plastic. For a moment it had his attention. He gazed down at it, his hands exploring.

I didn't wait for the inevitable question. Instead I asked another. "I meant, how did you know I was coming here?"

"Oh that," he said. His green eyes sought mine. "The second you left Thane's castle, I detected you. I've been waiting for weeks to catch you alone. That man is like a leech by your side. I don't know how you stand it."

"You're no better than Thane," I retorted. "You would keep me trapped like a prisoner just as he."

Cedric stared at me then. I could almost see the workings of him mind click over.

"Not so. At least, not now that I've had time to think things through. I merely seek to convince you that your place is with me."

He strode around the desks to face me. "It's time to come home, Rowena. Not here. Home with me to Castle Huel, where you belong."

No, I have to get you back to where you belong, I wanted to scream. I plunked down in the nearest chair.

Cedric wouldn't know what trouble he was in if he ever left this room. I knew him. He would blunder forth like a raider on a rampage, challenging every man who stood in his way. One crosswise look from a stranger, and he would use that dagger without a second thought.

I could just imagine the tactical squad taking him down in a hail of bullets.

Crap. He was far too dangerous. I had to get him back to Land's End.

"That gown is indecent," he said, staring at my legs.

Okay, *that* was the wrong thing to say.

"It's perfectly appropriate for this world," I snapped back.

Cedric snorted. "All the more reason to get you back to Land's End. How will the men keep their hands off you here?"

"*This is a test.*" A male voice came over the PA system.

A siren blasted through the air, so loud it hurt. I clapped my hands over my ears.

Cedric moved like a man possessed. Every muscle ripped to action. He bounded in front of me and pulled a dagger.

"Show yourself, Demon!"

I choked.

"It's okay," I yelled. "That's the fire alarm."

He turned to face me, eyes wild.

"What do you mean?"

I could hardly hear the words over the siren. I signalled for him to wait. It was too loud to talk over.

Cedric lunged to the door, opened it and charged out into the hall. The siren was even louder with the door open. He vaulted back in, then slammed the door and shot to the window. Shock crossed his face as he glimpsed the cars in the parking lot.

The siren switched off.

I sighed with relief. "Phew. Glad that's over. They're testing the fire alarm to make sure it works. It's awfully loud, so they do it when school is out."

"But that is foolish. Surely they know when there is a fire?"

I giggled now. "The alarm is connected to the fire station, where the firemen are."

He gasped. "You have men of fire here? This is surely hell."

My mouth flew open.

"No it's not. It's Arizona." Although in the summer it could be as hot as hell, but no need to further confuse him with that little tidbit.

He returned his dagger to the scabbard. "This world is madness. We leave *now*."

"I'm not leaving," I announced. "Don't even *think* you can boss me around in my own country. This is the United States of America and I'm an American citizen. We have rights." Oh yup, I was telling him.

He crossed his big arms and frowned. "Don't think you have erased my memory, Rowena. I know that you have moved time. And I know why you did it." His voice softened for the last bit.

I sat paralysed. But that wasn't possible! Val said he and I would be the only ones who would remember the weeks that were lost when we turned back time.

"How do you know?" My voice was breathy.

He smiled then. "The book remembered you."

What?

"I was in the cellar room. The book of spells was on the altar. It started to glow and I went over to examine it. The tome reeked with your scent. Did you know you have a scent that I can smell across a crowded room? It's tantalizing."

Not good. My cousin Jon had said the same thing to me, months ago. It had nearly been the cause of something tragic.

"So I knew you had held the book and even used it. But there was no time you could have done that. I acquired it after you left Huel."

He started to pace. "I reasoned then that most likely I was missing a block of time. Things had happened that I could not remember. *You* had been there and read the book, even performed spells from it. I did my best to conjure the past, to see what I had forgotten."

"And?"

He shook his head. "It's vague. Like dreams. I think I must have died."

The relief I felt was palpable. Cedric didn't remember everything!

"You did die," I said.

"And that's why you moved back time. To save me."

I gawked at him.

"It's a haze. I don't remember everything. But this part is seared upon my brain, Rowena—you looking down at me, frantic with despair, and you cried '*why didn't you teach me the magic to save you?*'"

I couldn't look at him. What was I to say? It was true. I *did* turn back time. I did it to protect Thane and Gareth too, of course, but even before that I had tried to save Cedric.

It occurred to me I could use this to my advantage.

"So you owe me, Cedric. I saved your life. Go away and leave me alone."

"I can't. Not until we talk." He moved closer.

The words were so simple. I met his eyes, compelled, as I always was when he stood close to me.

"This has to stop! Cedric, have a heart. I can't go on like this."

Cedric snorted.

"Have you given one thought as to how I have been affected?"

That confused me. No, I hadn't. It was uncharacteristic and supremely selfish of me, I now realized. I had never considered how this strange bond between us would affect anyone other than me.

Cedric stopped pacing and appealed to me with his arms. He was so close I could see the gold hair that covered his arms and legs. I flushed.

"Before you came to Land's End, I was content to lead my men, increase my mastery of magic, and maintain my fighting prowess. Now, I am only content when I am one with you."

The shock ripped through me.

"Harsh words, and even those are not entirely true. I am never content, not even then. Elated…euphoric perhaps, but not content. This thirst for you will never be sated. Rowena, know it now. You are my heaven and every minute I am away from you is hell."

I swallowed hard. "Then lift the spell."

"It is not mine to lift. I can no more mess with our destiny than my Lord Lucifer can turn night into everlasting day."

"I don't understand. I thought *you* invoked the draw between us."

"I merely make use of it to keep you near, so I am not in constant agony."

Wow. This was a confession I had not expected. Cedric was baring his soul to me. I sprung up from the chair and turned away.

"When you feel the draw, you are experiencing what I feel," he said. "That is all. My mind reaching out to yours."

This was far, far worse than I imagined.

"Are we never to be free of it?" My voice was strident.

"It is only unbearable when we fight it. Why won't you see that your place is with me, as the old gods have ordained?"

Holy freaking old gods.

"Now you carry my child. The circle is complete. There is no way for me to break free of it, Rowena. Not unless I am dead, and that can't happen now."

What did he *mean* that couldn't happen? Was he not human anymore?

But I was. He conveniently forgot to mention what would happen if *I* were dead. We would be free of it then. But that wasn't something I wanted to consider.

"I know they call me the Dark Lord. But I am not evil, despite what the others say. I would not keep you chained to me. In fact, I have a proposition for you. We need to talk."

The draw swept over me then, seeping in, enveloping my mind. I moaned with desire.

"Stop doing that, Cedric. I can't *think*."

"I'm not doing anything. Magic doesn't work here. You said so yourself."

Then what was this? I swayed, unsteady on my feet.

He crossed the distance between us in an instant and grabbed my arms. "What are you feeling now? Tell me."

"Get away from me!" I moaned. "All I want is…this is unbearable. We can't. This is a *school*."

"Ha!" He drew me to his chest. "Magic *does* work here. At least, the magic between us does."

The pain receded as I inhaled his scent. Already I was drunk from it and would have fallen if he hadn't been holding me.

"We'll go now." His one arm caught me under my knees. He swung me up into his arms.

"No!" I cried. "Not yet. I haven't phoned Dad—"

But he was already at the wall, and with one stride was through it.

Never had I entered Land's End this quickly. The air was ripped from my chest. I tried to cry out but nothing came from my throat.

Cedric landed firmly on his feet in Land's End. No unsteadiness, like Gareth and Thane had experienced on their first time through.

That figured.

He strode forward, away from the split oak, and into the small clearing where I had nearly been killed by brigands. Cedric had rescued me that day. Out of the mist he had appeared on his giant palomino, as if by magic, with several ghostly knights on horseback.

It *had* been magic. The brigands hadn't stood a chance.

Cedric held me firmly in his arms. The scent of him was driving me senseless with desire.

"Put me down now," I pleaded.

"Not yet," he said. "Not until we're safely away."

I felt a shiver at his words. He chanted something low and rhythmic. A swirl of dark mist started at his feet and wound like a cyclone around our bodies. I screamed as it whipped us up into the sky.

Chapter 2

No horse this time—Cedric had learned to *fly*.

He held me close to his chest with one arm as the other made a fist in the air. The tunnel of mist whooshed us toward Huel so quickly that rivers and fields became abstract below us, mere patches of blue and green on a haphazard quilt. In the distance, one grey square was visible.

I clung to him as he continued to chant, in that low, ancient tongue.

He didn't slow until the last minute. The four stone towers of Castle Huel loomed ahead as we skirted the raised wooden drawbridge in a blur of mist that no one would see.

He obviously couldn't walk through walls yet. We landed in the courtyard behind Castle Huel. He kept upright but the moment I touched the ground I fell in a boneless heap.

Cedric didn't offer to help me up. He was already concocting another spell. His eyes were glowing that eerie green.

At last he turned to me.

"I've spelled the outer walls. Nothing can get through here without me knowing," he said.

Nothing natural, I thought. I pushed myself up.

"We'll go to the tower. We need to talk."

"Can't I see Grandfather first?"

He hesitated. "Best we talk. Then you can see whomever you wish."

What? What game was he trying to play?

He took my hand and pulled me into the castle. We went the back way up the steps to his room atop the turret.

As soon as we entered the room, I pulled my hand out of his.

"Remember last time I was here? You spelled the door to keep me in."

"That was a mistake. I won't do that again."

"Come on, Cedric! Be honest."

He leaned back against the wall and folded his arms across his chest.

"Hear me out, Rowena. Just keep your mouth shut for one minute and *listen*."

Of course, my mouth flew open and was about to spill a retort. He held up one hand like a stop sign to silence me.

"I can't keep you here against your will. I know that now. You have powers just as I do. So what I plan to do is teach you the magic to protect yourself and our child. I need to know you are safe."

I stared at him, bewildered. How did he know this thing that haunted me, my need for freedom?

It was almost as if Cedric could read my mind.

He shrugged. "We are more alike than you can imagine. I tried to think of how I would react to being tied to the grounds of a castle with no freedom to choose where I go. You can imagine how long that would last." He smiled grimly.

I found myself pacing and waving my arms around. "That's it, exactly! I can't be protected like a child all the time. It's driving me insane. All I can think about is getting free."

He chuckled. "And you still don't think we belong together."

It was bitterly ironic. All this time, I had thought love would be enough. Now I was finding, deep down, that I valued freedom more.

Surely one could have both. Did it have to be a choice?

"I am offering you both love and freedom, Rowena. Can he do that?"

Bloody hell. "Stop doing that, Cedric!"

"What?"

"Reading my mind!"

He chuckled again, and the draw started up.

"You're playing with me again. *Stop* that!"

He laughed joyfully.

"Rowena, I have been alone so long. You can't imagine what a pleasure it is to have you here to 'play' with me, as you say."

Oh My God. Cedric was lonely. That's why he was so anxious to have me stay with him. Okay, and the sex, too. Let's be honest about that.

But I was getting him, finally. He could be himself with me. I didn't threaten him or consider him a monster.

I *understood* his fascination with learning magic. By God, I shared it. And he knew that. No wonder he wanted me around. A woman who shared his interests...

Not only that, but I loved Huel, our lands and castle, as much as he did.

I would try to be kinder to him. Regardless of what I chose to do, I would try to be kind.

He reached into a belt pouch and threw something on the bed.

"My bracelet!" I leaped forward to put it on. It wrapped around my wrist and clicked into place, almost without my helping it.

"It fell off your wrist at the portal. I picked it up," he said.

The gemstones sparkled scarlet and amber, as if pleased to be back where they belonged. This was the witch's bracelet that had been my mother's. It could channel magic, but not create it. I was just now learning how to use it.

And Cedric would help me learn. That's what he was telling me now, by giving it back to me.

"Thank you. This means a lot to me."

He nodded in satisfaction.

"So what do you want to do first?" he asked.

"See Grandfather. Then I want to have a look at the spell book."

His green eyes glistened. "I'll just bet you do. We have all day tomorrow for that."

First, I checked the closet to make sure I had some clothes here. Best I change into something decent for Land's End before I followed Cedric down the stairs.

I found a yellow linen day dress and pulled it off the wooden hanger. Yellow was not a color I generally liked, but it would be serviceable for work around the castle.

While I was changing, a bunch of men arrived unexpectedly to meet with Cedric. I think they were landowners from lands to the south of us.

I spent the rest of the afternoon with Grandfather. He was delighted.

"Cedric said he would bring you back. I begged him to."

I smiled and fussed with his bedding.

"Oh, he has a way of being convincing, all right."

"You'll stay here now, won't you child? You won't go back to that brother of Sargon's? He keeps you a prisoner there for his own pleasure." Grandfather's voice rose in anger and disgust. "How I would cut him down if only I could wield a sword once more. I rue the day they set eyes on you, that pair of brothers."

I held my tongue.

He was panting now. His voice became more feeble. "I should have challenged Sargon myself when he schemed to take you. Ivan wasn't strong enough."

He was mumbling now, thinking of earlier times. Had it only been barely six months ago?

"Never should have married you to Ivan. You should have gone to Cedric from the beginning."

So much for letting me choose my own husband, I thought wryly. He didn't let me choose then, and he certainly wouldn't now. The old earl would never change.

I didn't need to remind him that the deed had already been done. Sargon was dead. Ivan was dead, and Cedric was my legal husband in Land's End.

For better or for worse. No truer words had ever been said.

"We need you here, child. *I* need you."

I hesitated.

"I'm trying, Grandfather. But it's really too soon to tell if Cedric will be a good father. I must think of that."

Grandfather clutched my arm with his frail hand. "He will, my child. He will. You will see. He loves you beyond ken."

The way he used his left hand disturbed me. He was not left handed.

"Grandfather, I'm going to run a few tests. I think you may have had a stroke."

I knew the ways to test for stroke from my medical training. Even animals have strokes.

This was much easier to diagnose, of course, because I could give Grandfather specific instructions.

It was as I suspected. His one side was very weak. He couldn't hold a glass and he was having trouble recovering words and specific memories.

This made him very glum.

I was equally alarmed, but tried to hide it.

"There isn't much we can do for stroke here in Land's End. But there is a strong chance you will make a good recovery." I patted his arm. "I'll be here to help."

"Thank God for that," he murmured. "I hate being old. 'Twould be better to have died in battle with a sword in my hand."

"No it wouldn't," I said firmly. "I want you here with me, for as long as possible."

I bent down to kiss him.

"You are such a blessing, child."

I didn't tell him the other thing about strokes. That one often wasn't the end of it.

"Where are Richard and Jon?" It occurred to me that the castle was extremely quiet.

"There have been reports of activity to the south of us. Jon and Richard have gone down with troops to investigate. We are waiting for news."

While Grandfather slept, I thought about Thane.

He loved me, I knew. And he would be frantic when he found me missing. What was he doing now? Was he scouring the countryside for me?

I sighed. Likely not. Instead he would have scouts scouring the countryside.

Thane took his role as King seriously. He would never leave Land's End. If I went back to Thane, I would never again be allowed to leave Sargonia. Is that what I wanted?

I remembered our last conversation vividly.

Thane was about to leave with his war advisors for field exercises to the north. I sat on the bed, watching him pack.

This, in itself, was an eye opener. Apparently, 'packing' meant checking the cutting edge of his many weapons for sharpness and putting replacement armor in a sack.

"I still don't see why I couldn't go with you."

Thane laughed. "A woman in an army camp? Don't be ridiculous."

I wasn't happy to hear that last word. And I know it sounds childish, but I was sulking.

"It's not fair that you get to leave the castle and I don't."

"Three days we'll be separated. That's all."

I frowned. Thane was full of energy. He seemed almost jubilant to be making this trip.

Meanwhile, I was going stir-crazy.

"I could go to Castle Huel to see Grandfather while you're away."

That stopped him in his tracks.

"Absolutely not. I forbid it. The second you were through the gates, Cedric would make you a prisoner."

And I wasn't here?

We stared at each other. His handsome face was stern, the dark blue eyes particularly hard today perhaps in anticipation of physical challenge.

"He would never let you go, Rowena. Be sensible."

There was that admonishment again. I grit my teeth.

"I haven't seen Grandfather in over a month. Surely you don't expect me to go the rest of my life without seeing my family?"

Thane continued 'packing.' His broadsword was heavy, as were all his weapons and armor. His arm and back muscles rippled with the chore.

"I know this separation is hard for you. When I get back, we'll see about inviting him here. If you like, I could arrange to bring him here to live if he is still unwell."

I gazed at him in disbelief.

"He'll never leave Huel, Thane! He's the old earl. If anyone tries to make him go, he'll pick up his sword, no matter how sick he is."

I knew he would defend Castle Huel to his death. In fact, I knew this was the way he wished to die…defending Huel 'til the end.

"Besides, he wouldn't come here. He hates your family. Your brother killed his grandson Ivan, don't forget." *And you are preventing his granddaughter from leaving here*, I nearly said.

I remembered the words my grandfather had spoken to Thane in this very castle.

"You make my daughter a whore!" he had bellowed.

Thane had been furious then.

How time changes things. I didn't want to think it—and perhaps I was being overly sensitive—but at times like this it was almost as if Thane took me for granted.

I watched him finish packing.

Thane shrugged. "We'll discuss this when I'm back. I'm King now. I have important duties. This is the way things have to be."

And didn't I have duties as well?

That was the trouble.

It was one thing to live in this castle while I was married to Sargon. But Sargon was dead. I wasn't married to Thane, couldn't be while Cedric lived.

I wasn't Thane's wife. I was his lover. Lately, it had been haunting me.

My place was at Huel, where my grandfather lay ill, just as Thane's place was here.

He slung the sack over his muscular shoulder.

He was ready to leave. His eyes swept over me and softened slightly.

"God, you are beautiful. Even in your nightshift, with hair a-mess, you make a man want to forget his duty. But duty calls me. You must live with it, as I do."

I watched him leave, thinking I would do anything to get away myself.

Well, I'd gotten away and now here I was, in the very place Thane had forbidden.

I grimly reflected that it never paid to 'forbid' me anything.

I walked to the window and looked out upon the green fields of Huel. How gorgeous they were. Rolling verdant hills swept all the way to the river. Little sheep dotted the landscape like a picture postcard.

What was Kendra doing now? I had to think about what was best for her, as well. In fact, I knew what was best for her. She should go back to Arizona and finish her degree. But would she?

Not a chance. If I stayed here, she would stay with me. And I knew, in my heart, that I was leaning toward staying in Land's End. It was in my blood now. And my child was a child of Land's End.

"Don't leave me," Grandfather murmured. "Come back, daughter."

I felt my heart tear just a little. He was calling for my mother, who left Land's End, never to return.

I turned from the window and moved to his side. I lifted his weak hand between my own.

"I'm here, Grandfather, I'm here. You sleep now, everything will be fine."

Chapter 3

By evening, Cedric had not yet appeared. I, of course, was starving.

I ate a quiet meal in the kitchen with Bernard the cook. He was a plump little man with a monk's fringe of grey hair and a talent for making bread. He put me to work immediately tasting his latest creations.

"This is another reason why I'm glad to be back at Huel, Bernard. You are the best cook in the world." I munched away on soft rolls slathered with fresh unsalted butter.

He beamed. "For you, I will make a fruit pie tomorrow. And bread pudding."

Yum city.

Eventually I got around to eating some meat. And I took a vitamin pill, to make sure the baby got all the things my diet might be missing.

When I trudged up to the tower bedroom, the sun was starting to set. I decided to play it safe and divide up my vitamins. Half, I would keep in my fanny pack, in a baggie. The other half, I would leave in the tower bedroom in the bottle. I had enough to last me the entire pregnancy, assuming I didn't lose a bunch.

After that short task, I went to the western-most window and gazed out. I was just in time to watch the sky flash into vermillion streamers as the sun set beyond the green hills.

Soon the two moons would be visible. Night in Land's End was rarely as dark as at home, except that there were no street lights here, of course.

I sighed and took off my dress then hung it up in the closet. Gee, I had gone a whole day without wrecking a dress. Kendra wouldn't believe it.

I climbed into the high bed and pulled up the sheet.

Where was Cedric, I wondered.

Hours later, I felt him enter the room. My mind, which had been cleared of everything in a sweet slumber, was now overwhelmed with desire.

A wave of it hit so strong and swift that I startled awake. He was already on the bed and over me, seeking my mouth. I breathed in his air.

The tornado of lust swept through me like a living thing. He took me fast. My body arched to receive him, responding eagerly to the onslaught with frenzied animal cries. With each thrust, I felt myself falling more and more under his control, a slave to his every movement, with no will of my own. I could not separate my mind from his.

He consumed and I surrendered. When he climaxed, it was *his* voice that roared in my head…

Then quiet.

I drifted.

Cedric was kissing me. He was planting kisses all over my face, my hair, my breasts…

"Roll to your side," he said. "I want to hold you from behind."

I rolled without opening my eyes.

He wrapped his arm around me and pulled me against him so there was no gap. His hand found a breast and settled there.

I found my voice at last. The passion he bestowed on me was frightening and overwhelming. I tried to find the words to compel him to be less extreme.

"Can you be sort of sweet next time?"

"No."

"*What*?"

"No, I can't. I've tried. Rowena, I will never ever hurt you. But you ask me to go slow and sweet and I have tried. I will continue to try. But you don't understand the torrent that consumes me when you are within reach."

He kissed my hair.

"Even now, I am compelled to take you again. But I can hold it back for the next while. You need rest, I know. Sleep, my love."

This was the first time he had called me that. I lay in his arms, and the creeping tendrils of magic were sated and let me sleep.

When I awoke, morning light was streaming through the tower windows. Cedric was gone. The tapestry had been pulled back from the secret staircase and the plank door was open.

Cedric was inviting me down to his sorcery cellar.

I had to smile. The man was clever. This was the one bribe me that could tempt me to stay.

I got out of bed and looked for something decent to wear.

Jon had found a few dresses in an abandoned room when I was last here. The yellow dress from yesterday had been one.

I was pleased to see he had brought them all up to the tower.

I selected a light pink linen dress with a scoop neckline. It tied in the back, which was a bit awkward. It was also too short, but would have to do. Everything was too short for me here. Probably this was a good thing as I had a tendency to trip over anything and everything.

I put on my slipper shoes and hurried to the staircase.

This time it was not pitch black. Light from the bedroom lit my way down one turn of the staircase. It grew darker for about two flights, and then faint light showed ahead, becoming brighter with each half turn down the turret.

The steps were steep and narrower on the inside. I had to place my hands on the stone walls to keep my balance.

Cedric had left the door open for me at the bottom. When I entered the room, it was well-lit with candles. He sat at the altar, studying the book of spells.

His titian head lifted. "Ah! You are awake. Join me."

He pointed to a wooden chair opposite.

I plopped down into the chair.

"Look. We need to talk seriously," I said.

He cocked his head. Even in this candlelight, his hair shimmered. In another land, he might be mistaken for a Sun God.

"Continue," he said.

"If—and this is a hypothetical if at this point—I agree to stay here, how do we prevent Thane from declaring war on you?"

He closed the book.

"It must be your choice. You must tell him that it is what you want."

I paused, folding my arms across my chest. "He may not believe that. He would probably believe you spelled me to say that."

One eyebrow raised. "Is the man so vain as that?"

I shrugged. Probably, he was. They all seemed to be here.

Cedric rose to his feet. "Rowena, you carry my child. Any man of our time will recognize that it is unnatural for you to live anywhere else but with me. You tell him you are staying with me because of the child. He will believe that."

I wasn't so sure.

"To be frank, I'm not concerned with what he thinks. If you decide to stay with me, it will be. If I have to meet him in battle, I will."

"I don't want that," I said.

He stopped and smacked his right palm on the wall. "It's not natural for me to be—what's the word?"

"Rational?"

He glared at me. "Conciliatory. Usually I go after what I want, and I get it or I don't. Right now, if he comes for you, I will enjoy killing him. Does that make it plain?"

I gulped. "You're saying if I decide to stay here, you will kill anyone who tries to prevent it. But if I want to go, you'll let me?"

He leaned back against the wall. "I have no choice. You'll go anyway. You have the power to."

He started to pace. "Look. There is magic everywhere in this castle now. You have the power to channel magic. You can transport yourself somewhere else with that witch's bracelet of yours. I can null it for a time, but I can't destroy it. I also can't go dragging you back every single hour of every day if you decide to run."

It was true. Holy crap. This was the paramount difference between my living here or with Thane or Gareth.

There was no magic in Castle Sargon or Norland Fortress.

But there was magic here.

I would be protected, translate 'confined,' for my own good by Thane or Gareth.

At Huel, I would be free.

"Rowena, have you not realized yet that you are a child of magic, just as I am? You and I belong with our baby, here in this magical place."

His voice was seductive. "Think on this. Would you be so cruel as to separate me from my own child? And her from me, her true father? Think of what I can teach her!"

Her. I felt shivers. "You said *her.*"

"I did?" He stopped to consider. "That is...curious."

It was more than curious. Cedric didn't seem to know why he'd said it.

"But think of it, Rowena. Think of what I can teach *you.* Your mother missed her chance to learn the magic that was to be her destiny. You can become that powerful woman."

Oh, this man was cunning. He knew just what to tempt me with—knowledge.

He went over to the altar and opened the book of spells.

"This book...I've spelled it so it can't leave this room. As long as you are in this room, it is yours to explore."

He was clever all right. I could not walk away with the thing in my shoulder bag, like last time. No one could walk away with it, which was damned smart.

I had to smile.

His mouth was turned down in a frown as he flipped through the pages. Then he stopped. His eyes lit up.

"Here. I give you a small sample of what I will teach you. Rowena, I know you can communicate with animals. How would you like to be able to communicate with all living men?"

He put his hand over the page and started to chant. His eyes glowed neon green as they had many times before when he invoked magic. His voice grew louder and echoed, seeping into every perceivable corner of my mind. I was mesmerized...this must be what hypnosis is like. At the same time, I wasn't a bit frightened.

I floated, blind.

How long we stayed in that state, I do not know. Abruptly, the spell switched off. At first, my head was whirling. When my eyes could focus, they found Cedric staring at me, a small smile across his face.

"This is my gift to you. Tell me that you understand me. Repeat what I have just said."

"*This is my gift to you*," I quoted back. "What are you getting at, Cedric."

He closed the spell book. "I just spoke in our ancient tongue, which is known to only a few followers of the old gods."

I sat like stone.

He stood up, walked around the altar, and reached down with his hand to cup the back of my head.

"This is only the beginning, Rowena. I will make you the keeper of all the feminine magic that is natural to our world. And you won't even have to lose your soul to gain it."

I looked up to meet his eyes. They were normal-green again.

"What do you mean?" I whispered.

He frowned. "Forget that I said that." He reached down with both hands and pulled me up out of the chair. He held me to his chest and kissed the top of my head.

"Now do you deny that we belong together?"

Chapter 4

Okay, I was a tad seduced. The lust for knowledge that swept over me was something wild and scary.

"Let me try something on my own," I begged.

Cedric laughed joyfully. He had a clear tenor voice, smooth and seductive.

His hand hovered over the book of spells, and he raised it slowly. Then he beckoned me over to the altar.

"Put your hand here," he said and demonstrated. "Then think of what you would like to learn."

I did as he directed. I went to his side and placed my right hand about ten inches above the book.

The cover opened. I watched, mesmerized, as the book started to flip through pages beneath my hand, *of its own accord.*

It stopped.

I looked down at the page before me.

I gasped. Even though it was in a strange language, I could read it!

Cedric smiled. "The language spell works for the written word as well as those spoken. Let's see where you have landed."

He moved the book slightly to see it better.

"An animal spell. Of course! What else for my Rowena." He seemed amused.

"I wanted to see if I could conjure animals," I said happily. "How does it work?"

Cedric shrugged. "I'm not sure anyone knows that. But I believe you will summon them from other worlds, perhaps other times. You call them forth to this world and time."

"Let me try," I said eagerly.

He waved an arm. "It is not for me to permit you. You have the power just as I do."

Wow. That was something daring for Cedric to admit.

"Can I get into any danger doing this?" It suddenly occurred to me that I really didn't know what I was doing. Like not at all.

"Not with me here. I will stay with you, never fear." His eyes were soft, indulgent.

I remembered the last time I held the book. It was in the field south of Norland fortress, and I had inadvertently brought forth a Roman Legion in time about four hundred years. That had been rather a disaster. Their commander, Senias Cleva, had been fighting a war with the Celtic queen, Boadicea. Nice guy, in a really bad place.

Trouble was, my taking them out of time made it look like the legion had deserted. This was a terrible dishonor. Senias begged me to make it right.

I cried a lot when I had to send them back. Chances are they would die on that battle field.

Correction—*had*. It was several hundred years in the past. They would all be dead now.

Cedric wouldn't remember that. He hadn't been there.

This time, I would be more circumspect. Start with something small and work up, that sort of thing.

So I gazed down at the words on the page, added a few of my own, and chanted.

Poof!

A rabbit popped up on the floor on the other side of the altar.

"Oh! It's adorable!" I clapped my hands. "Can I keep it?"

Cedric chuckled. "Well done. Have you brought this forth for my dinner?"

I wacked his arm with my right hand. "Don't you *dare* think of doing that. It's far too cute."

And it was. A sweet little grey thing with a white tail. It was looking about the room, completely baffled. I wonder where it had been snatched from?

"Now see if you can send it back. Do you know the reversal chant?"

I nodded. "Val taught me."

Cedric raised an eyebrow. "Now, *who* is Val?"

I ignored him. Instead, I chanted the sounds that Val had taught me. Except...this had been before I had been given the language spell, and I must have gotten something a teeny bit wrong.

"Oh crap." The room was suddenly filled with rabbits.

There were bunnies on the floor. Bunnies on the altar. Bunnies hopping all around the room.

Grey bunnies. Brown bunnies. White arctic bunnies. Bunnies with long, droopy ears and those with shorter pointy ones.

Male bunnies and female bunnies, wasting no time doing what rabbits do best.

"Now stop that!" I scolded. I scooted forward, waving my hands to scare the male bunnies off, but they paid no attention.

Cedric was howling.

"Oh!" I cried, disgusted. "This is just a disaster."

He was doubled over with laughter now. "I can never ever predict what you will do next. It is a joy."

"Well, *do* something!" I pleaded. "Send them back! At least, send the males back." All those female bunnies looked so shocked and frightened. I felt terrible for them.

"You must do it, Rowena. It was your spell. Here, repeat this."

He gave me the incantation. I repeated it once, twice...

The rabbits disappeared.

I breathed a sigh of relief. "Thank God. I hope they all went their separate ways, unconnected. Does that reversal spell work for everything?"

"As far as I know," Cedric said. "But I really haven't used it much." He was wiping a tear or two from his eye. Nice to know I was so entertaining.

"Here, let me try it again." I was eager to see if I could bring forth something from the past.

Cedric stepped aside. "With pleasure," he said with a wave of his arm. "I don't know when I've had such fun."

Yeah, and it was at my expense, but I didn't care. Magic was *hot*.

I went up to the book again. For a moment I just stared at it, mesmerized. Elaborate Celtic scrolling bordered each page. The predominant colors were red, gold, and green.

The illustrations were beautiful. They ran down the left side of the left page, and the right side of the right, inside each border. Some of the symbols were similar to those woven into the tapestries that hung from the walls around us in this room.

I placed my hand over the page, not sure if I had to do that now since it was opened at the right spot anyway, and chanted.

There was a sudden ear-splitting shriek.

The room shook from the weight of, not an elephant, *a mastodon*?

"What the hell is that?" Cedric cried.

A great lump of brown fur shook and shivered in front of us. The creature shrieked again. It looked terrified and ready to charge...but where? Its back was smushed by the ceiling and its tusks were ripping the tapestry on the far wall.

Then it pooped.

"Oops."

Bugger. I quickly chanted the reversal words.

Pop!

Gone. Except for the poop.

"Sorry about that," I said to Cedric.

He was shaking from silent laughter.

"Do you want me to clean that up?" I walked around the altar, then stepped back.

Ick. Mastodons were a lot bigger than dogs or horses. And I don't know what they ate, but—not nice smelling.

He shook his head. "I'll get a servant."

Then he put his hands on my shoulders and said, "That's enough for now. Time for repast. Bernard will be livid that we have delayed the morning meal."

I accepted this cheerfully. Time enough to learn more magic, and besides, I was starving.

We were the only ones in the small hall beside the kitchen. I loved this place because it had windows to the outdoors and was much brighter than the great hall.

I could see chickens pecking the ground outside. And white geese moving in a small flock, everywhere together.

Bernard always had fresh eggs so I ordered a cheese and mushroom omelette. Cedric looked at me as if I were daft.

He was content with a pound of bacon and a dozen eggs, of course.

I was just getting into my meal when a runner was announced.

"From Jon?" Cedric asked.

The page nodded.

"Take him to the great hall." Cedric wolfed down the rest of his breakfast, drained his goblet, and left the room.

I kept on stuffing my face. One thing I had learned in this place—eat when the going was good. Who knew when I would get another real meal like this?

I downed a vitamin pill for the baby and another bun slathered in yummy butter for me.

After breakfast, I went up to see Grandfather. He was in a cheerful mood. Cedric caught up with me as soon as I had sat down in the chair by the window.

"I'm being attacked from the south," he said, from the doorway. His whole body was rigid and he looked distracted. "Strange boats are landing. I must raise more troops and join Jon immediately." His face was stormy.

Grandfather swore.

I rose to my feet. "Should I stay here with Grandfather?"

He swept his long ginger hair back with a firm hand. "For now. It should be safe here if we can prevent them moving north. If I am wrong…"

His eyes zeroed in to focus on me.

"If the castle is at risk, you move yourself. There is enough magic here to do it. Do not the risk yourself and the babe for the castle. Go where you will be safe."

I started. "Do you really think it could come to that?"

He shook his head. "No. But I can concentrate better on the battlefield knowing you can move yourself should it be necessary."

And there it was, proof indeed that Cedric loved me. He would have me go to another man—a rival even—for protection, rather than risk my life.

I met his eyes.

Take care of yourself, I thought.

"I will," he said out loud.

When he left, the room felt empty.

"I should be there with him," grumbled Grandfather.

"He needs you here for the defense of our castle," I said in earnest. "No one else knows what should be done."

We both knew that was a lie.

Chapter 5

With Cedric leaving to join Jon and his troops to the south, I was going to have time on my hands. Happily, I knew exactly what I was going to do.

To my surprise, Cedric had been true to his word. I was free to roam. Of course, there were always guards at the gates. I would not be able to leave on foot or horseback without his being told after the fact.

But he was clever. He knew I wouldn't leave right now, because something was even more tempting to me.

Knowledge. *The book of spells.* I could learn more about magic. So my plan was to sneak down into Cedric's secret sorcery cellar and do a little homework. The book would be there waiting for me.

I was sure Cedric wouldn't mind. In fact, I was pretty sure this was his plan. Hook me with magic. Then I would never want to leave.

I was just finished dressing to go down when a page knocked on my door.

"M'lady?"

"Come in," I ordered.

The page pulled open the door. The tower doors pushed out into the hallway of this castle for fire safety reasons. Fire was always a danger at Huel, because of the candles used to light rooms at night.

The young fellow was fairly short and finely built with thin shoulders. Definitely not warrior stock. But there was a place and calling for everyone in Land's End.

He stood nervously.

"M'lady, a runner has come for the Lord. He insists on an audience."

This was interesting. I wondered if it was from Sargonia or Norland.

"Take him to the great hall," I said. "Give him food and drink. I'll be down momentarily."

I checked my appearance in the rudimentary glass that served as a mirror. Not good enough. I threw off the linen day dress and opted for a more formal turquoise silk.

Whoever it was, we would do Huel proud.

I made my way down the corridor to the wooden staircase and into the great hall. I passed no one. The castle was deserted except for the two pages who tended Grandfather around the clock. A few elderly men worked the livestock outside.

The messenger was making short work of the simple food placed before him. When he saw me he leapt to his feet and made an awkward bow.

"My Lady," he said carefully, for it was clear that English was not his first language. "I come from the Prince of Gredane with a message for the Earl of Huel."

From Lars? I felt my whole body relax. Lars was allied with Gareth, and considered a friend.

"The Earl is not here," I said. "Give the message to me and I will relay it when he returns."

The young fellow nodded. "My Prince asks that the Earl meet with him at dawn tomorrow for parlay. I am to accompany him to the location, a two hour ride from here."

I stared at the fellow, who seemed familiar, but I couldn't place him immediately.

This news was not good. It sounded serious. Parlay was a formal term. And I wondered why Lars would want to meet with Cedric without Gareth there.

Cedric was not due back for three days. I could not get word to him in time for him to make the trip back for a meeting at dawn. I did not even know where he was exactly.

What was Lars up to? Many weeks ago he had talked about perhaps changing his allegiance from Gareth to Cedric. Was this his plan?

I was in a jam. If I told the young messenger that Cedric was far away, it could put the castle at risk. Our leader was not here. Never advertise a weakness. This is something I had learned in Land's End.

Yet if Cedric didn't show up—which he wouldn't—it could be seen as an insult and a challenge.

I made a sudden, reckless decision.

"The Prince of Gredane knows me. Let me return with you now. I will leave word for the Earl to follow when he returns."

The young lad looked startled. He clearly had never considered this option. I brought in the heavy guns.

"I am the Queen of Land's End, as I'm sure you know. So I do expect you to oblige me. Understand that I can ride like a man. I will not slow you down or be a burden."

He stood quite tall then. "I know, m'lady. I've seen you ride."

I looked more closely at him. He was a tall lanky fellow, about Kendra's age. "Sven?"

He nodded eagerly. "I remember you from the tournament at Sargonia. I was there with the Earl of Norland and Lars, our leader."

I gulped. If he had seen me ride, it would have been with Sargon, most likely. And yes, I had been riding hard. That was a time I wanted to forget.

Sargon died that week, by Cedric's hand. Beheaded no less.

I shook myself free of the vision.

Sven was gazing at me patiently.

"Ah! I am pleased to have you as my escort then." I gave him a sweet smile.

He blushed.

"Tell me, Sven. Would it be better if I dressed as a boy or young man for the trip? I could carry my dress and change into it when we arrive."

He frowned for a moment, thinking. "Yes. I think that would be safer."

"Stay here," I directed. "Eat your fill. I will return. We can pick up fresh horses in the stables and leave immediately."

I turned and moved swiftly out the hall.

Once on the second floor, I turned into another room, Richard's. He was younger and not as broad as Cedric. Hopefully, I could find clothing there that would fit me better.

I chose a brown tunic and cinched it with a cord tie. It was too warm for britches and most of the men chose to go bare-legged at this time of year. That's what a boy would do.

I used a ribbon to tie my hair into a ponytail and tucked it inside the tunic. Then I found a lightweight cape with hood on the wooden chair. It would be hot, but absolutely necessary when riding into camp. I could hide my hair and face.

I folded the turquoise dress carefully and looked for something to carry it in. A small sack could be hooked to the saddle. I had such a thing in the turret room.

Into the corridor I raced and up the back stairs, carrying the folded dress. Once there, I found a sack in the wardrobe. I placed the gown plus a few essentials inside and drew the cord tight. I strapped on my fanny pack.

Then I looked around for something to write on.

Cedric had played fair by not locking me in. I would play fair in return by telling him where I had gone and why.

The pen and small pad of paper were on the side table beside the bed, where I had left them previously. I wrote a short note in Latin, which I knew he could read.

I put it on the bed where he couldn't miss it.

He wasn't expected home tonight or even tomorrow. Who knows when he would see it. He wouldn't be happy, but at least he could be satisfied I was fulfilling my part of the bargain.

I took a last look around the room. I felt almost wistful. For some reason, I had a strange feeling I wouldn't be seeing it for a while. But that was pure fancy, I told myself.

I walked out the castle into hazy sunshine. Sven was waiting for me by the stable. He looked rather shocked when he saw me.

"Just pretend I'm a boy, Sven. I certainly ride like one."

He gave a crooked grin. I had to look way up to meet his eyes. The shock of blond hair fell all around his head in a shag. Darn, he was a good looking lad. If I were Kendra...

No matter. I had grown men to worry about.

I saddled Lightning and chose another horse for Sven. He seemed to know what he was doing, so I cooed to Lightning and tried to reassure her that this was going to be a fun adventure. She didn't seem to mind the gelding and was in a perky mood.

We trotted over the drawbridge past the sentries and onto a path going east. I hadn't been this way before.

"Sven, what is your place in all this?" I asked.

He pulled up. "Lars is my cousin. My father's first cousin," he said simply.

I nodded. That made sense. "We can travel more quickly, if you prefer."

He grinned again and kicked the gelding.

After a time, we slowed down to a walk. This land was beautiful, with green rolling hills, dotted with sheep grazing. I had been told that it was Huel land and therefore my family holdings, right up to the next river.

Funny that I hadn't been this way before. I made a promise right there to visit all our family holdings in the next few months and meet our tenants.

The farther we rode, the more it reminded me of Wiltshire, in current day England. This was prime agriculture land, very fertile. I understood now why everyone wanted to control Huel, or at least make an ally of us. You could feed yourself and all your troops here with little to no trouble.

I was starting to get weary when Sven pulled up next. He looked concerned.

"M'lady, just over that hill we enter the camp. We have to pass many men before we get to my commander."

"I'll put up my hood," I said. "Guide us through quickly, Sven. I'll keep up. The sooner I can get rid of this heavy thing, the better."

He watched me swing the cape over my shoulders, fasten it, and flip up the hood.

Then he turned and kicked the horse. I followed suit.

Up to the rise of the next hill, we cantered. At the top, I had to stop myself from reacting. Men were camped all over the valley. We kept to the ancient path and sped by them. I tried to keep my eyes focussed on the way ahead, rather than let them stray to the side.

But my insides were trembling with dread. Why were there so many men camped here? There had to be at least a few hundred. Previously, Lars had commanded a band of only twenty.

Sven slowed just before the crest of the next hill. He slid off his horse and gestured me to do the same. I dismounted, making an effort to hold the tunic down. Even so, I could feel curious eyes on me.

"Here, m'lady. This tent."

"Shhh! Don't call me that, Sven."

"Oh! Sorry. Let me announce us."

Sven called out to announce his presence.

"Indtaste," said a harsh voice.

It was Lars.

I felt my heart shift just a bit.

Chapter 6

Sven pulled back the tent flap and I entered.

There were two men in the room. One was Lars. My eyes found him and looked no further.

He was just as I remembered. Very tall, with shoulder length white-blond hair and light grey eyes. A pale face, rugged with carved planes. My vision of Hamlet, but Lars was not at all like that Danish prince in personality.

Usually, he wore clothes that were subtly different from the men in Land's End. This day, however, he was dressed for battle.

I threw back my hood.

"Rowena." His voice softened. Our eyes caught for a moment and held. I had to force myself to break free of his gaze, to find words.

"I knew Cedric would not be back in time to make your meeting. As the next in line at Huel, I came in his stead. It is good to see you, Lars."

"And you. I did not expect this. You honor me." He snapped a short bow.

I unfastened the cape and swung it to the floor. I untied the ribbon. My hair spilled out across my shoulders. "Do you have a place where I can change into something more fitting? I brought a gown, but as you can imagine, I did not think it smart to travel cross-country as a woman."

He seemed to shake himself like a man who has had a great shock. "That was cunning. Although the tunic does not disguise you well."

I was abruptly aware of other eyes on me. The younger man was grinning widely. He seemed to be a shorter, better-looking clone of Lars.

"So this is the woman who fires your blood, brother. I see. By Odin, I see."

"Be still, Soren. She is a Lady."

They were talking in a clipped harsh tongue. It took me a moment to realize that I could understand what they were saying. The language spell had worked!

Now I must be clever and not show that I could understand them. For some reason, I sensed this could be important.

The younger brother stared at me. His eyes traveled from my hair, across my body and down to my bare legs. His light blue eyes grew wide.

I saw his body become rigid and then shudder.

He laughed. "By God, it feels good to be a man today. I am fired, too. You didn't expect that, Brother!"

Lars growled. "Do not think of it, Soren. She is mine."

Holy hell! This was news to me. I struggled to keep my face from showing surprise.

The new man raised one eyebrow.

"The wife of your former ally? And yet you live?"

Lars's eyes narrowed as he fought for control.

A slow smile creased his brother's face. "Ah! He did not know. My older brother is treacherous. Perhaps he does not know even now. This Norland must be a fool."

Lars's face had turned to stone. I could almost taste the fury in this tent.

"Introduce me. Surely you are not afraid to do that," taunted Soren

All this time, I had worked to keep my face straight. I did not like this Soren. But they mustn't know I followed their conversation.

I decided to make it easy for them. "Lars, is this your brother? You are very much alike."

Lars strode forward then. He captured my hand with his own and kissed it.

"Not so alike, as you will find. Soren is the handsome one of my brothers. I am the ugly one."

I started. Lars was not ugly. At least, not in my eyes.

"You are very brave to come here today, Rowena. Braver than you can know. My Lady, this is my youngest brother Soren. He brings troops from my brother the King from across the sea."

I swallowed a gasp. More troops. And now Lars wanted to meet with Cedric.

My eyes shot over to Soren. I had not missed the inference, and worked hard to keep my composure.

"Soren, this is My Lady Rowena, granddaughter of the Earl of Huel, of whom you have heard. She was married to Sargon, King of Land's End, so still carries the honorary title of Queen here."

Soren moved forward with a merry look on his face. He managed a short bow.

"Enchanted, My Lady. Pay no attention to my solemn brother. You look fetching in a tunic." He spoke in English.

I blushed hard. It was daring and impertinent to say such a thing.

I could almost feel Lars growling.

"Soren, leave us." It was an order.

Soren eyed him. It looked like he was about to say something, and then he changed his mind.

"She will join us for dinner." He tossed the words over his shoulder on the way out.

Dinner? I hadn't planned to be here that long.

"Lars, may I change?" I took my turquoise dress out of the sack to show him.

"Yes. I will leave you. Then we must talk."

He stared at me once more. Then his thin lips curved into a small smile. His eyes flashed. It was the old Lars back once more. He strode out and closed the tent flap behind him.

Oh dear. I was feeling an awful lot like a fly in a web right now. What spider trap had I walked into?

No time to waste though. I threw off the tunic and pulled the silk gown over my head. It had small cap sleeves bordered with satin. I laced up the bodice, wishing that I had told Val to make the neckline just a bit higher.

I hadn't bothered with a necklace this time. It's never a good thing to risk travelling with valuables.

The witch's bracelet was different. I couldn't remove it from my wrist, in any case. Hopefully it would be enough to prove my rank in this strange wilderness camp.

I pulled back the flap. Lars was standing right in front with his back to me, like a sentry.

"Shall I come out?" I said.

He turned his head. His eyes swept over me with something akin to hunger in them. "Yes, come."

He gestured with his arm. I moved forward to stand with him on the hill overlooking the next valley.

A valley covered with troops and tents.

He stood very still at my side. I could see he was considering the words to use.

I decided to help him. "I've messed up your plans today. You had meant to have parlay with Cedric at dawn tomorrow. Now you are trying to figure out how to tell me what you were going to tell him, but in a way that won't terrify me."

Lars frowned. "You are extraordinary in how you anticipate."

I put my hand on his arm. "Then tell me straight, Lars. Don't spare me."

His rugged face held the ghost of a smile. "How fitting you would use that word. My concern has been exactly that—how to spare you through what is to come."

My hand dropped from his arm. I was getting a thoroughly bad feeling now. It had started up as soon as I caught sight of the troops below us. There were thousands of men making camp. Thousands.

"Shall I guess?"

He turned to me. His strange light eyes searched mine. He nodded.

I took a deep breath and stepped right into the fire.

"You meant to invade Land's End from the start. You allied yourself with Gareth to learn the lay of the land and the strength of all your opponents. Now, your brother the King of wherever you're from has sent you troops under the command of Soren to facilitate an invasion. And today..." I looked off across the field. "Well, tomorrow, you meant to make an ally of Cedric. He will stand with you or against you. You really don't care which."

"Oh but Lady, I do care," Lars said. "I care very much."

"Please elaborate."

"Not just yet." He was smiling slightly. "You are clever, Rowena. You make a formidable Saxon Queen. Everything you have surmised is true, to a point. And yet I wonder if you have considered the consequences for your own self."

"I've considered nothing but." My voice was shrill.

"I meant this day," Lars said. "You have admitted to me that you have guessed my plans. Surely you understand I cannot let you leave my side to tell others who would be my enemies."

For a moment I felt slightly faint. I found it hard to catch my breath. I wobbled a bit and Lars grabbed my arm to steady me.

"I thought it best we be honest with each other, Lars. We always have been."

He turned to face me. His eyes fixed on mine, and they were not smiling.

"Yes we have. And that is why I am being honest with you now." Both hands reached out to hold my shoulders firm. "You are my honored guest, Rowena. I shall treat you as such. But both of us know that you are now my prisoner for the duration of what is to come."

Chapter 1

And so I stayed for dinner. Lars kept me with him all the afternoon. I sat through his meetings with his generals, Erik and Karl.

They were startled to see me here in the camp. In any other circumstance, I would be equally disturbed to see them, because believe me, these weren't the sort of lads you'd want to meet in a dark alley.

Erik was at least six foot two, and built like a rock-face. His grey hair gave away his age, but his bulky arms and legs spoke of enormous power. I liked him. While his size was fearsome, his face seemed kind and he smiled easily.

Karl was equal in age, but of a more slender build. His face was narrower with the blue eyes close set, like most predators.

I was reminded of a chilling science study back home; how women with wide set eyes are often considered beautiful. Many celebrity names came to mind. But males were more likely to have close set eyes, designed for hunting down prey. Yes, prey, including those women with wide set eyes…

Karl stared at me that way. I had seen that look before in this world.

My instinct was to look modestly down or away. It must be a primitive reaction to avoid engagement.

Both men were bearded and wore skin tunics with fur across the shoulders. Their heavy leather armbands reached from wrist to elbow.

After the formal greeting, I lay down on the furs in the corner to have a nap. I closed my eyes and faced away. They did not know I could understand them. And did I ever get an eye opener.

Lars had another younger brother, Nial, commanding the troops to the south. They were engaging my cousins in battle this very day.

From what the others said, I was pretty sure Cedric had no idea that troops were also advancing on Castle Huel from the east.

This was a classic surround and capture strategy. I tried hard to keep the alarm off my face.

Also, it seemed everyone in the room accepted that I was already Lars's woman.

I definitely caught the political reason for my forced confinement in this camp.

"You did well, Lars. With her at your side, your position will be strengthened with the local lords and their serfs. But only if you marry her, of course. They would not forgive you for disgracing her."

"Will you marry her under our law?"

"That is the plan." I caught the smile in his voice.

Oh man, it was hard not to say something.

Erik barked a laugh. "You were clever not to remarry. It makes this possible."

"Methinks the gods had this in mind from the start. I have felt it since the day we met. Do not feel sorry for me. It is no sacrifice."

Erik chortled. "I do not think any man alive is feeling sorry for you, my friend."

Karl was not so jovial. "They say she is a warrior queen who can ride like the Valkyries. She is a Saxon, Lars. Will she obey you?"

Lars shrugged. "It takes a strong man to control a strong woman. She respects me, and I her. I will treat her well."

They returned to talk of troop maneuvers. More warriors from the east were going to come quickly and without warning.

Somehow I had to get away from here, the sooner the better. I had to warn Cedric and Gareth.

It was mid-afternoon and I was starting to get hungry when the meeting broke up. I feigned sleep as the men left. When Lars returned a short time later, he surprised me with horses.

"Come," he said. "The small fortress is not far from here. Our dinner and night will be spent there."

He helped me mount Lightning, then swung up onto his great white horse.

Lightning was frisky and definitely happy to be on the trail again. The white gelding was magnificent and very patient with her. It was obvious they had a rapport. I don't know if animals can understand each other in the way that I understand them, but it was clear that these two were simpatico. I might even say that Lightning was being a little saucy. She wouldn't know what 'gelding' meant, of course.

Mind you, if she were smart, she'd stick with geldings. They were a lot less trouble.

We rode north for a short while. I remembered this fortress—I had been there twice before. Both times, Lars had found me in his bedroom. Both times, he had reluctantly played the part of a gentleman. Funny how things come 'round.

As we approached the courtyard, men stopped to watch. Obviously, word of my arrival—aka capture—had been passed along.

I noticed a few familiar faces from the last time I had been here. I tried to smile and nod at them. A few smiled back. One young fellow attempted to bow. Mainly, they just stared.

Two older men were setting up the hall for dinner. Long rectory tables looked able to seat about fifty people. It was oddly quiet as we entered, and then voices picked up as soon as we walked by them. Lars whizzed me past everyone to the back bedroom.

Ah yes. That back bedroom. Cedric had nearly killed Lars in that bedroom. I had been the cause of that fight, but I had also been the reason Cedric *hadn't* killed Lars. I was fond of Lars, and Cedric was smart. He knew I would never forgive him.

I looked around the simple room. Nothing had changed since that day. The comfortable bed was against a stone wall, covered in furs. A single wooden table stood to one side of it. Sunlight poured in from the narrow windows.

"Will you be comfortable here for a short time? I have a few plans to make."

I nodded and decided to lay down for a real nap. Sleep overtook me until it was almost dark, and Lars came for me.

Dinner was a raucous affair.

I'd been to many banquets in Land's End. All had been loud and uncouth. Nobody used any utensils except their own small daggers. But this night made the others seem like a BBC period drama starring Maggie Smith.

I was already slightly nauseated. No doubt about it, first thing on my list when I got my hands on the book of magic was to find a spell to eliminate body odor. You can't imagine what it's like to be in a closed room with fifty burly warriors who hadn't washed in weeks.

But as always, when food was put in front of me, I lost the queasiness. The men might waste time talking and drinking, but I tore into the nosh. No need to worry about table manners here. I probably ate as much as any man there.

The noise in the room was punctuated by grunts of eating, rough talk, and relentless bellows of laughter. Often, I would look up to find eyes staring at me. I tried to ignore it.

Nobody knew I could understand their language, so nobody tried to engage me in conversation.

Soren was drinking heavily. They were all drinking heavily, even Lars. But the man across the table from me made me feel wary and uncomfortable.

Rarely had I seen such a change in one person. The young cheerful fellow who was so full of compliments had turned into a scary and unruly warrior. His eyes tracked my every move. He drank continually.

An unfortunate soused fellow walking behind the bench lost his balance and whacked into Soren's shoulder by mistake. He whirled and grabbed the other by the throat. They fell together to the floor. Several men yelled, fists flew, and the bench flipped over.

Erik roared as he hit the ground on his back. I could see clearly to the floor on the other side now. Soren was beating the other man senseless.

I could hardly believe my eyes and felt so helpless. There was nothing I could do.

Two other men leapt to pull him off the poor bastard. They held him back as more men moved in to grab the downed man's arms and legs to carry him out of the room.

The others righted the bench and returned to eating with hardly a comment.

I sat there stunned.

I turned to Lars to check if he had seen, but he was speaking to someone behind us.

I continued to keep my eyes trained on Lars, in the faint hope of feeling more confident about my safety here.

I liked looking at him. He may have thought himself ugly, but to me he had Nordic good looks. A thin face dressed with a mustache and goatee. White blond hair to his shoulders, mixed with grey. A tall, masculine build, but not as broad in the shoulders as either Gareth or Cedric. Very hard all over, with the kind of muscles that aren't for show.

His face was craggy with high cheekbones and deep vertical lines. I liked his eyes, which were a queer light grey. They could be mischievous when fixed on me. Or they could be hard as ice, which was fitting.

Lars was Prince of Gredane, a winter land of ice and snow. And now his violent younger brother had joined him in Land's End. We were in for stormy days.

I realized with a chill that I had never been in this position before.

Kendra and I had attended many banquets in Land's End. We had done so in Castle Sargon with all the heads of the houses of Land's End present. I had done so without her in Norland, with Gareth's men and the Roman commander Senias Cleva and his legion. In all those circumstances, I had been accompanied by family and men loyal to me.

This was different.

Lars was the only one who stood between me and the savagery in this great hall.

Thank God Lars was my friend.

When I turned back to the table, Soren was staring at me again. His tunic had fresh blood on it. His hair had fallen forward and hung limply. His eyes were bloodshot. He lifted the tankard to drink and ale spilled out the side of his mouth.

"I want Rowena." His voice slurred the words.

I automatically leaned back away, really frightened now. He had spoken in his native tongue but his meaning was clear in any language.

He slammed his tankard down on the oak table. "I want Rowena!" He pushed himself up from the table with such force that the table shook.

There was a roar from beside me, and another from across the table.

Lars grabbed my upper arm and roughly pulled me off the bench. He shouted orders to those around us while pushing me through the doorway. His men closed in behind us. I could hear the yells from the hall as he steered me down the corridor to the bedroom at the back of the fortress.

I moved automatically to the bed and sat down on it, like stone.

Lars closed the door behind him and pulled the heavy wooden bar down into place. A battering ram would be needed to get through the thing now.

Then he strode to the window and yelled orders to his man outside.

I was still so alarmed I could hardly think.

He swung around to face me. His mouth was turned down and his eyes were wild. He shook his head then started to pace.

"What is it?" I demanded. "Tell me the truth."

He stopped and stared at me with a haunted look. Then he looked away.

"I would never rape you, Rowena. Never. But my brother might. Nay, he most definitely will try."

I gasped.

He returned to the window and looked out to the rolling hills beyond. Both hands went on the sill to brace himself against it. I could tell by the hard set of his shoulders that he was warring with himself.

"I need to claim you. I told him earlier in our language that you were mine. I need to make sure he believes it is true."

"Why?" My voice was hoarse. It didn't sound like me.

"Because then he will know the consequences." He turned to face me. "If he tries to take you, I will kill him, even though he is my brother. That is accepted in our culture, expected. But it must be clear that we are already lovers."

I felt the blood rush to my face.

"I am married to Gareth, Lars."

He frowned. "That would not matter to Soren. We are preparing to declare war. You are counted among the spoils of that war."

I could hardly believe what I was hearing. Spoils of war?

Surely this couldn't be happening.

"But it would matter to you, wouldn't it?" I tried to appeal to his honor.

"That you are married to Gareth?" He shrugged. "We worship different gods. It is no sin. I have you under my protection, the captured queen. It is natural."

"I don't want to be a spoil of war. Say it straight, Lars. You are telling me…"

He moved closer. I could see the perspiration gathering on his forehead.

"You lie with me tonight, in here. Others will confirm it. Six witnesses are required."

I felt a chill. "You don't mean an audience!"

He smiled then. It was a gentler smile. Perhaps he knew that he would win this now.

"No. No audience. But they will know."

My hand flew to my throat in an age old gesture of…what, modesty?

He moved closer and stood rigidly before me.

"Rowena, I adore you. You must know this. I would not treat you poorly."

"Not as a 'spoil of war?'" I could hardly say the words.

He reached forward and captured my hand, pulling me from the bed. Then he raised the palm to his mouth and kissed it. It made me shiver.

"Harsh words for what I feel. But you are a strong, intelligent woman and I will not talk down to you. You must be made to see the reality of your situation here. You hold no power except that which I allow."

I pulled my hand back and turned away from him then.

"I know that, Lars. I've known that all along. I'm pretty savvy when it comes to war strategy, you'll find." I could hear my voice grow hard with frustration. "Sometimes I wish I were a man, so I could defend myself in open combat. Oh, how I would do it. I would take you on right now."

"I believe it," he said bitterly. "This is not how I would have wished it."

I sighed. Truly, I did believe him. Yet I also understood the gravity of my situation.

Yes, he wanted me and had for some time. I knew that. But I also knew that an unclaimed woman of my age and position was a dreadful burden on a leader. I would not remain unclaimed for long.

I tried to think of this from his point of view. Lars had always been honorable with me. He had protected me in circumstances where other men would have taken advantage. As much as he desired my body, I knew he must be loathing himself for forcing me into this position.

"I am not a monster, Rowena. I will not force you."

I turned to meet his eyes. "But you can't guarantee my safety if I don't cleave to you and make it obvious."

What a strange, archaic term.

He shrugged. "Men will be men. There are many who want you. They will come forward to claim you. But no one will touch my woman and live. They know that."

I felt a chill.

He looked away. "I have no time to bring you flowers, Rowena. This, I regret. It is night already. The men have had too much to drink."

He didn't have to spell it out. I got it. He was the only one who could protect me from the other men here. He had done so since the day we met. Even when I had been presented to him like a cake on a platter, in this very bed, he had done the noble thing. Even though I could have done nothing to stop him from doing anything he chose to do.

I liked him. My God, I liked him more than I wanted to admit.

One look at him, standing there, frowning with bitterness that he did not have the chance to seduce me like a cherished lover...

It would be easy to be kind.

I walked toward the bed.

"Do you remember the first time we met? I landed in your bed by accident."

"I remember," he said. "How could I not? It haunts me still in my dreams."

"You called me a gift from the gods," I murmured.

"That I did."

"You protected me then."

"As I will always. With my life."

I started to undo the laces of my bodice.

Behind me, there was a sharp intake of air.

"Do not distress yourself, my friend. I am not a silly fool. I will come to you willingly."

He moved so swiftly I hardly saw it. At once, his arms reached around me from behind. His hands crossed in front of me and gathered my breasts. His head moved down to kiss the side of my neck. I found myself leaning back into him.

"I will be gentle. I will not hurt the babe, I swear it."

I shivered as I found myself responding.

"I know you won't. Sex doesn't hurt a baby. That's not the thing that worries me," I murmured.

His hands continued to move all over me. I was reminded of that statement by a famous actress, *"Men are those strange creatures with two legs and eight hands."*

"Let me take off this dress. I can't afford to wreck it. It's the only one I have here."

He dropped his arms and stood back. I carefully pulled the gown over my head and placed it on the chair. Then I turned around.

Lars gave me no time to be shy.

He stripped his clothes in mere seconds and reached for me. His left hand held my head as his right arm wrapped around my back to pull me forward against him. His mouth sought mine and he kissed me deeply. I could feel the desire rip through his body.

"Oh my little bird," he murmured. "Let me make you sing tonight."

Chapter 8

Two candles burned on either side of the bed. The flames made dancing shadows in the dark room.

Lars moved above me like a man in possession of the greatest treasure in the world. His long torso barely brushed my body, so intent was he on keeping his weight off me. His arms cradled me on either side. His head dipped down to kiss me gently.

"Tell me if this is too much," he asked once more.

I smiled up at him. I had told him before. Sex wouldn't hurt the baby I carried.

The tenderness in his every move filled me with wonder. I reached to pull his head to mine and kissed him long and languorous. I felt him fight to keep control. He pulled out of me, then returned with a harder stroke and I sought to take him deeper. Now I was moving with him in a sweet, melodic rhythm, breathless. He picked up the pace, never once losing control.

The fire was there and I begged for that burn, fought for air, clung to him. I bucked against him and he covered my mouth with his own, this time deep and demanding.

I cried out.

Once more I was swept up into the clouds, and he held me there, floating, for one last euphoric moment.

I hardly felt him move off me. I was already sweetly dozing.

Sometime later, I heard his voice.

"Now I know. Now I understand Cedric."

"What do you mean?"

He kissed my shoulder.

"A woman who responds as you do? That is worth fighting for."

"Oh." I could feel the blush starting. "I don't seem to be able to control that."

He chuckled. "If I had only known this earlier."

"Probably best you didn't," I said dryly.

He was abruptly serious. He flipped on his back and locked his hands behind his head. "Not so. You remember that first morning I discovered you beside me in my bed. It was a sign from the gods. It could only be that. I knew this at the time. From that very day I have planned to take you to my home across the sea. Had I arranged it better, you would be there now, away from the battlefield. War is no place for a woman."

"Lars, I could not leave my land and people at a time like this. Not anymore. I did that once, and it was the wrong thing to do. I won't do it again."

I knew that now. If you run away, it only delays things. Face the world with your head high—that's what I intended to do from now on.

He turned his head to meet my eyes. "I admire you for that, although it may get you killed."

"So be it," I said firmly. "I can't help who I am, Lars."

He smiled then. "Yes, that is so. Perhaps we are well-matched in this, even though my instinct is to keep you far away."

His eyes drifted down to my chest. He leaned forward on his left side. His right hand came down to gently cup my left breast.

"You permit?" he asked.

I was momentarily taken aback. Surely the time for permission had passed. And then I kind of got it. Fornication was one thing to this man, a way of staking territory. He was asking permission to make love to me.

"Yes," I whispered.

He didn't wait. His head moved over me. His mouth found my breast, taking as much of it as he could. His right hand continued to caress the other one, rolling the nipple between his fingers and thumb.

Abruptly, his mouth moved from one nipple to the other and pulled hard.

I moaned with desire.

"I want to know all of you," he murmured. "I want to be able to say I know every inch of you, and remember."

His hand left my breast and moved down between my legs. I parted them willingly, my body pulsating with anticipation. His hand reached down to explore—

I arched.

"You are ready again," he said in awe. "So am I."

He moved swiftly this time, over me, in me, and I helped him, God help me, I welcomed it.

He wasn't as gentle this time. I welcomed that, too.

I awoke to a strange scratching noise.

Dawn light was streaming through the window. I was lying on my back on the bed. A fur throw covered me from mid-hip down.

Lars was sitting, still naked, on the wooden chair with his feet resting on the bed. He had something in his hand.

"What are you doing?" I asked.

He looked up. "I am drawing you." He returned to his task.

Lars, the great Viking warrior, was an artist? It was the last thing I could have imagined.

"I want to savor this moment. Who knows what war will bring and whether I will even survive it," he said.

"Don't speak like that. I can't bear it."

His eyes whipped up. "You have a big heart, Rowena. By rights you should hate me for what I have done this night."

"I don't hate you. I understand you have done this to protect me."

He snorted. "That shows you know nothing of men."

I was bewildered. What did he mean?

"You said that this...night in your bed would mean that I am claimed."

"Indeed it does." His hand worked furiously with the charcoal. "Which is what I want. What *I* want, Rowena, mark those words. I wanted you. I have for weeks. Do not make me out to be heroic."

"Ah," I said, swallowing hard. "Honesty, again. I trust, that is, I hope you will still want me after today, if my protection depends on it."

His hand stopped. His eyes shot up to fix on mine.

"Too much honesty. Now you are frightened. Never fear that, Rowena. I do not love lightly."

That word. What did it mean to him?

"You have the most beautiful breasts I have ever seen."

"May I see?"

He turned the wooden board toward me. On it was fastened a piece of parchment.

I blushed at what I saw there. It was me, there could be no doubt.

"You're very good," I said. "But I worry this could fall into the wrong hands."

He continued to draw. "The only ones to see this will be those I allow."

I sat up now. "Lars, no! You can't show this to anyone."

"Lie back down. I am not finished," he ordered. "This is a kind of proof, Rowena. Only a lover could create this with such accuracy. Soren knows that I draw."

I swallowed hard and did as he asked. "Oh please, Lars, don't show this to Soren."

"I do not intend to. It is—how you say—protection. In case of need."

"It's just that I worry if he sees this…"

"That he will covet you? Too late. That much is clear. I will have to kill him, I expect."

"Lars, no! Not your own brother. Cedric killed his brother Ivan. I can't be responsible for any more deaths."

He looked up from his work. "The wheel of fate is already turning, little bird. You can no more stop it than I can stop wanting you."

Chapter 9

The sun was fully up when I next awoke. Lars was dressing.

"You need to get ready, Rowena. We have a meeting to attend."

I moaned. "I know you said I must stay at your side, but Lars, I am with child. I need more sleep than you do."

"I'll make arrangements for you to nap later, guarded. But you must come now. I cannot miss this. You will see why."

I sat up and groaned.

A short time later, we had travelled by foot to a lone tent erected on the other side of the hill from the small fortress.

It was mid-morning now. Lars stood outside the tent with his hand on his sword hilt.

"He comes alone as instructed," he said to me. "That is good." He gestured for me enter the tent.

I could hear a single horse galloping furiously. It came to a sudden stop. I could hear a man dismount.

"Hail Lars." It was Gareth's voice. "Why this cloak and dagger nonsense? Why meet here?"

Lars held open the tent flap. He entered first and then Gareth.

"Rowena!" Gareth said. His face lit up. "You have found her for me. Good man. That's why the secrecy."

Oh Lord! Gareth thought Lars had rescued me on his behalf. I couldn't keep the shock off my face.

Lars had moved swiftly behind me. His hands gripped my shoulders—a deliberate act of possession.

I saw the change in Gareth's face as he came to realize something was very wrong.

"What is this?"

"Do not blame her. She rode here in Cedric's stead and walked into a trap. I cannot let her go now, of course. She knows too much." I could feel Lars's hands grip me harder.

"Rowena?" Gareth's blue eyes were hard as they focused on me.

"It's true," I said. "Lars sent a messenger to Cedric which I intercepted. He asked to meet at dawn. I knew Cedric wouldn't be back in time, so I rode here myself yesterday, in disguise."

Gareth cursed. "Foolish woman."

"Hey! Wait a minute—" I started to say.

"No more foolish than you, Norland. You came here yourself," Lars shot back. "Uncommonly brave for a woman to ride into this camp, do you not think?"

The admiration was clear in his voice.

Gareth looked furious, with himself and with Lars. He threw his butt down on the bench.

"Don't think this is over, Lars. You hold Rowena as hostage to ensure my cooperation. I get that and I won't forgive it." There was murder in his eyes.

Hoo boy. I didn't want to be there when Gareth realized it wasn't that, either. Lars wasn't holding me to ensure Gareth's cooperation. Lars had already claimed me as his own.

There would be hell to pay right here and now if Gareth figured that out.

I kept mum.

"So what is this about? Why am I here?" Gareth said.

"I attack Huel in four days. Are you with me or against me?"

I gasped. This was sooner than I had expected.

Gareth blanched. "What the hell do you mean?"

Lars moved out from behind me. His face was grim.

"Is there something wrong with your hearing, old man? I am preparing to take Huel from the east. My brother's troops are already engaging Cedric to the south."

Gareth exploded. "You support my plan to usurp the fiend and then you take over the battle to your own ends?"

"I need Huel." Lars's voice was cold.

"Okay, this isn't working for me. I'm really getting confused." I was also kinda peeved. "I take it you both want Cedric out of the picture. But can't you guys work this out some way? Both take on Cedric and then split the proceeds?"

Whoops. That was kind of loopy. Here I was advocating that my own castle be captured and looted.

They both stared at me as if I had turned into a squawking chicken.

"Okay, so that was a stupid thing to say. Of course I don't want you to sack my home. But I'm a pragmatist. What has to happen for that to be prevented?"

"I told you last night," Lars said. His jaw was set. "You here, with me, at my side. The castle will remain untouched."

"You take Rowena for yourself? I'll see you in hell," Gareth yelled. He started to pull his sword.

"No!" I leapt in between the two of them. "No fighting here today. I mean that, Gareth. If you kill Lars, I'll go back to Arizona. And vice versa. I mean that. Don't think I'm joking."

The testosterone building in that tent would choke a rhino.

"We have to come to some arrangement today," I said reasonably. "You can't be fighting each other and Cedric, too."

"I'll fight who I want," Gareth muttered.

I moved to the table and leaned forward. "Look at this pragmatically. Take me out of the picture. If I wasn't here in Land's End, what would you do, Gareth? Would you work with him to destroy Cedric?"

He grunted.

"But you *are* here," Lars said. "We cannot ignore that."

I glared at him. "I want peace. Huel is my home, and I'm next in line to it after Cedric, so I have the right to talk here. More than anything else, I want peace. How do we get that?"

Gareth snorted. "You don't. You never will."

"What? You're saying the natural condition is to be at war? That's ridiculous."

Lars cleared his throat. "It is the way of men. Each seeks to improve his condition. I seek fertile land for my people. I will take it from the man who has it, if I can."

Gareth growled. "Don't sound so blasted noble, Lars. You'll take it because you love to fight."

Lars turned to him. A faint smile played upon his face. "Yes, I do. That makes me proficient at accomplishing my goal. But it does not diminish my purpose in achieving it."

"Can you two not make temporary peace between you? Could we not come to some sort of agreement?" I was fed up. They were cousins of a sort. They shouldn't be warring.

Lars shrugged. "We could indeed. I seek Huel. The land is most fertile and I want the castle for my home. Gareth can keep his northern holdings. I have no need of those."

"You bastard. You are lying through your teeth." Gareth had risen from his bench. "You need the north to hold the south. How else can you land troops without a coast?"

Lars was not smiling now. "If Rowena were not present, I would call you on that insult. I do not need your north coast, Norland. I have the east."

Gareth vaulted up. He hissed like a snake.

Lars spoke again. "My brother Soren secured the east coast this past week. The castles are burning now behind us."

I gasped. "Lars! You wouldn't burn Huel!"

He turned to me, his face a mask. "I intend to keep Huel as my base in Land's End. I will not burn it unless I must."

He paused. His voice became softer. "I had always intended that. But now there is an additional incentive. You."

"You are mad, Lars. Cedric will not give her up, and he has all of hell behind him."

"Yes," Lars said. "I know this. But I have numbers on my side, and men who do not care if they go to their deaths as long as they take others with them."

I felt stony cold now.

"You're all insane," Gareth sputtered. "Every last one of you Normans."

Lars shrugged. "We believe in a different kind of afterlife, that is all."

"Now just a cotton-pickin' minute here," I intervened. "You two are conveniently forgetting about what I want. Don't I get some say in the matter? No, don't answer that. Let me reword it. I will choose where I end up. Believe it. I'm not without power, remember. I can move myself with magic."

They both looked at me as if I were simple.

"Yes, you can," said Lars. "But you cannot control that we war against each other. Rowena, for as long as you live, there will be war among us."

I felt struck in the face. "So I should die? That's how we get peace?"

Lars moved forward to pull me to him.

"No, no, little bird. No one is suggesting that. Your death would not bring us peace. It would make us more war-like, if that is possible. Each would blame the other. It would be personal."

I pushed away from him.

"So what *are* you saying?"

"He's saying that nothing you can do will stop the fighting between us." Gareth's voice was strong again. "It's natural. We will fight over land and we will fight over you. The strongest, for now, will win. At best, we will establish new boundaries and guard them for a time."

I had a sudden idea.

"Then you should let me ride for Cedric. If this all comes down to establishing boundaries, let's skip the fighting and go directly to negotiations. We can settle this now. Let me get Cedric here."

Gareth burst out in laughter. Apparently I was quite entertaining. He rocked back on the bench and slammed the palm of his hand on the table.

Lars did not laugh. "You are not going anywhere," he said firmly.

I looked him in the eyes, and what I saw there was scary. This was not the lover of last night. This was a powerful man and warrior from another land who sought to conquer *my* land and *my* castle.

"So this is how you settle battles in your future world? By negotiation?" Gareth was still chuckling.

I was silent. Oh dear. How could I answer that?

"Tell me, Rowena. I am curious."

I turned away. "No. We don't do hand to hand combat much anymore. We have developed powerful nuclear weapons that can destroy entire cities by the mere flick of a switch." Actually, they could destroy entire worlds, but I didn't think it good to mention that.

"Cowards!" Gareth uttered. "A real warrior faces his enemies. He will triumph or die."

Lars nodded. "Triumph is better."

That's another thing I hadn't thought of. How these men would consider modern warfare.

But I had one more thing to say. I pulled myself up to my full five foot six inches.

"Lars, you realize that by attacking Huel, you are attacking me and my home. Huel is *my* castle, my family seat. You make war against *me*, not just Cedric."

He looked weary now. I could see the movements of his mind reflect upon his face.

"Little bird, yes, as you are second in line to the Huel fortunes, we are indeed enemies. You are my prisoner here, and while so, are under my control. My behaviour with respect to your castle will be a result of what you choose to do. I know you have some power to move yourself. So let me be honest, as we always are with each other. Stay with me for the course of this war and the aftermath, and I will not destroy your home. Leave me, and there is no reason for me to spare it. The choice is yours."

We stared at each other across the room.

All that he said was true, except for one thing. I didn't have the power to move myself right now. There was no magic for me to channel in this war camp.

I was stuck here. And my goal for the next few days would be simply to survive.

Gareth laughed without mirth. "This is how you Gredanes romance a queen? You threaten to burn her home?"

I turned in anger. "Tell me you were not prepared to do the same, Gareth. Tell me!"

He glared at me. "Of course I would! I will destroy Cedric and the whole bloody castle and everyone in it if I can get to them. You seem to forget that Ivan shot an arrow through my shoulder and killed my cousins in my own fortress grounds. I hate the Huels."

That shocked me. And scared me.

He was forgetting that I was a Huel.

"Why did they not finish you off?" Lars asked.

"*She* stopped them." Gareth's voice was softer now.

Dear God, I remembered my Grandfather's words when we had returned to Huel. "You should have killed him when you had the chance," he had said grimly. At first, I had been alarmed. Now I saw the wisdom of it.

Ivan was already dead. But Gareth would not rest until he slaughtered Richard and Jon, just as his own cousins had been slaughtered by them.

How naive of me not to think of this before.

Lars gestured to me with his arm. "One final word on this. You forget, Rowena, that I called this meeting with your cousin, not you. Oh, I will not deny that your arrival has been vastly superior for me in many ways. But understand in letting you stay for this parlay, I am treating you as I would a man. Do not mistake this for a change of heart."

"I get it. You're saying don't penalize me for treating you as an equal."

He nodded. "Exactly."

I considered that. It was interesting—and so very ironic—that of all the men I had known in Land's End, Lars the barbarian from across the sea was the one who awarded me the most consideration of an equal.

No secrets. Cards on the table. Respect. I had to admire him for that.

"You are very clever, Lars," I said finally. "I don't think anyone quite realized that. Certainly, I hadn't until now."

Lars smiled. He folded his great arms across his chest.

"Why is he so clever?" Gareth demanded.

I glanced at him and shook my head. "It appears I have some serious thinking to do."

In the end they managed an uneasy truce.

"Let me speak to her alone," Gareth said.

Lars hesitated, then nodded and left the tent.

Gareth came up to me and put his hands on my shoulders. His blue eyes look directly into mine. "Do not think I am abandoning you to him forever. Understand that I could not get us away from here without getting us both killed. He has too many men."

I nodded. "I understand. It would be foolhardy. But Lars won't do anything that could hurt the baby. You know that."

Gareth pulled me in for a hug. "I hate this. But I'll get you back, and when I do, that man will wish he had never been born."

Gareth rode off without me. I was not surprised to see that Lars allowed him to leave, although I think deep down Gareth was.

I stayed with Lars in the tent. He watched me, waiting.

Curious, how the present had a way of triggering the past in one's memory. I was grimly reminded of a television documentary on the early history of Scotland.

"A Norse-Celtic alliance against the Brittons. My God, this is the battle of Brunanburh all over again."

"Explain," Lars said.

I searched my memory for the date. "937 AD, I think. The Vikings aligned with the Gaels to stand against the Anglo-Saxons on the western shore of Great Britain. In my world."

"Did they win?"

I shivered. "I can't remember. But it was a bloodbath."

I did remember, but I didn't want to tell Lars the outcome. It wouldn't help.

Instead, I changed the subject.

"He may stand with you for now, but he will never forgive you for this, Lars."

"No, he will not." The ghost of a smile graced his face.

It was funny that we didn't need to speak the reason. We were oddly simpatico in ways of the mind.

"I will miss him. He has been a good comrade."

"Can you not still reconsider?"

Lars shook his head. "My path is already part of destiny. The damage is done, in any case."

I plunked down on the tent floor.

"You would really burn Huel." I still couldn't believe it. My gorgeous fairy-tale castle.

He watched me. "It is what we do. We raid. Surely you know that. You must have heard the tales."

He put one foot up on the bench and leaned his arm against his knee. "I can keep the men from destroying Huel if I parade you as my consort. They must see that you are tied to me and know of my intensions to make this legal and permanent."

I got the picture. My 'alliance' with Lars would save the castle. But there was one thing even more important.

It was my only chance of saving Grandfather.

I swallowed hard. My choice was clear for the next while.

"At home we have a saying, 'take one day at a time.'"

"You are holding up well."

I drew my knees up and wrapped my arms around them. "Only on the outside. I'm trembling inside."

"That, I can imagine. A woman alone in an enemy war camp. But you came to me, Rowena. I did not force you."

"When I rode here, I did not know you were my enemy, Lars."

"I know, little bird. I know. But you are blessed with great intelligence. Surely you understand that I cannot let you go free."

Of course I did. I was just kicking myself for being such a fool. Lars didn't even set a trap. He didn't have to.

I was such an idiot.

"Do not fear that you will be seen as a collaborator by your people," he said. "I will make it known to all that you are being held against your will."

I started. "You have to stop doing that."

"What?"

"Reading my mind."

His eyes crinkled as he smiled. It was a gentle expression, but also tinged with satisfaction.

"You and I, we are very alike, my lady. I have no doubt you would lay down your life to save your people. I have no wish for that. I will do all in my power to prevent it."

Nor do I wish for you to die, I thought grimly.

What a colossal mess. "So what now?"

"Today, you will see how a Prince prepares for war. We will ride to meet the troops."

I shivered. He was watching me. I know he was waiting to see if I would crumble under the strain.

That convinced me. I vaulted up. "Then let's get started."

Chapter 10

He held the tent flap open and gestured for me to follow him through.

"If I ride astride in this gown, my legs will be uncovered. Is that a problem?"

"Ride in your gown," he said. "You are a queen, and they need to see that you are unafraid. Can you act that way?"

I nodded. I would act the proud queen if it killed me, which it very well might someday.

We continued down the path that led to the small fortress. He walked on my right and he didn't hold my hand. I noticed that he always kept his sword hand free.

"This is a trust thing for you, isn't it? At least partially."

He nodded. "Yes indeed. I know you cannot speak our language and that our ways seem strange to you. You would be a fool not to feel fear, and I know you are not a fool."

We came around a hill. The small fortress was directly ahead.

"You will need to trust me to protect you when I am with my men. Have no fear, I will."

I brushed my hair back with a hand. "It is spooky how you keep reading my mind."

A short time later, I was mounted on Lightning. I got a kick out of how gorgeous my turquoise gown looked against her dark coat. Val would approve.

I probed her mind to see how things were going. Not bad. It seemed they treated their horses well here.

There actually weren't many. Most men were on foot.

Lars cantered toward me on the huge white gelding. "Stay at my side, Rowena. Do not venture off. Shall I take your rein?"

I shook my head. "No need. I won't stray."

He nodded. His eyes swept over me, as if in approval. "I need to show myself to the men. We will travel from camp to camp. Do not dismount until I am there to help you."

"I understand. Are we going to walk the horses all the way there?"

He grinned then, with big white teeth. "I think not. We will ride hard in approach."

I met his eyes. They were sparkling.

I knew what he intended of course. The sight of a young Saxon Queen roaring into the camp astride a horse was bound to shock. I would earn the title of Valkyrie today.

"Is this not dangerous?"

He shook his head. "Word has made its way through camp. They will be curious. We will give them a show, yes?"

There is nothing, absolutely nothing I love more than taking a swift horse on a full gallop. Lars kept to the outskirts of the camp, at first turning north and veering across an open field. When he saw I could keep up, he took us up a hill.

It was a beautiful day, warm without being humid, and clear. The last four weeks in Land's End had been too rainy for my liking. I know the frequent rain made it lush and green here, but I found grey days depressing. Of course, I came from the Sonoran desert and was used to almost constant sun.

When I came to his side, Lars bid me to stop. Below stood the main camp of several hundred men. Many had turned to watch us. Others were pointing and signalling to still more.

Lars kicked his gelding and we galloped along the top of the ridge, then slowed to canter down the far side.

He was showing me off, of course. I did my best to do him proud.

He took us right to the edge of camp at a gallop, and pulled up hard. I did the same, and Lightning was panting as we drew up to his side. I was also grinning from ear to ear.

Lars looked back at me, smiled and nodded. Then he signalled me to walk my filly at his side.

I liked that. He didn't insist I walk behind.

Two broad-shouldered men in full armor came forward from the crowd to greet him.

Lars nodded his head.

"Ejnar. Henning."

The shorter man with the dark beard grinned.

"So this is the Valkyrie we've heard so much about."

Lars nodded. There was pride on his face.

"Does she fuck as well as she rides?" said the other.

Holy shit.

"Mind your tongue, Ejnar. She is a Queen."

He didn't sound too upset, which surprised me. Later I found out they were boyhood friends.

"You know I joke, Lars. She is magnificent."

I had to work hard to keep my face straight. It was most important that no one knew I understood their language.

"She is also a wise woman with great courage," Lars said. "You will see why she is a Queen worth fighting for."

"You intrigue me," said the blond man. "But it is good to see you happy."

Lars turned to me. His eyes sparkled.

"Yes. That I am."

"A battle to look forward to and a Valkyrie in your bed. It doesn't get much better than that," Ejnar said.

The other men laughed.

"Until tomorrow." Lars nodded. He kicked the big horse forward and I followed.

We walked around the edge of the camp and then Lars guided me up the hill to a rise.

He dismounted and signalled for me to do the same.

We walked to the edge and gazed over. What I saw made me gasp.

The line of men on foot went on for miles and miles. Camps dotted the landscape. I could see the smoke from fires burning way in the distance. They didn't look like campfires.

Lars came up behind me and wrapped his arms around me. His hands cupped my breasts and settled there.

"Should you be holding me like this in front of the men? Some might be able to see from there."

"Now that I have known you, it is impossible for me not to touch you." He kissed my head. "It will do no harm. They know that I have taken you."

I blushed like crazy. "What did you do, send a telegram?"

"I do not understand you."

I sighed. "I'm sorry. I'm just a little embarrassed."

"Ah. Have no fear. No one considers you a harlot. They know you have no choice."

Crap. I just couldn't get used to my sex life being a topic of conversation for strangers.

I decided to change the subject. "These are your men?"

Lars bent down to kiss my neck. "As you see, I hold the east."

This was very, very scary.

"When do you march on Huel again?"

"Four days." His right hand traveled down my belly to my—

"Lars, stop!" I turned around in his arms and his mouth came down hard on mine. I struggled for a moment and finally gave myself up to it.

This man could kiss me so that I would forget the world.

Clip clop. Clip clop.

"I see you have taken your prize already."

Lars's head shot up. He released me and stood tall. I was alarmed to see one hand go to his sword hilt.

A single rider had come up behind us.

"Take care, Gustav." Lars didn't seem to like this man.

I didn't like him either. He had light brown hair and broad shoulders. His armor and sword showed him to be of the upper classes. An ugly scar ran from the top of his cheek to the corner of his mouth.

He had the most unhappy eyes I've ever seen.

Gustav shrugged. "Is the child yours?"

There was a stunned silence.

"It is now," Lars said coldly.

I held my breath.

Both men stared at each other across a space of ten feet. One was mounted and the other wasn't, which was a great disadvantage for fighting, I knew. I prayed for Lars to keep his cool.

"When is the council?" Gustav asked finally.

"Tomorrow before the banquet."

"I'll see you there." Gustav turned his horse and cantered off.

"What's wrong with him?" I asked.

Lars's head whipped to me. "We have a history. I gave him that scar."

Holy hell. I needed to find out about that.

He signalled for me to follow him.

We went back to the horses. Lars helped me into the saddle and then vaulted up on his own steed. I turned Lightning and we trotted to reach his side.

I could tell he was still furious. His mouth was turned down and his face had set to hard planes.

I decided to address it.

"You are angry, but you can't do anything about it because I am here."

His head turned slowly to me. "You are starting to think like a Norman."

Interesting. Lars didn't consider himself a Viking. He used the old term, from the original Northman. Maybe 'Viking' wasn't in use yet?

I continued. "Normally you would engage him because of whatever he said back there. But you can't because then I would be unprotected."

"I never lose," he said darkly. "But I can't protect you and fight at the same time."

That's exactly what was worrying me about the battle to come.

We walked our horses in silence around the outskirts of the camp.

The smell of roasted mutton was almost overwhelming. This was sheep country. Most of the meat we ate in Land's End was mutton or venison. What I really missed was a good old hamburger.

Or a hot dog. Man, could I go for a baseball stadium hot dog right now.

"Lars!" someone called.

I looked over. Lars had spotted the man and was vaulting off his horse. I held my breath.

They embraced and slapped each other on the back.

"Jory, you old dog! How are you?"

"Ha! Lars, we'll have a good one this time, won't we?"

I stared at the man who embraced my captor. He was a burly fellow, much broader in the beam than Lars, but not as tall. His red hair and beard were both braided.

"So this is she?" He looked straight at me.

Lars had his arm around the other man's shoulder. He thumped his back and then turned to me.

"I will help you down," he said in English.

I lifted my right leg and swung it over the back of the saddle. Lars caught my waist and I slid gracefully to the ground.

"My Lady Rowena, Queen of Land's End. Meet my good friend Jory. None can beat him with an axe. "

"I am honored." Jory smiled. His eyes were warm. "Lars, is she yours?"

"Most definitely," he said.

"Good man. Keep her close, or I'd be takin' her myself."

"Do not try." The words were strong, but he was still smiling.

"Be still, man. I'm not a fool."

"Come to the banquet, Jory. Sit with us."

"I would not miss it."

They clapped shoulders.

While the two leaders conversed, other men filled in around behind us.

I found many eyes upon me. I tried to smile, but it was uncomfortable being this close to so many strangers. These men towered over me, so I kept my head high and concentrated on my surroundings rather than the faces.

Not all of them carried swords. Most had axes and spears. It occurred to me that maybe they didn't have access to good metal. Perhaps only the wealthy could afford fine blades.

I also had this Hollywood idea of what a Viking helmet should look like, with horns on either side. None of them had these. A few had simple helmets made with four parts fixed together with a metal rim that crossed the helmet on the top and around the edges.

They weren't pretty.

Someone touched my hair from behind, picking it up to let it fall through his fingers. I shivered and moved closer to Lars.

I don't think I have been so uncomfortable in my whole life. To be a lone woman surrounded by rough strangers who don't speak her language is terrifying.

A fire was going not far away. I could see a side of mutton roasting over it on a spit. The smell was not appealing. I could hardly bear to look at it. The men at the fire were watching me. They looked unkempt and didn't speak.

There were plenty of small kegs around. I think they were called firkins and held ale.

One younger fellow came forward. He had a full head of white-blond hair and dazzling blue eyes. He smiled shyly and bowed his head.

"You are beautiful," he stammered.

"Thank you, you are very kind," I said back.

Crap. I wasn't supposed to know their language! I had to be more careful.

There was a commotion from behind. Men were yelling and pushing their way through the crowd.

Lars was at my side in an instant, blocking me from the two men who were forcing another one forward.

"Jory, a hand."

Jory came to his side, axe ready.

Two men pushed their way through the yelling crowd and threw another to the ground at Lars's feet. He landed hard.

I gasped. The man was dirty and badly beaten. One eye was swollen shut. His nose was broken. Blood streamed down his face. One arm was fractured and hung limply. He had numerous surface knife wounds on his face and arms.

My instinct was to rush forward to attend him. A fortuitous sense of self-preservation held me back.

"This bastard killed my brother," said the older one of the two captors. "Murdered him like a dog when we were supposed to be fighting the enemy." He spit on the body.

"Why would he do that?" Lars's voice was harsh.

"He wanted my sister!" The second man said, disgusted. He swiped stringy brown hair out of his eyes. "He always wanted her. But she chose Jens. So he killed Jens on the battlefield to make it look like he died in battle."

Lars glared down at the man on the ground.

"Is this true?"

"It was self-defense, m'lord. He was coming for me."

"Liar!" The first man kicked him hard in the side.

The downed man screamed.

"Enough!" ordered Lars. "Let him speak."

He turned back to the man. "Why did he attack you?"

Silence.

"He didn't," the brother said. "I saw it. You swung from behind and axed him when he was engaged with the locals."

The rumble of voices increased.

Lars grunted. "Did anyone else see this?"

A dozen hands shot up.

"I saw it." An older grizzled warrior came forward. "Could do naught about it as I was up to my arse in cursed Saxons."

"You saw it, Axel. Then it must be so." Jory nodded. He turned to Lars, frowning. "Not the first time a man has taken out one of his own on the killing fields."

All eyes were on Lars.

"This is most serious. What is his name?"

"Bardo," said the younger man.

Lars looked down. "Bardo, you are accused of murdering a fellow Norman with no provocation. There are witnesses here who swear you did it. What do you say in your own defense?"

The crowd grew silent. The man said nothing.

All waited.

"Kill him," Lars said. "Make it quick."

I gasped. The crowd roared.

"Get her away," Jory urged.

Lars turned and coaxed me to the horses.

"Move quickly," he said.

I put my left foot in the stirrup and he practically threw me onto Lightning. I fell forward across the saddle, nearly blacking out.

Lars cursed. "Slide down. You'll ride with me. Jory?"

I slid off Lightning into Jory's arms. Lars was already mounting his palomino. Jory carried me over and the big man easily lifted me up to Lars.

"Up you go, pretty lady" he said.

The crowd was rabid behind us. Men yelled and cheered. I tried to block out the sound, but then all went hushed. There was a great thwack and the men roared.

I closed my eyes tight.

Lars had me across his lap with one arm wrapped around my back. Both my legs hung over one side. He kicked the gelding and we cantered away.

He didn't speak until we were up on the rise, well away from the camp. Lightning followed us.

"It is unfortunate you had to witness that," Lars said.

"Why was it necessary?" My voice was breathy.

"He murdered another. I cannot have my men killing their own side on the battlefield."

I was silent. Lars didn't know that I could understand their language and had followed their exchange. An innocent woman had been the cause of this. I wondered how she would feel when she found out. Poor soul.

Now that woman had no husband. The other man who wanted her was dead as well. What would she do now?

"I am their leader, Rowena. They expect me to be fair. This was not a time for mercy."

Lars seemed to sense my angst. But he didn't know the source.

And I had seen in action how ruthless these Normans could be.

Chapter II

Lars kept me away from the men for the next few hours. I was profoundly grateful.

After returning to the fortress, we went immediately to the back bedroom. I lay down on the bed for a nap. I don't know how long I slept or where Lars went.

When I awoke, Sven was sitting by the door, whittling a piece of wood. His eyes shot up at my movement.

"You are awake," he said in English. He lurched to his feet.

I smiled and sat up. "Thank you for guarding me."

He blushed. "I go tell Lars."

I watched him leave. What a nice young fellow. I bet Kendra would like him. No doubt, he would adore her.

I wondered what she was doing now. Damn, I had to get word to her that I was okay. How could I do that?

I rose from the bed and walked to the window.

Twilight was beautiful in Land's End. The two moons were rising, spilling gentle light onto the rolling hills below.

I gazed into the distance, lost in thought.

Lars entered the room carrying a tray of food. He placed it on the small table.

"Feeling better?" he asked.

I nodded. "Thank you. The nap helped."

"That was too much for you today. I will remember this."

He gazed out the window, and that worried look came back to his face. "This did not accomplish what I intended. I shall have to do more."

"What do you mean?" I stared at the food.

"I wanted the men to see you were with me. We did not reach as many camps as I had hoped."

We sat on the end of the bed with a small table in front of us.

You would think the traumatic event I had witnessed would affect my appetite. Not a chance. I lit into the food like a famished wolf. Kendra would laugh if she could see me now. God, I missed her.

Lars watched me with amusement. Nice to know I was a constant source of entertainment.

"What?" I said, picking up a chicken drumstick.

He shook his head.

"I can't help it. This baby makes me ravenous." I continued to munch.

He frowned then. I watched him drink from the goblet. Something was on his mind. He drummed his fingers on the table. I could almost see the gears turning.

"Something is bothering you," I said. "What?"

He glanced at me quickly then rose to his feet and looked through the window again. "Is Gareth truly the father of your child?"

I hadn't expected this. "No," I said truthfully. The thought made me sad. "It's very unlikely. I am almost positive it is Cedric."

He nodded. "I thought as much."

Lars appeared to lighten then. His whole body seemed to release a great weight.

"Would that make a difference?" I asked. I licked my fingers as there didn't seem to be anything to wipe them on.

He took his time considering this. "Only to my conscience."

He crossed both arms and turned to me. "I am not in a position to change my plans, Rowena. I was sent to this land for a purpose. I will see it through."

I nodded. This was an interesting position for us both. I was acting as his trusted confidant, yet he had become my enemy.

Whatever he felt for me, he would not back down on his mission. This was a man who would keep his word. But I couldn't help worrying about how it would all play out for us.

"Lars, I know you intend to keep me by your side until you are ready for battle. But what will you do with me when the fighting starts? Where will I be?"

"I have not decided. You are an unexpected complication."

I wondered if he was thinking the same thing I was. That in another time and place, I might be treated as a prisoner and put in chains, or even killed.

What I had witnessed today did not make me feel sanguine.

"How long before you give birth?"

That startled me. "I'm four months pregnant."

He looked thoughtful. "So in the winter. I can take you home to my mother before then. Never fear. You will have help."

Holy crap.

I stared at him. "I'm going through déjà vu."

He raised an eyebrow.

I tried to explain. "You said this once before, I remember, when we were with the Romans."

His face looked blank. "What Romans?"

"Remember the banquet at Gareth's fortress that turned into a brawl? You were teasing me most of the night, until it became more enticing to beat the others silly. Then Cedric appeared and you left the fighting to defend me. I'll never forget that. You wrapped your arms around me so he could not pull me—*Oh My God.*"

I just realized. I had turned back time.

I could remember this part of our past, but Lars wouldn't.

It was true. It *had* happened. I remembered the words he spoke at that banquet, and the feel of his strong arms around me as if it were yesterday. But *he* wouldn't remember it. In turning back time, I had caused everyone's memory of the missing weeks to be erased.

And now I had blown it, big time.

He stared at me now like he was watching a vision take shape before his very eyes.

"I dreamed of this." His voice was hushed. "You vanished from my arms at Norland and reappeared at this very fortress. So that was real?"

I stared with my mouth open.

"Rowena, is this true? Did you give me some potion to make me forget?"

Oops. "No, not that. I…um…I kind of turned back time."

I saw several emotions play across his face. What settled there surprised me.

He burst out laughing.

"How in all of Valhalla did you do that?"

"It wasn't just me. I had help. And it was just a little bit of time, honest. Hardly worth mentioning." Perhaps I could leave it at that. Really, I wasn't in a position to betray that confidence.

There was a glimmer of a smile left on his face as he shook his head. "Hardly worth mentioning." He folded his arms. "And what else have you erased from my memory by turning back time? Were we lovers before, like I have also dreamed?"

"Oh not quite," I said truthfully. "Although…"

"Yes?"

I watched him now, watched him take off his armor, his belt and weapons. My eyes followed his sword to the floor.

"At the banquet, you said the gods were playing with us."

"And so they have been, by my mortal soul. They put you in my very bed. You have haunted my dreams at night for weeks."

His eyes bore into mine. I felt my breath catch, and my face flush. I looked down, away.

How did I feel about this man? It was more than just liking now. Not only did my mind respond to him. My body did, too.

I was so confused by all that had happened. No, I wouldn't think of Thane. I couldn't.

When I looked up, Lars was watching me.

"In my land, women can hold property. They can divorce their husbands."

I was baffled by this sudden change of subject.

"What are you getting at, Lars?"

He moved to the side of the bed and sat down. "You need to think about your future, Rowena. You have a choice now. You can live the life of a pampered Queen with Gareth or Thane in Land's End. Be tied to a castle like a brood mare. Or you can roam the world at my side and see a thousand different things with me. Each day a new adventure just waiting for us both to explore."

I couldn't help it. Excitement rose in my breast. This man took my breath away.

"I am a prince. Marrying me would not degrade you."

So here it was. He did want to marry me. Not just for the castle. I was no fool, though. He would have that with or without me, if he could defeat Cedric.

No, this was the *man* speaking, not the Viking Warlord.

And the man was reassuring me that I would not lose status by agreeing to be his wife.

Funny how he thought this important. I remembered that the word 'degradation' came from the Norman practice of forcing Saxon noblewomen to marry beneath their rank when they were widowed. It was seen as a despicable thing to do to a respectable woman.

I almost smiled. Nothing about this man would make me feel degraded.

"All men would want you for their bed. I don't deny I am the same. But there are many beautiful women in my land."

He paused to let the words sink in. It sat there in silence, the rest of the sentence he didn't say.

He didn't need to. Lars was not married. He had not chosen any of those women. His eyes watched mine to see that I got it, and he smiled in that knowledge.

"There is a wildness in you that calls to me, little bird. I never knew a woman could be so intrepid and quick witted. Hear me clearly, Rowena. I would never crush that which I so admire in you. I would not tie you down."

Now I gasped. This man was a master marketer. He seemed to know exactly what to say.

Maybe you wouldn't tie me down, but a baby would. Or would it? How did Viking women care for their young? Did they travel with them?

I got up from the bed with my mind focussed on the future.

His mother was still alive. I would need help. She would know how to birth a baby in this primitive world.

I groaned. But no! I was hoping to have the baby back in Arizona, in a hospital.

Lars cleared his throat. He looked vulnerable without his warrior trappings.

"Oh. You're waiting for my answer." Whoops. I hadn't planned to say that out loud. Why did I say it?

He shook his head.

"It is too soon for that. Not tonight, little bird. One day at a time, as you say. Tonight let me demonstrate why you should stay with me."

A tingle of desire shot through me. Not the desperate kind fueled by Cedric's depraved magic that made me feel so trapped. But the stirring of fire that can grow between a man and a woman who see only each other in a room full of people.

Memories of last night flooded my mind. For the first time, I was truly in awe of him.

I sat down on the bed to catch my breath.

Soundlessly, he approached me.

He wore only his tunic now. I could smell his musky male scent, like earth and hay. It was unique. His hand cupped my chin and raised my face to meet his eyes.

"Do you want me tonight, Rowena?"

It was painful to look at him. I tried to turn my head, but he prevented that. "Would it make a difference?"

"Answer me."

I closed my eyes. "Yes." I barely breathed it.

A sharp intake of air.

"My honest lady. How you honor me."

Here is what I have learned about men: when a man has you the second night, he knows you better. There is a confidence in him that makes him stronger and more self-assured.

I was coming to understand this strange Viking warrior. I had responded willingly to his lovemaking the night before. This time, he would make me surrender absolutely to the demands of his body. I knew this, and so did he. It was in his eyes.

Anticipation made me breathless.

Shall I describe the way he took command of our tryst? The arms that forced me back upon the bed, the knees that pushed apart my thighs, the shaft that entered me without help or hesitation, the eyes that watched me all the while his torso found its own solid rhythm to rock me.

The mouth that reached down to cover mine when I cried out...

Fire whipped through my loins, rushing me into euphoria. Delicious caramel flowed in my veins.

And then, too abruptly, I was brought back to the present.

I wanted to scream at him in frustration. *Stop moving.*

The stroking hadn't stopped. Perspiration dripped down his face onto my own, but he didn't stop.

"Not again," I murmured.

"Yes, again," he said firmly.

I groaned, begging for sleep. Instead, my wayward heart started to follow his rhythm and pound in response.

Tireless, relentless, gaining strength with each thrust forward, he rocked against me, controlling me like I was a wild mustang in need of a master.

A Saxon queen in need of a Warlord...

His eyes gleamed, his mouth was set in a triumphant smile. I grit my teeth and closed my eyes, refusing to look at him. My head thrashed from side to side as the need for release built in me. He reached for my hands and held them down with his own.

"You devil," I whispered.

He chuckled but did not stop. Over and over, he did not stop.

When at last I cried out his name, he laughed and closed his mouth over my own.

Lost, lost. I was lost to this man, who surged twice more and then fell on me.

Hours later. Or was it ten minutes?

I lay in his arms, deliciously weary.

"You have such control," I said.

He kissed my hair.

"Forgive me if one day I do not."

I felt a shiver then. Such an odd thing to say. Could he sense the future in some mystical way? Certainly, he had been convinced we would be together like this. I was truly bemused, but felt it best not to pursue this any further.

"How old are you, Lars?"

"Thirty-four."

I thought about that. He looked older. At first I had put his age at forty. But men aged early in this violent land. I grimaced. And if childbearing didn't kill the women, apparently the men did.

"Tell me something. Assuming you win this, what will you do when the battle is over? Will your people settle here and farm this land?"

"That is my plan. Most of the common men with me are farmers. That is why you see many of them carry axes instead of swords."

Ah. I understood this now. Axes were farm implements, readily available.

"Will you bring women over?"

"Yes, of course. Most of my men are married. A land is not civilized without women."

"I'm glad of that." It gave me hope that Land's End would have a future. Children would be born here again.

Wow. I needed to think about that. This could be the best solution to all our problems in Land's End. An invasion by the Vikings would bring families, children, and hope. A future for everyone.

Ironic, that an act of violent invasion could be our salvation.

That made me think of something else.

"Why are you not married?"

A pause. "I was. She died of a fever."

I felt awful. Why had I asked?

"I'm so sorry."

"Do not be. There were no children. It was long ago and not a love match."

I relaxed against him. I shouldn't be feeling this relief. It was dangerous.

He kissed my hair and then my cheek. "I have not been in love before now."

Several emotions hit me at once.

"Oh dear. That is so not good for either of us."

"You are wrong. It is most important for you that I love you. Your land is being invaded and you are its queen. Can you imagine what could be your fate?"

I lost it then. All the fears of the last two days, all I had seen today, the family I had lost and missed, Thane, Kendra—all this came tumbling over me.

Tears started slowly, then built quickly to a crescendo. I shot to a sitting position and sobbed uncontrollably.

"Rowena, no!" Lars sat beside me and tried to take me in his arms. "I am an accursed fool. Forgive me. Forgive me."

I couldn't stop. My body shook with violent tremors. And worse, they didn't have tissues in this world. What the hell was I going to use?

Lars handed me a square of linen. I didn't stop to look if it was clean or ask where he came up with it. Instead, I blew my nose like a little child.

He wrapped his long arms around me and gathered me to him. "No one will harm you. Believe me. I will not let them." He rocked me back and forth.

Slowly I calmed. My breath was coming in little gasps. I buried my face in his warm chest.

He started to sing, a slow lullaby in his native language. It was sweet and beautiful.

All the time, he rocked me and held me close.

"I try to act brave, but really I am so scared," I whispered finally.

"You are as brave as any man I know, and I have been a fool."

He woke me in the middle of the night.

I was lying on my side with one knee up. A hand delicately stroked the inside of my thighs.

He kissed my shoulder.

"Rowena, I am on fire. Let me have you."

The candles had burned down. It was very dark in the room. I felt him raise himself from the bed and softly roll me to my back. I could sense his head close to mine, his hair falling on my face and in that instant his mouth closed over mine.

I parted my legs. He gently forced his way in.

I let him rock me in this way until the switch kicked in and then I bucked against him like a fevered animal in the dark.

Chapter 12

When I next saw Lars, he was fully dressed. Light streamed in from the window. He walked into the room and threw something large on the bed.

"Here. I had the men collect some clothes for you. Some of these may fit."

I shot to a sitting position and attacked the sack.

"This is so great, Lars! I really need to keep that one dress fairly clean. It's expensive and the only one I have here."

He smiled and folded his arms across his chest.

"What is it about a woman and her gowns? Never are you more beautiful than when naked."

I shot a look at him. "You really don't want me wandering around here without clothes on."

He chuckled. "In this room, yes, always."

I pulled out a fine copper colored dress with gold thread shot through it. "Oh, this is pretty. Wonder if it will fit?"

I pulled it on over my head and then stood up.

Lars burst out laughing.

Oh dear. The front bodice laces wouldn't close by at least three inches.

"That gown would start a war among my own men."

"I can fix it. Honest. I just need to get some extra material to sew a false chemise into it."

He shook his head, amused. "Choose another for today."

He pulled a few more from the sack. A cream one fell on the bed.

"Try this," he said.

The dress he held was a dark emerald green. It was high-waisted and the sort of thing you would wear over a full-sleeved blouse. Unfortunately, there were no blouses in the pile, but the thing might do as a summer dress on its own.

The bodice was square and a little deep for my taste, but it was trimmed with ivory lace and very pretty.

I whipped off the copper dress and shimmied myself into this one.

"It fits! I can even do it up."

Lars nodded with satisfaction.

"I will find more for you. Word will get around."

I reluctantly met his eyes. "These were looted, weren't they."

He shrugged. "I pay a small amount to each man for his contribution."

Lars missed my point. While it was interesting that he would pay his men for 'donating' clothes, I was concerned about the poor women who had lost theirs.

But then I realized…these clothes had no owners. They had all died in an earlier war.

I shivered.

"Here is a shawl if you are cold."

He held something made of ivory wool.

"I'm not cold. I'm just—the women who wore these—"

He came forward immediately and took me in his arms.

"You are brave for a woman, Rowena, but you have a woman's heart. This pleases me very much."

I clung to his chest and felt better for it. In fact, it gave me confidence to ask a favor.

Of course, I should have waited until right after he had made love to me. Men are usually in a generous mood then.

But, as usual, I blundered forward.

"I have a favor to ask."

Lars gazed at me. One eyebrow raised.

"I want to get word to Kendra. She thinks I went through the portal to my world for just an hour and must be worried sick about me. It's been two days."

"Kendra is where?"

"Castle Sargon."

He nodded. "I can send a messenger."

"Will it be safe for him?" This was sort of like the wild west stage coach days, where messengers had to dash through Indian territory.

"It will be if I send him now. Our plans are not known."

"I would really appreciate that, Lars."

"I do not recommend that you invite her to join you here. It would not be safe."

I paused for a moment. "And speaking of safe, I have another request."

He frowned. I was pushing it.

"Teach me how to defend myself."

Now he smiled.

"That I will do gladly, woman."

Chapter 13

Lars left the room.

I took the time alone to contemplate my position here.

Lars planned to take Huel. If I stayed with him, he would spare my grandfather, and hopefully, any family that was left. I was thinking of my cousins, Jon and Richard.

What were the chances he could get through to Huel?

Cedric was strong and could produce a thousand ghost warriors. But Lars had surprise on his side. Could Cedric get back in time to save the castle?

He would be fighting invaders from the south *and* east at the same time, and if I knew Gareth, he would attack from the north, just when Cedric was at his weakest.

What would Thane do? Would he come to our defense?

Even as I thought it, I knew the answer.

He wouldn't. Not a chance. Not for Cedric. Not for Huel.

I tried to be pragmatic and leave my personal feelings aside.

What course of action could I take to save the most people? And especially, the people I cared about?

This assumed I could actually escape from here. It was unlikely. There wasn't a chance in hell I could steal a horse or go on foot with all these men watching me. My bracelet could only channel magic.

There was no magic around here.

Even if there were, where could I go?

Gareth would leave me back in the castle keep up north while war was raging.

Thane would force me to stay at Castle Sargon, a virtual prisoner for my own safety.

Cedric...I didn't know what Cedric would do. But I wanted to get back to Huel so I could learn more magic and maybe help our cause. Besides, I was a Huel. I should stand with the others.

Lars came back into the room with his hands full. He held a brace of daggers.

"These were mine when I was a boy," he said proudly. "This is how I learned to be a warrior. Now, I give them to you."

I sucked in air. They were about 14 inches long and not pretty. No delicate carving. No markings at all. Just deadly blades that meant business.

"Here is how you will wear them."

He picked up a belt with two scabbards attached. He swung the belt around my waist, buckled it, and separated the scabbards so they hung on each thigh angled out at the bottom. Then he placed a dagger in each.

"You pull from across like so." He stood in front of me and demonstrated. "I will give you lessons."

They were heavy on my hips.

"You already know how to hold a dagger. I saw you demonstrate that when we first met." He smiled in memory.

So the big Viking had a sense of humor. That particular attempt at self defense hadn't gone well for me. Regardless, I smiled and shrugged.

"I'm an animal doctor. Believe me, I know where to strike to inflict the most damage."

He barked a laugh and removed one dagger from the belt.

"Yes, little bird, I was lucky that day." He was teasing me. We both knew he would have easily disarmed me.

"One holds it with the blade facing up. You are shorter than most men. Shove it up, so the blade goes behind the ribcage." He demonstrated, striking through the air.

I nodded, knowing full well that I would never use them as long as I had my Derringer. But I wasn't about to reveal that to Lars.

No, even though Lars protected me and professed to love me, I couldn't show him my one ace in the hole. But I vowed to myself right then, that never, ever, would I use it on him.

"Be careful that you hold the blade firmly when you strike. Do not let it be knocked from your hand." He passed it to me. I held it in the approved way, and then Lars took a downward swipe at my hand. The dagger fell to the floor.

Oh dear. He hadn't even struck hard. I was going to have to work on that.

"Wear them when you ride. These are not ornamental, and that is good. Men will know by looking at these that you mean to use them." He nodded in satisfaction and retrieved the dagger from the floor. Then he returned the blade to its scabbard.

"Thank you." I was touched by this gift. He was giving me something he treasured.

"Lars, why do you call me little bird?"

He smiled. "Because you sing all the time. Little songs. You have a lovely lilting voice. And because you are like a rare and pretty green-eyed bird that flies away from me when I try to catch you in my arms." He was referring to those times when he tried to protect me from Cedric, and I had vanished.

He reached forward with one hand to pick up my hair. I watched it fall through his fingers.

"So beautiful," he murmured. "I have never seen this color before."

"They call it dark auburn. My mother had the same."

"It is odd," he said. The look in his eyes was something almost religious. "Most times when I look at you, my body throbs to lust. But other times, you are so beautiful it takes my breath away. I see you as a thing of splendor, too precious for any man to touch. It calms me just to feast my eyes on you."

My voice caught in my throat. This was the most stunning thing a man had ever said to me.

"M'lord?" It was Sven at the door.

"Yes?"

"We can't awaken Soren." He looked frightened.

Lars turned. "The fool drinks too much. I'll come."

"Let me go, too," I said earnestly. "I'm a healer.

He nodded. I followed him out the room.

Soren was lying on the floor against the wall in the great hall. It was a fact of life in these times. Only the very elite had the luxury of separate rooms. The rest of the people would sleep in the hall on the floor or in the corridors.

Soren hadn't moved from where he had fallen. Lars looked down and shook his head in disgust.

"Bring him to the back room," he ordered.

"Let me look first," I said.

I dropped down to my knees beside him. It was hard to get close, because of the smell. He had obviously vomited.

I took his pulse. It was steady, although slow.

"He's alive, thank God," I said, rising to my feet. "You can move him now."

Sven and three other young men lifted him by arms and legs and carried him down the corridor.

I rushed after them.

Lars pointed to the small room beside ours. *Good lord, did I just think 'ours?'*

They lay him on the floor and stood back, obviously waiting for me to do something.

I sighed and plunked down beside him again.

"It's probably alcohol poisoning." I slapped his face gently. "Soren! It's Rowena. Open your eyes if you can hear me." I slapped him twice again, harder this time.

His eyes opened wide. They fixed on me and started to glow. His right hand came up and closed on my wrist in a death grip.

"The magic woman," he said.

I gasped and tried to move back. He held me firm.

This wasn't Soren.

I could tell by the eyes that glowed bright blue. Eyes like Cedric's.

"Let her go, Soren," Lars said.

He didn't let me go.

Lars snorted in disgust.

"I will break your arm if needed." He moved forward.

"No!" I yelled. I put my left hand up to stop him. "Don't come any closer. Lars, remove the others from the room. Close the door."

He stared at me.

"Please," I said again.

"Out," he said to his men in his native tongue. "Close the door but stand by."

They were reluctant to leave. I could hear voices arguing. But I couldn't see their faces, because the eyes before me compelled me to focus on them.

The door closed with a bang.

"What is it?" Lars was impatient.

I swallowed hard. "This isn't Soren."

Lars cursed. "What do you mean?"

I jerked my head to the left to free myself of the compulsion, and as I did, the hand gripping my wrist pulled me down closer to his face.

"You set me free." The voice was low and harsh, the accent unfamiliar.

Lars growled.

"Stay back, Lars!" I cried.

The eyes glowed neon, like Cedric's.

"This is your consort, Witch Queen?"

"Yes. Don't hurt him," I pleaded in a language I couldn't name. "He protects me."

"As you wish."

"Rowena, what are you saying?"

The man released me suddenly. He vaulted up to his feet in one smooth unnatural action. He turned to Lars.

"He is your brother and a warlord," I explained rapidly in that strange language.

"Brother," he spoke to Lars, in English. It still sounded odd.

A slow smile spread across his face. He flexed his arms and turned back to me.

"This is a good body, very strong. I like it." He reached his arms up to the ceiling and stretched.

"Rowena?" Lars was just barely holding it in. He came over and held out his hands to help me up.

"I should have done that. How remiss of me," said the creature in Soren's body. "What did you say my name was, beautiful witch?"

I swallowed. "Soren. And mine is Rowena."

"Row-e-na," the creature mouthed. "Exquisite." His eyes continued to glow as they observed me. "I am feeling a man again. It feels good."

I instinctively backed away.

"So, Brother," the creature said in his own tongue. "This is your woman?"

Lars stared. "Have you gone mad, Soren?"

"It's not Soren," I murmured again.

"My apologies. I should speak your tongue. This is your woman, Brother?"

Lars looked dumb-struck. "Of course she is. You know that. Stay away from her or I will kill you."

The creature looked amused.

"So violent. I like you. This woman has magic. Did you know? It is all around her."

Hoo boy. This wasn't good. Only another supernatural creature could detect that, and one at least or a lot more powerful than Val or Cedric.

He turned to me then. "I honor you." He bowed from the waist.

"Why?" I was almost afraid to ask.

"You worked a spell that weakened the barrier between your world and the underworld. It set me free."

Crap.

This was the price. Val had said there would be a price for turning back time.

"What is your real name?" I asked in that foreign tongue that Lars couldn't understand.

"Some call me Baal," he said, never taking his eyes off me.

I almost fell then. Lars caught me as I wavered.

"You know me. How gratifying. You have been waiting for me."

His eerie blue eyes danced.

I remembered the words spoken at my Satanic wedding to Cedric. I had been drugged at the time, but even so I remembered that the name of Baal had been spoken and called to.

Something changed. The eyes no longer danced but fixed on me. "And I know you." His hand reached over to touch my hair.

My heart raced in my chest.

I shook my head.

"Soren, what are you playing at?" Lars growled.

"It's not Soren," I repeated. "Look at his eyes."

I backed up against Lars's chest. His big arm wrapped in front of me.

"What do you want?" Lars demanded.

Baal spoke in English.

"I want the woman. You can have this child. I want the next."

Chapter 14

Lars flung me to the floor and reached for his dagger. Baal raised his hand and Lars went flying into the far wall.

I screamed as he fell to the floor, limp. I ran across the room in a second, dropping to his side.

He was conscious, staring up at me in horror.

"What is that?" he whispered.

"A demon." I felt for his pulse. It was racing.

"Do not distress yourself, brother. We can share her." Baal's laugh was an eerie tinkle.

He turned back to me. "I think I shall stay in this body for now. It suits me and it gives me access to you."

Baal turned to leave the room by the back door. Lars was still slumped on the floor, paralysed.

I made a split second decision, putting all my strategic thinking to work. I rose to my feet and raced after Baal.

He was standing on the steps looking over the green hills when I reached his side.

"Baal, a word."

"For you, sweet witch, anything." He had a predatory smile.

I took a breath. Here goes nothing.

"I am thinking of strategy. You may have a more enjoyable time if you make Lars think you are not a demon, but rather his brother but with some new supernatural powers. Then he will invite you to be with him in his inner circle. He is a prince, as are you, in this body."

He stared at me. "Go on."

I tried to remain steady. My heart was beating frantically. "If it were me, I'd make a friend, rather than an enemy of Lars. For one thing, it will be more fun for you if you have friends. If you want enemies to fight, we have plenty to share."

A different kind of smile spread across his face this time. A considering smile. A not-quite-sure-I-believe-it smile.

"Why, aren't you amusing! Imagine, thinking of that. I think I shall do as you say. How do you suggest I correct the situation?"

"Simple. Why not erase his mind of the last few minutes. As long as you don't threaten me, he will accept you. Especially if I call you 'Soren' still."

There was intelligence behind those blue eyes. I could see the wheels turning.

"Clever witch. I know what you wish to accomplish. Do you really think it will protect you from me?"

I shook my head. "Of course not. If you decide to destroy me, I can do nothing. I don't have your sort of power."

He cocked his head. "You know I didn't mean that kind of protection."

My face flushed. I caught my breath. "Allow me a little female modesty. It is hard enough being in my position without having to discuss what awaits me."

He chuckled then. "Always, you surprise me with your words. This is most delightful. We shall have fun together, you and me."

He turned back to the room and swept a hand in front of him. "That is done. He will not remember."

"One more thing," I ventured. "Lars does not trust you alone with me."

"Nor should he." Soren twinkled.

"This could be inconvenient," I said cautiously. "You don't know our ways here. You might, at some time, want me to act as your guide. Is there any way you could relieve his mind on that issue?"

He looked at me

"You think of everything. Consider it done. Shall we return to my dear brother now?"

I followed him through the door, hoping like hell that I had done the right thing.

I had the next hour to myself for female ablutions. It was a relief to be in a room free of testosterone.

I was missing Kendra badly. She would head for Huel after receiving the message, I was sure. I just prayed she would be safe until I could get there myself.

Whatever happened over the course of the coming battle, I had to make sure we were together in the end.

And then there was Soren. Who knew what he had planned for us?

Oh crikey! That gave me a new thought. Was Baal the only one, or had I set others free by moving back time?

I had to get up the courage to ask him.

Lars returned later with Sven and Soren. We were having a midday meal in the adjacent back room. Eric and Karl joined us.

All the men dug into the food with gusto, except Soren. I expect the others took his silence for the effects of a hangover.

I watched him. He stood by the east window looking out upon the camps, deep in thought.

I fixed a plate with meat in a bun and brought it over to him. "Here. You must eat, Soren. Your new body demands it." I spoke softly so the others wouldn't hear.

"Why aren't you sweet!" he said, waking from his reverie. His blue eyes danced. "Brother, our lady is kind-hearted, did you know?"

"Of course I knew," said Lars. He turned back to talk with Eric.

I watched Soren try the bun. First he nibbled it tentatively. Then, as if remembering pleasure in eating, he took a big bite and chomped it enthusiastically.

I took a bite of my own and enjoyed it. His pleasure in so simple a function was contagious.

I decided it would be smart to know him better.

"Tell me how you came to choose Soren as your body."

He shrugged. His blue eyes fixed on me. "Easy. I sought the source of my release. That was you. And I looked for a soul close by that was already part way to hell. It is easy to appropriate the body of one so lost to evil."

"But—" I had better not say it.

He smiled. "I know what you are thinking."

I stopped thinking it immediately.

He laughed. "You are such fun, sweet witch. I think I shall stay on with my violent brother after this battle. And with you, of course, as you set me free."

This was my chance to ask the question.

"No, just me," was his response. "I expect that is good news for you."

I didn't know what to say.

"It is certainly good news for me," he said with satisfaction. I wondered what he meant by that.

Lars left us to consult with his guards, with instructions that I was not to leave the fortress without his brother.

At first I was flabbergasted. Then I shot a look over to Soren, who had a merry glint in his eye.

Damn and blast. He had taken me up on my impulsive offer and managed to plant the seed in Lars's mind. Exactly who else was he able to influence?

I didn't want to know.

Soren stayed at my side for most of the day, and what a surprising day it turned out to be. I was almost afraid to admit it to myself, and I certainly would never say it to Lars, but he was actually a lot of fun to have around.

The first thing we did was seek out his belongings. They were in a corner of the second room, the room to which he had been carried.

"Such an odd shield," Soren said, reaching down. "Have you ever seen such a thing?" He hefted up the round wooden shield with his left hand.

"Are they heavy?"

"Very. But I am gifted with great strength, it appears." His grin flashed. "Here. Try to lift this."

He put it on the ground first. Good thing. If I'd tried to take it from him, the darn thing probably would have fallen and broken my foot.

I tried with both hands to lift it by the edge. He brushed me aside.

"You slip your arm through the strap there and grab the hold." He demonstrated again, with his left arm. "Your forearm takes some of the weight of it."

I smiled and shook my head. "I can't even lift a broadsword beyond my knees."

Soren laughed. "No, you were made for other things, beautiful witch."

He reached for the sword with his other hand and hefted it easily. "This is good. Much better quality than I have known before."

"Flemish forged, I believe. Jory told me only the rich carry swords like these."

Soren's eyes dazzled me. "I chose this body well, Row-e-na." He pronounced each syllable as if testing his tongue. Then he nodded, satisfied. "Better to be a rich, powerful man than a poor one."

"Do you know how to fight with these?" I asked. Who knows what occupation this demon had held in an earlier life.

He shrugged. "I have wielded weapons. This body will be well-trained, I imagine. I will let it act from experience."

Now that was something I hadn't thought of. Was it like driving a car or riding a bike? Did your body automatically know how to respond on its own if you were a trained warrior?

The medical professional in me was keen to find out.

He belted on the scabbard and replaced the sword within it. The movement seemed natural to him.

More weapons were piled in the corner of the hall.

Soren lifted a huge axe with one hand, the kind with a curved blade.

"What is that for?" I pointed to the metal spike on the other side of the cutting edge.

"For stabbing through armor, I imagine," he said easily. "You strike with the spike side and rip." He demonstrated in air. "Then you kill."

I shivered and turned away.

Soren laughed. He deposited the axe where it had been.

"What shall we do now, Row-e-na?" His blue eyes sparkled. I could only imagine the mischief he could bring on us. Or on me.

I thought quickly. "Why don't I tell you the recent history of this land, so you will be well informed for the war council later."

He cocked his head. "Clever witch. That is indeed wise and useful. Shall we go outside and enjoy the sun?"

I hesitated. "Wait for a minute. I need something to draw on."

I raced back to Lars's bedroom. Yes! His drawing paper and charcoal were still on the small table. I sifted through the paper to find a blank piece.

"What is this?"

Rats. Soren had followed me back to the room and had spotted the drawings. I dashed to grab them, but he caught my wrist with his left hand.

His other hand went to lift the parchment. His eyes went wide.

"This is you," he said. His voice was hushed. He dropped my hand.

I felt the blood rush to my face.

"Brother is a master artist." He leafed through the drawings.

"Please don't tell anyone," I pleaded.

"Oh, I won't." His hands whipped through the pile of architectural drawings and came back to the top one. I could feel the heat radiating from his body, he stood so close.

"Find me a blank page and I'll draw you a map of the kingdoms of Land's End," I said. "Then you can know where we are and who we face in battle."

His eyes lifted to mine. He smiled. "Fair enough. I can wait to discover how good an artist Brother really is."

"Stop that," I scolded. "You're making me feel uncomfortable, and there's really no need for it."

He lifted one blond eyebrow.

I threw up my hands. "We were having such a good time, and then you go and spoil it all by threatening me."

His face twisted. Had I gone too far?

"I expect you to cower in fear, yet you scold me," he said slowly. "I am not accustomed to females who speak their minds. It is unexpected, but…refreshing. And somehow fitting for the witch who set me free."

He nodded at that. "So. Show me your world of Land's End."

Phew. One potential calamity avoided. Or at least, postponed. I sat down on the bed and started to draw.

Soren was easy to teach. He had a thirst for knowledge that pleased me inordinately. I gave him the family history of all the Saxon and Celt houses in Land's End and their holdings. I filled him in on the recent wars and his own Norman family history, as I knew it.

He was sharp, I'll give him that. It didn't take him long to pick up on the finer points.

"So you are indeed a queen, but not *their* queen. Or should I say, not *our* queen," he said. "In fact, you are a prisoner here."

I swallowed hard. "I walked into a trap. But you have to understand that I knew Lars quite well from before. I counted him a friend."

Soren stroked his chin. "And he has taken you for his own."

I felt a flush creep over me. "If you knew our history—"

"Then I would know he intended this from the start. Tis obvious, that goal of his, sweet witch. His reaction to me was most violent when I threatened you."

It was odd sitting next to Soren. His body odor was similar to Lars's, and I found it familiar and comforting, yet also disturbing in that very fact.

"Are we camped on your land?" he asked.

I nodded. "This is Huel. You can see why I didn't hesitate to ride here. Let me show you where my Grandfather's land ends and where the King's begins."

I drew maps to show the boundaries of Sargonia, Norland, and Huel, carefully positioning the main river Sargon and the rugged mountains and badlands to the north and east. I knew the cliffs off the west coast of Sargonia, and the fertile lands to the south of us, down to Port Town.

The only region I really had no experience of was that to the east of us. How far did it extend? I would have to ask Lars about that.

I told Soren what I knew of his homeland. It wasn't much. I assumed the landscape was similar to what I had learned in high school geography class of Scandinavia.

Time flew. We were still sitting on the bed, hours later, when he dropped the bomb.

"But you are not from here originally," he said finally.

I looked over in surprise. "How did you figure that out?"

He shrugged. An enigmatic smile creased his face.

I told him then about the curse of Land's End. How some cruel and ignorant men had burned a witch, who, when dying, cursed the land so that no female babies would be born for a generation. My generation.

Soren looked thoughtful. "So that is why you are the last."

This wasn't the reaction I expected.

"The last witch." He nodded with satisfaction.

"My mother was from here," I said. "She was the Earl of Huel's second daughter, as I explained. But she left for another land far away before I was born."

"I thought as much," Soren said.

"But really, how could you tell?"

Footsteps and men's voices were coming from the hall. He shot up from the bed. All his movements were swift and deliberate.

"You don't smell like the others of this world," he said, his arms reaching in a stretch for the sky. "You smell...of honey and fruit. And sweet, sweet magic." He held out a hand to me. "Shall we go meet the others?"

Chapter 15

After the evening meal—more mutton and bread, grumble—Lars excused himself to meet with new arrivals. Troops were pouring in from the east. Their leaders needed to be briefed.

Soren seemed restless. I suggested we look around outside. It was a beautiful evening, just perfect for a walk.

He brightened immediately. "Have no fears. You'll be safe with me," he said.

As if I hadn't figured that out. He was decked out in every weapon imaginable.

Still, it was marvelous to step out of the fortress and breathe fresh air. I was feeling cooped up again. Being a prisoner in an enemy war camp was a lot like being an upper class woman confined to a medieval castle. But better, actually. At least in the war camp, I got to go outside and see some action.

We left by the postern door, away from the great hall where Lars and the others were gathered.

I giggled. "We're like two children, sneaking out from under their mothers' skirts."

Soren's gaze flicked to me.

"My big brother would probably not approve of you leaving the fortress grounds. No matter. We shall have our brief excursion while he is otherwise occupied."

The hills out to the back of us were sparsely populated. Most of the men were camped in the east valley by the stream. A lone sentry stood on the ridge to the north of us.

"We'll stick to the perimeter of the camp. I'd prefer not to start a riot with you at the center."

I felt myself blush.

His icy blue eyes surveyed me. "Oh, I will keep you safe. But numbers might prove to overwhelm this mortal body. I would prefer to protect you without resorting to our, shall we say, otherworldly ways."

I looked him over. He was extremely broad-shouldered. His upper arms were thickly banded with muscles. My eyes drifted from his solid chest down to thighs like tree trunks.

I could not imagine a man better built for battle.

He watched me watching him. Then, almost as if he had read my mind, a slow smile crossed his face.

He shrugged. "Remember, I haven't tested this body yet in battle. I do not know its level of skill."

I gulped. "Were you planning to find out during this stroll of ours?"

"Not if I can help it." The smile had gone from his face.

Okay. So I learned something more about Soren. He was fearless, but not foolhardy.

He was also rather clever.

The sheep had made trails through the meadow. We followed the paths to the north, below the ridge. Of course, all animals were gone from these fields now. An army marches on its stomach, and Huel was like one big restaurant supplier. Rich fields provided plentiful feed for livestock. I didn't want to think about what had happened to those animals.

Soren was content to tramp through the grass. He seemed to be enjoying the last sun of the day and the quiet buzzing of insects. Every now and then he would stop and reach down to touch a stem of grass, or pick a wayward wild flower to sniff.

They were blue here and reminded me of the chicory that lined the dusty highways at home during summer months.

When we came to a drumlin, he paused. At first I thought he was going to race to the top. Instead, he turned away from it and looked west across the open fields, with his face to the sun.

"Do you know how long it has been since I have felt the sun and experienced this green earth?"

I shook my head. He didn't answer, and I didn't press it. His eyes were closed and his whole face relaxed.

"Is it this green in your homeland?"

"Not where I grew up," I said. "I come from a desert, the Sonoran desert, not far from the Mexican border. But still beautiful, with craggy red-rock mountains and buttes. I miss it."

First time I had admitted it. I actually missed the dry air and hot sun of the American Southwest. It rained too much in Land's End for my liking, and it had been especially wet these last few weeks. Of course, August was our wet month in Arizona, too.

After a few quiet minutes, Soren sighed. "Why humans long for heaven, I will never understand. There is no more beautiful place than earth."

He turned and resumed walking with purpose toward the war camp.

At the outmost edge, a training exercise was in progress. Soren seemed curious, so he gestured me to move forward with him and then to stay still by his side.

A sergeant, or whatever you called them in the Viking army, was trying to instruct a group of newbies in the skill of archery.

"They're dreng and he's a Lithsman." Soren pointed. "This should be fun."

Later, I was to find out that dreng were young warriors, and Lithsmen were mature professionals. We stood behind them, close enough to hear, but out of their sightline.

"Bloody stone me!" the big sergeant said. He looked like a wrestler with thick unruly greying hair. "Where in the lowest hell did that one go? Snorri, you are without a doubt the worst archer in the entire army. Ulf, did you see where that one went?"

"Half way up the hill to the left, Bard," Ulf answered. He was tall and unusually slender for a warrior.

"Half way—" The sergeant rubbed his gnarly face with his hand.

"Sorry, Cap. I'm a sailor. Didn't join the raids to be a sodding archer."

Bard put a thick arm around the younger man's shoulders. "The Saxon bastards have a shite-load more archers than we do. So the big boss told me and Ulf he needed more archers." He poked Snorri in the chest with a stubby finger. "Now, I'm telling *you* that you and these others are going to become archers. Do you understand?"

The young lad scrunched up his face. He didn't seem too bright. He wiped his nose on his sleeve and then scratched his crotch with his pull hand.

Bard pushed away in disgust.

"Ulf, did you see that? Did you bloody see that?" He snorted. "Make archers out of these clods. Next he'll be wanting them to do a bloody harvest dance."

Soren was doubled over in silent laughter. His hands were on his thighs and his whole body shook.

"Be careful!" I fussed about him. "You'll hurt yourself on your sword."

He straightened, sweeping his eyes over to me. Tears were running down his face.

"Sshhh…" he said.

I returned my gaze to the action. Things had revved up a bit.

"What did you say?" Bard yelled.

"Yes, Cap."

The sergeant glared about. "I didn't hear you."

"YES, CAP!" they shouted together.

"Better. Now, let's try this again. Notch goes on the string. Pull the string back to your cheek. Sight along the arrow about a hand span above the center of the target. Let the string roll off your fingers."

We heard a dozen bow strings snap.

My eyes whipped to the straw bales set about thirty paces down range.

Two arrows had hit the targets.

"Snorri, tell me one of those arrows is yours."

"One of those arrows is mine, Cap."

The tall man called Ulf crossed his arms, spit, and shook his head.

"Now tell the truth."

"Sorry, Cap," Snorri said.

The sergeant sighed long and loud then put his hand on the arm of the nearest man. "Give me your bow and an arrow."

We watched the exchange take place.

"Notch goes on the string to the bits of thread that mark the center. Arm extends as you draw the arrow back to your cheek." He drew the bow then held the string to his cheek without the slightest tremble. "You sight along the arrow at a point a hand span above the center of the target. Hold your breath as you let the string roll off your fingers." The string twanged. The arrow thudded deep into the center of the target.

He handed the bow back to its owner.

"Now, let's try it again, shall we?"

Everyone tensed.

"Draw. Aim. Release."

Twang-ang-ang.

All eyes followed the arrows.

"Better, Bard," Ulf said. "Eight in the targets."

"One of those is mine, Cap!" Snorri crowed.

"Will wonders never cease. Well, if you're all done marveling like ponsie-faced arses, let's go at it again."

Soren grabbed my wrist and gently coaxed me back. "The young lad over there has spotted us. See how he watches you. Let's make our retreat."

I let him guide me through the meadow out of earshot.

He was still chuckling. "Odin help my brother if this is the best we have to offer our enemies."

I said some words I was quick to regret. "I've seen your brother fight. He is formidable, believe me."

Soren met my eyes and twinkled. "Oh, I have no doubt of that, beautiful one. He would be dead by now if that were not so. In fact..."

He paused.

"I would like to see him in action. I have a mind to challenge him, just for fun."

"Oh Soren, don't!" I gasped. "You mustn't do that. He would have to meet you. You know the rules."

Bile rose in my throat. I guess it showed on my face.

He raised one eyebrow. Both hands went to his hips. "So you really do care about him, then? I know you have acted the part, which is a clever strategy in your position. But I did not know your true feelings."

His blue eyes bore into me.

"Fear not, Rowena. Your man is safe from me. I was testing, you might say."

I nearly stamped my feet.

"Soren, you are the very devil."

He laughed merrily. "Not quite, but close enough."

Chapter 16

Late that night, I remembered Soren's words.

Yes, I cared about Lars. But how much did I care?

I was afraid to think about that. He might be killed in the next few days, and there was nothing I could do about it. Fate had us all in her grasp.

Better to focus on the now.

We were lying together on the bed, wrapped in each other's arms.

I could tell Lars was preoccupied. I waited for him to speak.

"Rowena, do I hurt you?"

"You mean physically?" I was startled. It was such an unusual thing for a man to ask. "No."

He kissed my forehead. "I am astonished at the punishment women are able to take from us."

For some reason, a little sadness poked its way into my head. It spilled out in a peculiar way.

"Here I am living my very own fairy tale, except for one big difference."

I felt him squirm. "Tell me."

"The prince didn't wait for a priest before plundering me."

He stiffened. "No. I did not. Of course this will bother you."

I was quiet. It was hard to put my thoughts into words, but it seemed important to let Lars know that this passion we shared was not something I treated casually.

"In my land, I would not be in your bed like this. You would need to court me."

"Good that we are here then, for I could not have waited."

Oh dear. This wasn't the answer I was looking for. I needed to think. Quite against the mood, he chuckled.

"What?"

"When I was a young fellow, my uncle once said to me, "If you want a happy life, choose a wife who likes sex.""

"Oh." My turn to blush.

"The dilemma is, in most courtships, one does not have the opportunity to test out the wife before the ceremony. That is why I am so fortunate with you."

I rolled my eyes. "Meaning you got to test the pudding before you purchased it."

"Benefit of being a warlord."

I lifted my head. "There you go again, wrecking my fairy tale."

He laughed. "I love to tease you. It is so easy."

"But…what would you have done if I had not been to your liking?"

I should have known by the grin. Sometimes you just shouldn't ask some things.

"I would have passed you on to my brother."

I tried to whack him with my hand, but he grabbed it. "You wouldn't!"

He laughed again. "Of course I would have."

He moved like a wildcat then, grabbing my other arm and flipping me up onto his chest.

"Let me tell you how happy I am, Rowena. There is not a man alive who can keep me from marrying you. Not Gareth. Not Cedric. Not any man you have back in your land, as long as I can hold a sword. Do you understand me now?"

He pulled my head down to his and kissed me deeply.

I pushed away finally, fighting for air.

"Wow. I appreciate the sentiment, really I do. But, Lars, do you have to be so bloodthirsty?"

"You had a man in your land. What was he like?"

I thought about Steve and grimaced. "Point taken. He was a ruthless financial trader. Made millions."

"I do not know what that means, but I understand ruthless."

I rolled over on my back. "He used to shower me with jewels."

"Is this something you value?"

I took a moment to think. "They are beautiful, of course. And I love sparkly things. I suppose it is more the gesture. That a man would spend a lot of his wealth on you."

Lars grunted. "It is a way of fighting for you, if he can give you more than other men. We are not so different."

"I am beginning to see that." And I was. Men weren't so different in Land's End and America. They just used different weapons.

Lars stood up abruptly. He walked over to the corner of the room and picked up the saddlebags that lay there.

I loved to watch him move. For such a tall man, he had an exacting grace that reminded me of a big cat. I watched the muscles harden across his back as he swung the bags up across one shoulder. When he turned around, my eyes went to his chest, which looked almost carved into marble planes.

He balanced the bags on the bed and opened one flap. Then he dumped the contents on the bed.

I gasped. This was a pirate's treasure trove of jewelry.

"All that is mine, is yours," he said with determination. "Would your man at home say that?"

I sat up in a shot. My hands went automatically to lift the jewels.

"Pick one to wear now," he said.

"Oh no, Lars, I shouldn't." My hands sprung away. I was ashamed at how drawn I was to this treasure.

"I insist. I want everyone to see how I value you. Pick something or I will do so for you."

I let my hands sift through the thick chains of gold and silver. Some were so heavy, I couldn't imagine wearing them.

One necklace caught my eye.

It was a more delicate thing of gold, silver, and colored gemstones. Beautiful oval topaz, garnets, and amethysts the size of dimes winked at me. The necklace made a V, and then more gems dropped from the point in a line. I put it up to my neck.

"Let me fasten that," Lars said.

His hands tickled the back of my neck as he worked the clasp. I shivered.

"Stunning," he said. "Very like your bracelet."

"Thank you for this," I whispered.

He kissed the back of my neck. "I am pleased you like it. You cannot imagine how erotic this is to see you wearing my necklace and nothing else."

His hands reached around to cup my breasts. I heard him moan softly with contentment. "You will have much more as my bride."

I shook my head. "You probably don't want to do that."

"What do you mean?"

"Marry me. Haven't you heard? I'm hell on husbands."

He snorted. "Explain." Still, his hands kneaded my breasts.

"Cedric killed my first husband, Ivan. Come to think of it, he killed Sargon, too. Do yourself a favor, don't even think of marrying me before you go into this battle with him. It's the kiss of death."

"Humph. I am not superstitious."

He pulled me back down to the bed. We stayed cuddled like that for a few minutes in silence. Lars broke it with a strange comment. He had obviously been thinking about my world back home.

"So the men in your homeland still make war. But not all do. How do they express their aggression?"

"Through sport. Violent games. Although some just watch."

I could feel his warm breath on the back of my neck. "We are the ultimate predators. We hunt and fight for food, chattels, women."

I stiffened. "I see a condition of my staying."

I could feel him tense behind me. "Speak it."

"No *women*. Just me. Touch another, and you're dead."

"Ha!" he yelled. "My bird has talons." He laughed with joy.

He flipped me over on my back and sprang over me. "You have made me happier than I imagined possible."

Why had I said that? Even now, I am amazed that it came out so quickly and easily.

His eyes sparkled. "So, my lusty wench. Are you ready to receive your prince?"

Have you ever had a tickle fight dissolve into a sudden feast of lusty sex?

I had never seen him act playful before. None of the men in Land's End had been playful with me.

Thane was sweet and considerate, but always serious. Over the last few weeks, I discovered that Thane was not a man who took anything lightly.

Gareth treated me like I was a wonderful prize, to be enjoyed and cherished.

With Cedric, I was always drowning in a shadowy pool of lust.

But Lars…

He had me giggling and begging for mercy, and then the mercy he offered up was hard and slick.

His hands linked with mine and held them down on the bed. His tongue explored my neck, my breasts, my underarms…

"I am going to ravish my captured queen," he murmured. "Try to stop me."

I giggled and fought against his hands. Not an inch could I move them. He grinned widely, supremely confident of his own strength.

"So this is what Vikings do to poor, naïve virgins," I accused.

"Neither poor nor a virgin, wench. You are more luscious than ripe fruit. I think I shall consume you."

I groaned under his powerful body. I purred and yelled and egged him on like a back street tart—notice the food metaphors.

What a meal he had of me that night.

I sped him through appetizers and begged for the main course.

"Meat," I told him sternly. "I want meat on the bone."

He chuckled and gave me a serving I could hardly contain and will never forget.

He demanded seconds. I was all for it.

"Dessert," I whispered after. "Something sweet."

He groaned and said, "Wait until I digest this last bit."

I slapped him lightly. "What kind of a Viking Warlord are you? Finish the job."

He growled. "So this is how you plan to kill me, you clever Saxon queen."

He moved over me once more and used his tongue.

Gods above, I was a thoroughly ravished and compliant captive.

"Ask me for anything," I murmured. "I have no will left."

He chuckled again and kissed my shoulder.

"So you were wrong." Lars wrapped his long arm around me.

"What. I'm never wrong." Even then, I smiled.

"You said the gods had made a mistake when they put you in my bed those weeks ago. They did not. I should have taken you then."

"No. You had to earn me. The gods are funny that way."

What was happening to me? I was falling for this very primitive man—no, warrior. How could this be? I wasn't even sure he could read.

And yet here I was, prepared to leave my modern world to witness this invader from afar plunder these ancient lands. Ready to share my castle with a Viking Warlord who would be my captor. Correction, he already was my captor. How primitive is that?

And why did it feel so right?

It felt right because I had made a decision. Something Lars had said made all the difference.

He had called me a 'clever Saxon queen.'

This was my land. These were my people. I was the granddaughter of an Earl and the widow of a King.

Land's End was where I belonged, where my birthright was a given. I was second in line to my Grandfather's lands and castle. It was time for me to step up and accept my responsibility.

Seeing the invading army camp today had compelled a change in me. My presence here could make a difference.

I would not walk away for good as my mother had done. I would do everything in my power to protect this land and my people. I would do what was best for *them*, even if it meant eventually allying myself with this Viking Warlord.

"Are you nearly finished your strategy meetings?" I asked.

"Not yet." He was uncharacteristically short.

For some reason, that made me feel grumbly.

"Sargon used to include me in his war meetings. He sought my advice."

"Yes, but you were on his side, little bird."

That's right. I had to remember that Lars was my enemy.

"You think I would lead you astray?"

He kissed the back of my head. "I would be shocked if you did not."

So Lars didn't trust me. He loved me, but he didn't trust me. Good for him—he shouldn't. My first loyalty was to Grandfather. If I could prevent this invasion, I would.

Not that there was much hope of that.

I had to marvel at our strange relationship.

Three days remained. And then Lars would become a warrior once more. I had seen him fight before, bare-handed, when we had been with the Romans. I feared for him then, as I had watched, fascinated. He was quick as a panther, extremely skilled, and very, very violent.

Everywhere around us, men were preparing for battle.

What would happen then?

"Lars, I'm frightened."

He wrapped his arms around me tighter.

"Tell me."

"You go to war in three days. What will happen to us?" I started to shake.

Lars stroked my breast. "Rowena, I have spent my entire life working up to this battle. The gods have prepared me well, and in their cunning way, have provided me with one final inducement. Can you guess?"

I shook my head.

"With you as my reward, I cannot fail to win this battle."

What do you say when a man tells you that?

He kissed my hair. "You will never lose me now. You have my heart forever."

Lars fell asleep quickly. I lay awake, fighting down panic, my thoughts centered on one person—Kendra. Where was she now? And how could I ensure her safety during the violent days to come?

PART 2: Kendra's Story

Chapter 17

So here I am, writing in a frigging journal, like I promised Row I would do if we got separated.

Which just goes to show, you should never promise to do things with the thought that—what the hell—who cares? Like *that's* ever going to happen.

Again.

Row claimed that writing would keep me focused and give me something to do instead of panicking.

Well, I have news for her. She was wrong. I can write and panic like a pro simultaneously.

Row had been gone for a full day and I was frantic. A measly little one hour trip home to Phoenix had turned into 24 hours of who knows where she was.

This wasn't like her. Something had gone wrong. She would never stay in Arizona and not tell me. And she would always send me a message somehow, if she were still here in Land's End.

I wanted to put my head out the castle window and howl.

No doubt about it, I couldn't wait any longer. She might be in real danger. Thane and Logan wouldn't be back until tomorrow. I needed to act fast, before they could stop me.

There was only one thing to do. I had to retrace her steps.

Ten minutes later, I was in the stables, saddling Blacky. I know. Very original. But black goes with my Goth gear. And yes, she is black.

Since Logan was up north, no one would wonder where I had gone. Row and I were always taking the horses out for rides.

Only difference today is I was alone and in disguise. Meaning black tunic, leggings, leather boots, Goth armbands, and a black fanny pack loaded with travel essentials.

Alfred the farrier raised an eyebrow.

"Riding alone today, so I decided to dress like a boy," I said.

He nodded and helped me to mount.

"That's clever. Don't wander too far."

Men were working in the castle courtyard, like always. Ducks and geese wandered about in little groups, making a racket.

I walked Blacky through the huge iron gates, nonchalant-like. Then I ran her like the devil when we got out of sight.

At least it wasn't raining. The last few weeks had been stormy and major dreary. The mud had dried, thank God. You don't think about it much when you live in a city full of asphalt, but these dirt roads turned to mud pretty quick in a downpour.

As soon as I could, I turned Blacky off the main road and we followed a path through the forest.

I knew this path. We had walked it many times to get the time portal. Actually, it wasn't a time portal, to be exact. More like an alternate world portal.

Would it be open now?

I dismounted from Blacky in the small clearing and tied her to a tree. Then I stepped over to the path along the edge of the ridge that led to the split oak.

Everything looked normal. In other words, very green. I'm not much on green. I'm a desert girl. Forests are not my thing. All sorts of scary, creepy crawly things live in forests.

I looked down. Her magic bracelet wasn't on the ground. That could mean a lot of things.

Row couldn't take it off herself. It was, like, welded on with magic. But I knew, before, it had automatically fallen off the second she entered the portal, because it didn't like to leave this world.

I know. Sounds crazy, even to me. A lot of things in this world defied logic.

There was no bracelet on the ground here. That could mean she had already come back through the wall and picked it up.

Or someone else had. That was the most likely explanation. Row had gone through the wall and someone else had come along and found the bracelet.

And then I had a chilling thought. There was another possibility. What if she never made it to the portal? What if she had been abducted before she even got here?

I heard nothing, I swear. It was just a feeling. Someone or something was standing behind me. I moved my hand casually to grip the dagger at my waist, and turned.

Val and a big black wolf stood there.

Loki broke from Val's side and lunged at me. My arms swept down to hug the black furry beastie.

"Loki! And Val." I breathed out. "That's a relief. I didn't hear you."

Of course I didn't. He would have used magic to appear there.

"Greetings little Kendra. Her animal sought me out. She is not back?"

I straightened up. Loki leaned against me, snuggling. Amazing that Val knew Row was missing. Perhaps Loki had told him in some kind of wolf-talk, or perhaps they shared a bond like Row and Cedric did?

I shook my head. "I'm not even sure she got this far."

"She did," he said. "The wall was breached. We shall have to go through it to discover if she is still there." He reached down to stroke Loki. "Our animal friend here will track her."

I tilted my head. "I'm game. I had planned to do just that."

Val smiled then. "I know, little princess. I know."

Princess? How could I be a princess? Row was still Queen, as left over from her marriage to Sargon. I used to kid her about being the old 'dowager.' I was her cousin here, but that didn't make me a princess, did it?

What exactly did you call the granddaughter of an Earl anyway?

Val laughed then. "No, you're not a princess—it is a term of endearment. You are a Lady. But you certainly aren't dressed as one now." He tched-tched.

Val himself was dressed for the stage. When I first met him a few weeks ago, he had shimmered like the walls of his crystal cave. Right now, he was in plain clothes, if you took that to mean burgundy doublet, white hose, knee high boots, and a wondrous sweep of cape that is. There was lace at his cuffs and throat, but not a rhinestone in sight, thank God.

I wondered how he would fare in the scorching heat of Arizona.

"Shall we?" Val waved his arm at the place beside the split oak where the portal should be.

I gulped.

"Sure," I said. "I'll go first." Never show a weakness is my motto. At least until I throw up.

But I took up the challenge. With a fearless grin, I turned and strode through the portal.

It swallowed me up whole and spit me out the other side.

"Shit," I mumbled, tumbling forward on my hands and knees. The room was spinning like it always did, and bile rose up my throat.

As the nausea subsided, Val and Loki appeared before me. Loki stuck his face up close and licked my mouth and nose.

"Ick."

He wagged his tail and tried to flop into my lap.

"Let me get up, Loki."

He sat down with a thump.

I pushed him off and looked around. The classroom was empty, as I figured it would be.

"What is this place?" Val asked.

"This is Row's classroom," I explained, pushing myself up. "It's part of a large school for higher learning. You know Row is a teacher, right? She teaches animal medicine. The room is empty now because we don't have classes in the summer."

"Why ever not?"

Good question. I paused to think. "I think in the olden days young people were needed back on the farms to bring in the crops. Now, we use the summer to work in order to earn money to pay for school."

Loki had his nose down to the floor, sniffing. He walked straight to the window, where he snuffled around in a four foot radius, whining. Then he sniffed his way back to the wall we had just walked through. He sat down facing it and waited.

I sighed. "Looks like Row made it this far, then something made her turn back. She never got beyond the classroom."

This sucked. But it had to be so. Loki would never give up the trail. Row was definitely not still here.

Val had walked forward and was touching everything he could reach.

"What a strange world," he said. "The colors are all wrong."

"What do you mean?" I asked. I wanted to skip. It felt so good to be back here!

"It's rather faded, isn't it," Val said, almost sadly. "Like it's been left out in the sun too long. Come, Loki." He reached down to pet the wolfie.

Loki wasn't alarmed at all by our new surroundings. Of course, he had been in Arizona before.

It's true that colors in Land's End were more intense. I had to smile. "It has, Val. Wait until you see our sun."

I dragged him to the window. There, I worked the stick thingy to open the Venetian blinds.

"Oh!" Val exclaimed. "It's shiny!"

He had both hands on the windowsill and was gazing out to the parking lot. Sunlight bounced off the car windshields.

"I take back my words. It's dazzling here!"

"You won't believe how hot it is. This is summer here, but we get it hotter than almost any other place on the planet."

"What do you call this land again?"

"Arizona. It's across the ocean from Land's End, to the west." Well, not exactly, but sort of. It was also across a dimension of time, but I didn't have the science to describe that.

"What do you call that funny red animal moving there?"

I giggled. "That's a car, Val. It's a machine to move people."

"Amazing. Rowena told me about those. Can we try one?"

I thought about it. Since Row wasn't here, I really didn't have an excuse for staying. Yet it seemed a shame not to show Val some of our modern world. Surely we could spend an hour or so here. It would only delay the search for her a little while.

Row would understand. In fact, I could practically hear her insisting. Except for the fact that she didn't know I was even looking for her. Best not to think about what she would say about that.

But I had an idea.

I nodded. "I'll call Janet and see if she can pick us up in her car." I reached for the cell phone in my fanny pack.

"Who is Janet?" Val asked. He was running his hand up and down the glass of the window.

"Row's cousin. Our cousin," I corrected quickly. Jeesh, I had to remember that. I was supposed to be Row's cousin from back home. That gave me a place and protection in Land's End. "Janet's great. You'll like her."

I congratulated myself for putting her in my address book last time we were here. Hopefully, she'd have her own cell phone handy and some time available.

She answered on the second ring.

"Janet! It's Kendra. I'm in Phoenix. Are you free by any chance?"

"Are you at the school?" She sounded excited. "I'll be there in ten minutes!"

I had a sudden thought. "Oh, and Janet? Wear a maxi-dress if you have one."

A pause. "Now you've got me intrigued. Make it fifteen."

I clicked off.

Val was watching me with bug-eyes.

"May I see that?" He reached for the phone.

I explained how to use it.

"No wonder you don't use magic here. You don't need it," he said sadly.

Chapter 18

So everything was set. Val would get his little tour of the modern world, and I would get my coffee and drugstore essentials.

There was just one problem.

"Loki, I'm not sure what to do about you." He circled in front of me, panting in the heat. This was summer holidays, so they hadn't bothered to air condition the classroom.

I turned to Val, who was feeling the white board with his palm.

"Val, I'm worried about Loki being mistaken for a wild beast here. We don't have wolves in the city. Can you do something?"

Val turned around absent-mindedly and waved a hand. *Pop.* Loki shrunk to a quarter of his size.

"Oh! You're so cute!" Our fearsome wolfie was now the size of an adorable puppy. I reached down to pick him up.

He wiggled and waggled in my arms and licked my face.

"But Val, I thought magic didn't work in this world?"

Val shrugged. "Whoever told you that?"

To be honest, I couldn't remember. Maybe we just thought it didn't work because we'd never met anyone here who knew real magic.

Maybe it wasn't a lack of magic, but a lack of knowledgeable practitioners?

I needed to talk to Row about this.

In the meantime, it was time to roll if we were going to meet up with Janet at the college entrance.

With Loki still in my arms, I signalled for Val to follow me.

We clambered along the long hallways of C wing, and then to the corridor that opened to the main entrance. I heard cleaning staff talking in a foreign language out of sight, but otherwise, no one was around.

In a few weeks, the place would be hopping though. This window of summer opportunity was small but perfect.

I pushed open the door. Val followed me into the blazing Arizona sun.

"Oooo," he exclaimed. "This is magnificent!"

Too damned hot, in my opinion. I liked winter in Arizona best. Maybe I'd become acclimatized to the cooler temperatures in Land's End. Which led me to another concern.

"Will you be too hot?" I said.

Brown curls bounced as he shook his head. "I can regulate my body temperature."

Wish I were a wizard, I muttered to myself.

"What are these fluffy bushes over here?"

"Don't touch that!" I yelled.

Too late.

"Ouch!" Val yelped and jumped back. "It bites. Nasty thing."

He raised a hand and *ZAP!* The plant collapsed into ashes.

I sighed. Then I looked around furtively to make sure nobody saw that.

"Okay, you probably shouldn't go zapping things here."

Val was staring down at his hand. "But think of poor Loki! That evil animal could injure our poor companion."

"That was a plant, actually. A teddy-bear cactus," I said. "They only look fluffy. Let me look at your hand."

Yup. Lots of icky thorns.

"Do you want me to pull them out, or can you take care of it?"

He sniffed. "I can do it. But really, Kendra. Plants shouldn't bite. It's not natural."

"Maybe you should just ask me before you touch anything outside. For instance, scorpions. You don't want to go touching scorpions." Nor spiders or snakes, but I figured he'd know that already.

He held his head up high.

"I shall heed you and avoid these scorpions and biting plants. But truly, Kendra. This does not seem like a very nice place."

I really hoped Janet would show up soon.

We didn't have to wait long.

Janet rushed along the sidewalk. I had to smile. She wore a long halter maxi-dress that sparkled in the sun. It shimmered in vibrant jewel colors of fuchsia, purple, and sapphire blue, like stained glass.

I gave a sigh of relief. Good for Janet. Val might not understand the concept of a respectable woman in shorts or mini-skirt, and I wanted him to like her.

Her gorgeous dark hair swung down her back, and she wore the prettiest jeweled sandals. She looked just like a runway model, which she had been until a few years ago. You could tell Row and Janet were related, but where Row was all Playboy curves, Janet was Vogue magazine.

"Kendra!" She nearly knocked me over with her hug. "Is Row here, too?"

"Nope," I said. "My turn. But I brought a friend along I want you to meet."

I turned to introduce Val. Val?

"Earth to Val," I said, poking him in the ribs.

He was a man entranced. Can a wizard be entranced? I thought they were above mere male emotions, but I guess Val had never seen anyone like Janet before.

He snapped out of it and swept into a low bow.

"A goddess! Kendra, you didn't warn me. Beautiful deity, I am honored to be in your presence."

"Oh please." Janet's laugh tinkled like silver bells. "I'm no more goddess than Rowena is. But I'm delighted to meet you. Valentine, isn't it?"

Val straightened. "You know of me?" He sounded delighted.

She nodded. "Row told me all about you. You love fabrics and fashion just as I do. I feel as if we are already friends."

She smiled brightly. That's when I thought Val might melt into a puddle.

"Are you here for long?" she asked.

I shook my head. Row wasn't here, so I really had no excuse to stay. "Just an hour or so. Thanks for coming, Janet. I need to hit a drugstore, but I thought we could show Val some sights on the way."

"Forgive my forward nature, Lady Janet. But where did your acquire this magnificent gown?"

"Nordstrom. It's a Vera Wang. Would you like me to take you there?"

The skies might have come down from the heavens and offered him the stars. He bowed again, shorter and more clipped.

"It would be the epitome of my poor life for me to accompany you to such a place, dear lady."

Janet smiled sweetly. "I can see why Row is so fond of you, Val. Okay, well, I brought the Outback so we can take everyone easily.

Kendra, they have a drugstore at Scottsdale Fashion Center, so we can do that at the same time."

"And get coffee," I added.

"God forbid we forget coffee," she agreed. "How adorable! Is this a puppy of Loki's?" She reached down to pet him.

"Kind of," I said. "One of the pack, for sure." So it wasn't a total lie. But I didn't know if Val wanted his magic to be known. Wizards are funny that way.

Loki squirmed happily at her touch.

Janet turned her gaze to us. "So what do you want to do first?"

Val cleared his throat. "Could we possible ride in one of those magical animals?"

"He means your car, Janet," I said.

She smiled. "Of course. I parked over here. Please come."

She turned to lead the way. Val scooted up beside her. I could see him engage her in conversation, but I couldn't quite here everything.

Loki struggled to get down from my arms. I let him scamper around, sniffing along the pathway to the parking lot. So many VIS's—Very Important Smells.

Janet's car had four doors, which was handy. She was a savvy kid; she walked around to open the passenger door for Val, so he wouldn't get bamboozled by the strange handles.

"You'll need to put on the seatbelt." She instructed him how.

"Lady Janet, this animal must travel very fast to warrant such harnessing."

I grinned. He was right about that. Janet had a thing for speed.

Loki scampered happily into the back seat. I opened the window for him so he could stick his head out.

Janet got herself in and adjusted, then switched on the ignition.

Both of Val's hands flung to the dashboard. "Kendra, you didn't warn me. This beast roars!"

Janet giggled. She shifted the car into drive. Off we sped through the empty parking lot.

Val was wide-eyed. "Truly magical," he said happily.

"Actually, it's engineering. My dad is an engineer," she explained.

"You are fortunate to have such a powerful mage for a father." Val nodded his head in respect.

"Oh no," she started to explain.

"Forget it, Janet," I said. "Val, we have lots of engineers here, but no mages. You'll see lots of cars like this on the road. Different shapes and colors. They aren't animals, but they do eat gas."

I smirked at the pun.

"Where to first, Kendra?"

I considered. "Are you hungry, Val? We could go to a drive-through."

Val looked back at me. "I would be honored to partake of your local faire for luncheon. What say you, Lady Janet?"

Her dancing eyes caught mine in the rear view mirror. "McFood, Kendra?"

"Sure," I said. "Do you have any cash on you? I need to go to a bank machine."

"No problem," she said. "My treat."

She whirled us through the streets of Phoenix.

"Wooo," said Val, when we passed some cars in an intersection. Then, "Eeep," when another car pulled in front of us.

Gasp. "That animal is out of control."

"Here, play with this radio," Janet coaxed to distract him.

She pointed to buttons. Val pushed one and a voice came blaring over the speakers. He snatched back his finger.

"This beast talks our language," he muttered, enthralled.

Loki kept his head out the window like a pro. That was the nice thing about dogs and wolves. They didn't question what things were, or why. They just enjoyed the moment.

I needed to be more like that.

Janet pulled a right turn into the drive-through lane and pulled up to the speaker. "Normally, we'd go inside, but I don't think Loki would be welcome."

Val stared at the speaker box. "We could all fit in there?"

I grinned. "Sure. It's like the Tardis."

Now Janet laughed. "Kendra, that isn't fair. Val, pay her no mind."

Janet ordered three quarter pounders with cheese meals.

"Don't forget a hamburger for our puppy," I said.

She laughed and added a hamburger.

The car moved forward to the collection window. A young girl poked her head out. Money exchange hands, and at the next window, Janet was handed a bag of hamburgers and French fries.

Loki was standing up now with his head through the gap in the two front seats, very interested.

Janet pulled out of the drive-through lane and into a parking space. She stopped the car and reached into the bag.

"Here, Val. This is a hamburger. And here are some French fries."

Val was clearly astonished. "How do they cook them so fast, Lady Janet? You just gave the command. Surely it is magic."

I grinned. "Who says we don't have magic in America? Wait 'til you taste it all." True, too. There's something scarily addictive about that ground meat and special sauce.

She handed me the same, and then unwrapped a hamburger for Loki.

I took it from her and put it on the back seat. Loki was on it in a flash.

"Loki approves," I said.

Val took a bite of the hamburger. Janet was watching him intensely.

"Oh! This is very tasty," he said. He finished it before Janet had taken one bite. The French fries were also a hit.

"I must learn how to make these," he said as he munched. "From potatoes, you say?"

I nodded. "We use vegetable oil here, but you'd probably cook them in lard."

A few minutes later, we had finished every bite of food. Loki had eaten half my French fries as well as his own hamburger. Janet took all the wadded up wrappers and put them in the paper bag.

"I'll drive over to the garbage can, and you can pop this in, Kendra."

She backed out of the parking spot and shifted the car into drive.

A late model mustang whipped around the corner of the building, just as a little boy ran out of the restaurant. He bolted across the parking lot.

Someone yelled, the mustang screeched, the driver slammed on the brakes. But it was not soon enough.

The two collided.

Chapter 19

Someone gasped. A woman screamed.

The boy flew off the bumper, lifting into the air like a weightless dummy.

Time held still for one second as we all watched in horror.

He landed hard on the pavement, twitched, and then fell still.

A woman continued to scream and scream.

Val was out of the car before I could move. He dashed to the boy's side.

I glanced at Janet. Her hands covered her face.

I threw open the car door and raced to Val's side. He was on his knees beside the boy. His right hand hovered about 10 inches above the body. He was running it slowly up and down the length of the body, chanting in a language I didn't know.

A woman with long black hair fell to her knees on the other side of the boy. She moaned and rocked back in forth.

The driver was out of the car now, a young guy about my age.

"I didn't mean to!" he yelled hysterically. "I didn't mean to!"

It was horrible. Someone else left the car and grabbed the driver's arm to keep him back.

I could hear Val clearly now. It was almost as if he was in a spiritual trance. His eyes were closed and he seemed not to notice the crowd gathering around us.

What I am about to recount is something I would never have believed if I hadn't seen it.

The air above the boy seemed to glow. It reminded me of the way the portal gleams just before you walk through it.

There was blood behind the boy's head. At first, it had been spilling from a split in his skull, into an ever-growing dark red puddle. Now the film reversed. I watched as the puddle decreased in size and the red finally disappeared from the pavement.

A leg that had been shattered and twisted, unwound and straightened of its own accord.

Arms moved from their awkward positions, jerking into place.

The boy opened his eyes. They were dark brown, and they darted around.

"Ouch," he said. One hand reached up to stroke his forehead. "Mommy?"

"I'm here," she cried. She started to sob.

The glowing subsided. I watched it fade, then dissipate.

My eyes shot to Val. He was still on his knees, smiling gently. One hand reached forward to pat the boy on his shoulder.

"You will feel a little woozy, but then quite well after a short while."

The boy stared at him, wide-eyed.

"Val, what did you do?"

"I couldn't let the poor lad die," he said, rising to his feet. "Not when it was within my means to save him."

The mother lifted her head. Her brown eyes were wide with relief and worship. "You're a saint," she whispered. She made the sign of the cross.

Val shook his head. "No, no, dear lady. I am a simple mage, is all."

Adults in the parking lot were silent and still. A group of young kids stood on the sidewalk. They looked about preteen age and had seen the whole thing.

They were all chattering and pointing. I was getting an uneasy feeling.

"He must be a superhero!" one of the girls cried out.

Bugger.

"No really!" said the original girl. "Look at his cape."

They started to creep forward. Then the cell phones came out.

Janet was at my side now. "Oh no," she groaned. "They're taking photos."

"What's a superhero?" Val asked.

He looked immaculate, of course. No blood...not a spot of dirt on him. No one would ever believe that he had just been down on his knees on the filthy pavement resurrecting a dead body.

Except a whole gang of strangers had seen him do just that.

"It's Superman," said one boy. He looked star-struck.

"No it's not," countered another. "He died."

"Then who is it?"

"He doesn't look like any of them. Must be a new guy."

"I know! I know! Look at the cape. And the weird clothes like in Robin Hood."

"It's Robin Hood?"

"Nah. Robin Hood always wears green."

Everyone looked, of course. Val was wearing maroon; a very medieval-looking maroon doublet and cape.

Then one older boy gasped.

"It's...MEDIEVAL MAN!"

Startled cries went up from the crowd.

Every cell phone was clicking photos now. Before long, Facebook would be loaded with pictures.

I said a really bad word. But this was serious. Val, my medieval wizard friend, mistaken for a modern day superhero. Performing miracles right on the streets of Scottsdale. In a fast food parking lot, no less. Could this get any loonier?

People had been watching from the restaurant window. They poured out of the place now.

"What are they doing?" Val asked.

Then he seemed to get it. He was a celebrity! He whooshed the cape back and stuck out his chest, placing his hands on his hips.

I groaned. He looked just like Superman in that pose.

He smiled and waved at the cameras.

"Val, this isn't a good idea," I said.

"Why? Are those little boxes dangerous?"

It took me a moment to realize he was referring to the cell phones.

In the distance, I could hear sirens.

Shit! How could we explain Val?

"Janet, I think we better get out of here before the cops come."

Janet was staring at Val with reverence. She put a hand on his arm. "Are you sure the boy will be okay?"

I glanced over. He was sitting up now, with his mother's arms around him.

Val nodded. "He is as he was."

"Then we must leave. His people will take care of him."

Val smiled. "My work is done. I am happy to be of use."

We rushed him back to the car. Some kids followed, still snapping pictures. In that moment, I started to hate cell phones.

Janet put the car in gear, and drove us away in a hurry. A cautious hurry.

Val was another thing. It was hard to get him to shut up.

"Kendra, you can't imagine how satisfying that was. All this time, I was thinking how useless a mage is in this world, with nothing to do." His voice held a happy note.

"You did a good thing back there," I said with feeling.

"It was nothing. Truly, it did as much for me as for him."

Sort of like volunteer work, I thought. And helping animals, like Row does. These things just make you feel good.

"It has been a long time since I have seen children." His voice was wistful.

"You like children, Val?" Janet asked.

"Oh yes. They are magic for one's soul. Just live in a world that has none, and you will find out."

The car grew quiet. It was almost a relief to sit back and feel the adrenalin drain from my body. Would I ever get the sight of that poor boy landing on the pavement out of my head? I sighed. At least the story had a happy ending.

"Funny thing about today," I said finally. "If we hadn't made this trip through the wall, you wouldn't have saved that little boy, Val."

He would have died, for sure.

"Tis true, Kendra. I had not thought of that." His voice was quiet.

"So we did some good today. Row will be pleased." Even if we hadn't managed to find her here.

When would I be able to tell her all that had happened?

I watched the other cars go by. Loki cuddled onto my lap and lay his head down. My hand reached to stroke him automatically.

"Where to now?" Janet asked me. "Scottsdale Fashion Square?"

"Drop me off at the mall entrance, and I can meet you in Nordstrom, or wherever. I can take Loki. I won't be long."

There was a pause. "Loki?"

Whoops—caught! "Yeah, about that. You can explain that one, Val."

Chapter 20

Twenty minutes later, I had made it to the drug store and finished my business there.

Next, I stood in line at a takeout coffee kiosk. Thought about taking a brew back for Val, but then decided it would be too tricky with Loki in my arms. Besides, it would be way more fun to take Val to Starbucks itself. Watch him deal with the espresso makers and the tattooed baristas.

"That's a cute puppy!" exclaimed the woman behind me in line. "What kind is it?"

Loki preened with the attention. I had to think quickly.

"He's a miniature Wolfie-poo," I explained. "Twelve weeks old."

"Is that a new breed?" We had a small crowd around us now.

"Where did you get it? I have to have one!"

"You can only get them in Canada," I said quickly. Why Canada? Why did I think of that?

"Oh, are you Canadian? I have a cousin in Toronto." She gave a name.

I didn't know the cousin.

No shit.

"They have lots of wolves and bears in Canada," someone said knowingly. "But I didn't know they were breeding them with poodles."

"Maybe they're good in the cold," another voice piped up.

Holy Freaking A-mazing.

Hands reached out to pet him. Loki wiggled adorably in my arms. Probably, I could have sold him right there for mega-bucks.

Not that I could use those dollars for anything back in Land's End.

Time to mush—that's Canadian sled dog talk.

I nursed my coffee all the way back to Nordstrom, carrying the pup under one arm. I dumped the empty cup into a recycle bin and went in search of Janet.

It was easy.

I found them—where else?—in the couture evening wear department.

Janet was modeling slinky gowns, and an audience had formed.

"This is perfection." The sales clerk clapped her hands together. "That dress is made for you."

"Actually, it sort of was," Janet explained softly. "I know the designer."

I rolled my eyes. Only Janet could say that and still sound modest.

Meanwhile, Val was giving dress advice to a bunch of girls my age.

"Whatever are you wearing?" He waggled a finger at one in shorts and tank top, and his head moved like a bobble-head doll. "Do you *want* to be taken for a scullery maid? No, no, no."

He gestured to Janet, who had paused in a three way mirror to view the dazzling gown from all angles.

"Now observe Lady Janet. Always wear long, my dear young lasses. See how the gown drapes across the body, accentuating the figure but never revealing it? That is how a goddess dresses."

A few silly girls giggled. But they didn't move away.

He pulled a white Grecian number from a rack. "Now you." He gestured to a tall dark-haired girl with mocha skin. "In this style, you would be deserving of the cover of—what is the name of that fashion book that comes out each month, Janet darling?"

"Vogue Magazine."

"Yes, Vogue, sweet thing. Now I ask you—why would you want to dress like a slattern when you could look like you walked off the cover of Vogue?"

"There he is!" yelled a voice.

"There's Medieval Man!"

My head whipped around. A crowd of people with cameras surged through the glass doors that led out to the parking garage. Children and parents, teens holding cell phones…I could count at least ten running toward us, and there were more behind them.

Loki yipped.

"Holy hell!" I yelled. "We have to get out of here!"

We had maybe thirty feet on them, but they were closing in fast.

Janet had already grabbed her purse and leapt to the door beside the three way mirrors. She gestured madly. "Follow me. I've done fashion shows here. I know a way out the back."

I held Loki tightly in my arms and pushed Val past the bewildered sales clerk and other shoppers.

"But they want me." He looked back at the descending camera-wielding crowd of fans and would-be journalists. Or maybe they were real journalists. How could you tell?

"Get moving." I pushed him again. "I'll explain later."

Through the door we sped. Janet clicked the deadbolt home from the other side.

Thud. Someone tried to turn the knob. Then knocking. Then pounding and yelling.

Val started.

"See what I mean?" I said to him. "That crowd is dangerous! And you're a rock star now."

"That doesn't make sense, Kendra. I am not made of stone. Nor am I a star."

We rushed along the back hallway, past racks of clothing and boxes piled to the ceiling.

"You're still wearing that dress," I yelled to Janet.

Janet laughed. "I have an account here. They'll just add it."

She was in high spirits, racing down the concrete steps to the ground floor. We swept through a warehouse area that seemed deserted and out a steel door by the loading dock that led to the back parking lot.

Janet had parked close by. I finally breathed when we piled into the car, and could lock the doors. Janet turned the key and moved us briskly out of the shopping center.

"But why was it so important we leave just then?"

Val seemed to like the limelight. His face was a study in disappointment.

"Because you don't have the correct papers," I explained. "If the newspapers hear about Medieval Man, the reporters will go ape to research you. They'll try to find out where you're from, and you won't be in any databases. They won't find anything. You don't exist here. So then the cops will get involved, and—"

"Cops?"

Frig. How do I explain what cops are?

"She's right, Val," Janet said. "We can't take a chance. They could detain you for questioning."

"Meaning lock you up," I added.

Val frowned. "But I could convince them otherwise."

"No!" I insisted. "No more magic. It frightens people."

"But I only do good magic. You have seen that. They have nothing to fear."

Val was sitting in the front passenger seat. I saw Janet pat his thigh with her right hand.

"Dearest Val. Try to understand. People here think that magic doesn't exist. If you prove to them that it does...well, imagine the bad men who would seek to control you and your powers."

Val shivered. "Just like in Land's End."

I nodded. "We need to get back there. I still have to find Row."

"So I should drive to the school?" Janet asked. She pulled out onto Scottsdale road at the lights.

"With one short detour."

Maybe I shouldn't have taken the time. But how could I resist stopping for ground coffee at Starbucks? I left Loki in the car and dashed in to buy two pounds of Kenyan AA, and a pile of those disposable one-cup filters.

Didn't bother to pick up fresh drinks. No time to spare.

When I got back to the car, it was clear that Janet and Val had been in deep discussions. They went silent at my approach and looked slightly guilty.

Janet glanced in the rear view mirror. "So off to the school now?"

"Roger, Roger," I quipped.

"Who is Roger?" Val asked.

It was evening and still a sweltering furnace outside when we arrived at the classroom wall. I put Loki down on the floor.

Janet surprised me by sitting down in a chair.

"We really need to get back now. I don't want Thane and Logan coming back early and missing me," I said.

The silence made me turn around. Val looked nervous. He glanced swiftly at Janet, who met his eyes and held them.

Wait a minute. For Chrissake. What had they been cooking up while they were in the car alone?

Janet clasped her hands together and looked down at her lap. She looked guilty as hell.

Val cleared his throat. "Kendra dear, I'm not going back with you quite yet."

I stared

"I knew it," I blurted. "I frigging knew it." Don't ask me how.

"It's just..." Val pleaded with his arms. "I want to see more of this world. And Lady Janet has kindly invited me to be a guest in her abode for a short time. Never fear, she will keep me hidden from the rapacious hordes."

I nearly guffawed.

"I will return to Land's End. But this opportunity is so tempting." His eyes switched to Janet. There was something holy about the way he gazed at her.

And then I got it. This was about a lot more than seeing this world. This was about Janet.

I gulped. "Sure, I guess. You'll just keep the portal open?"

He nodded. "I can return anytime. When you find Rowena or Gareth, tell them where I am and for them to have no fear. I won't come to harm here with sweet Lady Janet as my guide."

More like his siren, I thought to myself. But I was cool with Janet. If these two wanted to share their worlds for a short time, who was I to interfere.

The practical side of me was working hard. I turned to Janet. "You'll have to get him out of those clothes and into something that doesn't scream Medieval Man."

She nodded. "I was thinking of that. What do you suggest?"

I gazed at Val for a few seconds. He wasn't the sort who would go for casual. Then it came to me. "Bond. James Bond."

"A tux or white dinner jacket?" Janet jumped up from the chair. "Oh! A shirt with ruffles."

I nodded. "And maybe cowboy gear for day. The flashy country singer kind. Boots with spurs, hat, silver belt buckle, and bolo tie. He'll go for that. We are in the wild west, after all."

Janet clapped her hands together. "This will be FUN! Val, we have shopping to do."

Val looked puzzled, but he gazed at her indulgently. Then he turned to me.

"Young Loki can guide you back to Castle Sargon. You will be safe with his companionship."

Val raised a palm, chanted something low, and…

ZAP!

Loki was back to his former wolfie size. Or wait. I looked again.

"He looks even bigger." I patted his back with my hand. Didn't have to bend down at all.

Val smiled. "A small precaution. Now, none will bother you."

I'll say. The critter was a *beast*.

Loki gazed up at me, expectantly. Those shining black eyes looked so intelligent, sometimes I forgot he wasn't human.

"So, we're off then. Goodbye and thanks for all the fish."

Val looked at me as if I had gone loony.

Janet laughed. I was pleased to see she got it. "It's an expression here, based on a book by a famous author."

Val tilted his head. "I shall have to read this book."

Now I grinned. Val reading *Hitchhiker's Guide to the Galaxy* was somehow freaky-fitting.

This was the first time I had gone through the wall alone. Okay, not exactly alone. I gripped Loki's fur to make sure he made it through with me. I wanted no part of that middle world. It scared the crap out of me.

"Take care, little one!" Val's voice rang out after me.

I took a step forward and colors danced wildly about me. I shut my eyes tight to block them out, and lost my footing.

Of course, I landed in a heap on the other side with the worst hangover ever. Loki sat patiently and licked my arm.

My bag sprawled on the grass about five feet away. All that precious cargo of coffee and drug store essentials spilled out. At least the trip hadn't been a complete waste. I stuffed it all back in the bag.

Then I gathered myself together and spoke reassuringly to Loki. Yet even as I mounted Blacky to make my way back to the castle grounds, the big question still plagued me: *Where the hell was Row?*

Chapter 21

She didn't come back the next day. I searched all over the castle property for signs of her, and outside the castle walls as far as I could go without raising suspicion. That night, I went to bed in a black mood.

She wasn't back by the time I woke up the following morning. I tried to busy myself in the stables to keep the panic down. Physical work would sop up some energy. And Alfred was happy to leave the mucking out to me.

That worked for most of the morning. Blacky was always glad to see me. I gave her a nice rub down. After an hour or so, I went back to the castle to clean up. After that, I sauntered to my next favorite spot, the kitchen.

George was glad to see me. His wide face beamed and he wiped his hands on the soiled apron that strained against his girth.

"Try this," he offered, pointing. George was always trying to fatten me up.

I reached for the honey cake and took a bite, thinking how wonderful this would go with the coffee I brought back. How many times had we shared coffee and cakes back home, Rowena and me? I mourned for that little ritual now.

Henry the page stuck his head into the doorway.

"They're back. He wants to see you."

Whoops. I knew who he meant. Here was showdown time, and it was gonna hurt.

I hoofed it into the great hall. As expected, fireworks.

Logan was already seated. They had been away for two days, and riding since mid-morning. The weariness was in his face. He rose to his feet when he saw me and his eyes lit up. I grinned back at him. A nervous sorry-about-this grin, for what was to come.

Thane and Rhys were removing their sword belts. Thane spotted me and his face went hard.

"Where is she?"

I gulped. "I'm not sure exactly." Which was true. I wasn't. And I was worried as hell.

"I mean it, Kendra. I've been riding for hours and am in no mood for tricks. They say she's been gone for two days. Tell me where she went."

I sucked in air. "Arizona. She went back through the wall. But she was only supposed to be there an hour. I don't know what's happened."

Thane cursed. He made a fist and drove it into the palm of his other hand.

"Why? Why would she go? And why are you still here?"

I gulped. "I was covering for her. She only meant to be gone a few hours. She wanted to call her Dad, you know, talk to him on the phone. Then she planned to be back here in time for dinner. No one was supposed to know."

"Why now?" he demanded.

This was the tricky part.

"Because she knew you were up north and wouldn't miss her." *And because she was going crazy here.*

The room temperature dropped about ten degrees. "Row knew you'd try to stop her."

This was the crummy truth, but Thane had to face it. He never let her do anything outside the castle without him.

"Her horse is here. The fast filly Norland gave her. I saw it in the stables when we rode in," Rhys said.

Of course. Rhys was the horse guy. He would notice.

"It came back alone two days ago," I said. "She never ties them up. Doesn't have to."

Thane slumped down into a chair. He looked incredibly weary. "Would she stay there?"

So that's what he was worried about. I shook my head. "No way. Not without me. She'd never leave me behind. I know that for sure, Thane. We have a pact."

He nodded. "So something has gone wrong. Either there or here. What do you think it is?"

I looked down at my hands. "I don't know. At first I wondered if there was something wrong with her Dad and she had to stay in Arizona longer. But I'm pretty sure it's not that. She would come back to let me know."

In fact, I knew that wasn't it. But I wasn't going to tell Thane and Logan I had gone back through the wall myself yesterday to check.

Thane started to unlace his gauntlets. "This is grievously inconvenient. I haven't time to go after her. "

"I could try," I said, knowing full well they wouldn't let me.

"No you won't," growled Logan.

I glared at him.

"This won't happen again," Thane stated. "We'll post a guard next time."

Now that got me bristling.

"Thane, are you nuts? You can't hold a woman like Row captive in this castle."

"What do you mean, captive? This is her home. She should want to stay here."

"Actually, Thane, it's not her home. It's *your* home. Castle Huel is her home."

There was an uncomfortable silence. No one wanted to say it, but we were all thinking the same thing.

Row wasn't married to Thane. She was married to Cedric. Thane had no legal right to keep her here at all.

In fact, Row was the granddaughter of the old Earl of Huel. She was second in line to all the Huel lands. For Chrissake, her baby was a Huel, sired by Cedric.

But it went deeper than that, and got a whole lot trickier. It started over a month ago when Cedric killed Ivan, his own brother. The punishment for that was banishment. Cedric would lose everything, including his castle, title, and lands.

Except that Row interceded. She had ridden to Sargonia and offered herself in return for Cedric's freedom. It was a fair trade, as far as primitive rule went.

But this is where everything went topsy-turvy. One night a month, it was supposed to be. Rowena would have to return to Castle Sargon one night a month to do Thane's bidding. Cutesy way of saying 'to share his bed.' That was the payment to buy Cedric's freedom.

But here's where it all went wrong. Thane changed his mind after that first night. He never let her return to Huel.

Thane broke the deal. It startled everyone. Nobody knew what to do. He was supposed to be an educated man, a truly benevolent leader. That he would keep a noblewoman prisoner indefinitely, for his own pleasure? Unthinkable.

Everyone was shocked.

Yes, we all knew he loved her. But that didn't change the facts.

Thane didn't have a single case for keeping her here one hour more, if she wanted to leave.

She had kept her part of the deal, even though she was married to someone else.

And Thane felt it. There was nothing that got him angrier than being reminded that Rowena was married to Cedric.

Thane leaned forward on the table with both elbows and put his head in his hands. "I can't go chasing after her all the time. I have a kingdom to run and defences to plan. She must start to act responsibly."

Now that pissed me off.

"Holy cow, Thane—you talk like she is a child. She's been here a whole month and she hasn't gone anywhere before now. You have to remember that Row is used to getting in her car and driving where she wants whenever she wants. You can't expect her to sit in this castle all day waiting for you to come home."

He threw one gauntlet on the big oak table. Thud. "She is a woman with child. She should start acting like one."

Hoo boy. I could just see where this was going, and I wasn't gonna like it one bit.

"Kendra, think," said Rhys. "She can't go riding all over the countryside with a baby."

"It isn't safe." Logan looked right at me.

Thud. Another gauntlet hit the table.

"If she's in Land's End, she'll try to get in touch with me," I said helpfully. "You can count on that. But if you like, I could ride to Huel and check if she's there."

"You're not riding to Huel," Logan stated. He crossed his heavy arms.

Yeah, I didn't think they'd go for that.

"Richard would never let any harm come to me," I said sweetly.

Logan was out of his chair, storming around aimlessly.

That was mean of me. Richard used to be Logan's friend, but when it came to me, they saw each other as rivals. No way would Logan want me within a mile of Huel, even if it was supposed to be my home, too.

Funny how everyone had forgotten about *that*.

"Rhys, have the scouts alerted. I want someone posted right by the portal as soon as possible to catch her when she passes through. Logan, you know where it is. Show them."

Logan nodded, obviously happy to have something concrete to do.

"But Thane, you've got to come to terms with this. Rowena isn't going to be happy here if you make her a virtual prisoner. She'll just run away again. You need to accept that."

He looked at me coldly. "I don't *need* to do anything. I'm the king here."

Well, goody two shoes for you, I thought. *Smug son of a bitch.*

"So what are you going to do? Make her a prisoner for life?"

I stared right back at him until he looked away. There was a long, awkward pause.

"You know I would never do that." His voice was calmer now. "And things would be different if I were a common man. But I have duties here, Kendra. My people and kingdom must come first."

"But that's exactly it, Thane! Rowena gets it. She is feeling it, just as you are." I paused. I had their attention now. "But the trouble is, her duties are not to you. They are to her family and the people of Huel."

The room was heavy with silence. I didn't need to remind Thane or anyone else with us there, that he had broken the deal. The silence said it all.

Row would have kept to her part. She would have come back once a month to Castle Sargon to fulfill the obligation for Cedric's freedom. Then she would have returned to Huel for the rest of the time, to be with her family. But Thane prevented that.

I tried again. "Don't you see? She is being torn in two by her guilt. And then you try to confine her here so she can't even tend to her grandfather when he is gravely ill?"

It can't last, is what I was trying to say.

Everyone averted their eyes.

I softened my voice. "It doesn't matter how much you love her. This can't go on."

Thane's face had gone stony. His eyes were shut and his mouth was a grim line. I had finally gotten through to him.

Two men entered the room. I knew them to be Evan and Thomas, two of the lesser lords, but good leaders, respected by their men

"A scout has arrived. You need to hear this," said Evan, the bigger one.

"Bring him," ordered Thane. He got up from the table and threw himself into the throne chair.

Logan waved a hand at me. I was being dismissed.

Cripes, that made me mad. He was going to hear about this later.

I left my chair and went out the side door. But I didn't close it. Instead, I backed up against the wall beside the opening to listen.

"Boats are landing on the north coast, leaving hundreds of men." I didn't recognize the voice.

"An exaggeration, no doubt."

"Let the man speak, Rhys."

"I heard he has ten thousand men," said the scout.

"Norland?"

Several exclamations.

"Any news of Huel?" That was Thane's voice.

"There is fighting on the south coast by Port Town. Their second, Jon, is commanding."

"Do we know who they fight?"

"Strange colors. Big men wearing furs and leather. They carry round shields."

Someone cursed. "Sounds like the same as up north."

"Is Norland fighting them?"

Silence.

Then a curse.

"Crafty bastard." Thane's voice. "I'll bet he's behind the south, too.

"He's boxing them in." Rhys's voice. "Do we know what's happening to the east?"

No one spoke.

"You may go," Thane said. "Find food and drink in the kitchen."

I had to say this about Thane, he was thoughtful to his men.

So. Gareth was planning a full-out attack on Cedric. And when he captured Huel—if he did—would he turn on Sargonia?

I wasn't the only one with that thought.

"Huel is our traditional ally," said Rhys.

"No more. They broke the treaty when Cedric killed my brother Sargon. I'll not defend them."

"But Thane, if we join them now we may be able to defeat Norland. If not, and Norland takes Huel, we'll face him alone."

Thane cursed again. "I don't want to weaken our forces by dividing them. We need every last man to defend Sargonia."

"Better to fight the invaders now on Huel land than wait for them to appear at our castle gates," a deep voice said determinedly.

"Cedric won't honor us for supporting him." Logan spoke now. "He'll turn on us as soon as he's free of Norland."

"We should make an ally now." The same deep voice I couldn't recognize.

"I need more information," said Thane. "We need to know who is attacking from the south. Make an ally of them, if possible. Rhys, send an envoy. Find out why they are here and who funds them."

"We should have kept Cedric an ally," Rhys grumbled.

"Impossible! Sargon destroyed that when he took Rowena from Ivan. He humiliated and then banished the man. The Huels will never forgive that."

And you've perpetuated the whole thing by keeping her for yourself, I thought.

Thane loved her, I had no doubt. That's why he was so angry now. I could forgive him for that. It was an impossible situation.

Row might have loved him too, but that didn't change the facts. Rowena was born a Huel and married to a Huel. Thane was neither. As far as the old Earl was concerned, Thane was keeping Rowena hostage and treating her like a whore.

So much for respecting allegiances.

"Can we pull troops from the north?"

"I don't recommend doing that until we know the strength of Norland's allies. We've always had an uneasy peace with the north." This was Thomas talking, I think.

"Then we wait out Huel's battle to the south. Evan, your opinion?"

"We can hold Sargonia. But there won't be much of a Kingdom left if we lose Huel and the south."

"This is maddening." Thane's voice again. "I need to know what is happening to the east."

"It is folly to wait."

"Then it is my folly," Thane said angrily. "I need more information. Who is the enemy and do they threaten us as well?"

Very soon, I was to find out.

Chapter 22

Logan left on his secret mission. I spent the night alone, fretting in the room.

The next morning, Row still wasn't back and I was frantic. Not only that, I was really bored.

Trouble was, without Row around, I didn't have much to do.

That was the thing about her. She was so much fun. We would spend the whole day together doing stuff until we separated at night to go with the guys.

Row was always making me do things. I mean, she was teaching me crap. If it wasn't Latin (*you've got to learn Latin, Kendra—all the books here are in Latin*) then it was how to make fairy cakes or frittatas in the kitchen. And of course, we spent hours in the stables where she taught me more about how to be a good vet.

Not only that, but she was just so nice and cheerful to be around. And she hummed all those crazy songs all the time. I used to think it was weird. But now I understood how the men felt.

You just felt good being around her.

This was like being in mourning in a way. It didn't feel right, our not being together. I'd never had a close friend like this before.

So I was moping around the stables, wondering what to do next, when I heard a familiar voice.

"Hey, Kenny." It was sort of a whisper, but also a yell. Make it a 'stage whisper.'

A slender fair-haired fellow waved at me from the side doorway.

"What's up, Howard?"

"Come outside with me. Don't tell anyone."

I looked around. Nobody here but us horses. But Howard was always one for drama. Which is why he got all the good parts in the travelling rep theatre company.

The good parts, meaning the female ones. Howard was awfully pretty.

I followed him outside to the back of the stables.

"This fellow," he pointed, "has been asking for you. He has a message from your friend."

From Row! "Tell me," I said eagerly.

The runner looked exhausted. He was extremely tall and thin, with a shock of white-blond hair. I hadn't seen him before.

"I am to tell no one but you. She is safe with my leader, and headed to Huel."

Huel! I should have guessed. Row had been waylaid by Cedric, as before.

"Your leader is Cedric," I stated.

The lad looked confused. "Prince Lars."

Lars! What the hell? He was up north with Gareth, wasn't he?

Or was he?

Curiouser and curiouser.

"Thank you," I said to the runner. "Howard, go get some food and drink for this guy from the kitchen. I'm going to Huel. Don't let anyone know. I mean that. Row would have a fit."

He nodded. "Tight as a clam shell."

I turned to go. "Do you want to come with me?"

Howard shivered. "No thanks. I have a new play to rehearse. You should see the gown I get to wear. Besides, you'll make better time without me."

I grinned. It was true. "You're a good friend, Howard."

While I would never trust him to cover my back—he was, after all, 'Howard the Coward'—I knew he could be trusted not to tell a soul.

My mind was whirling as I scampered back to the castle. My way was clear. I had to get to Huel. No way Thane and Logan would let me go if they knew. So I wouldn't tell them.

The sun set later these days. I could get there before the worst of nightfall if I rode hard. Could I risk taking a horse?

Guess I'd have to. Chances are, they wouldn't miss me until dinner. The guys were all closeted up together planning how to rule the world. I would be forgotten, as I was earlier until they discovered Row was missing.

I sauntered back into the castle, slipping by the great hall nonchalantly. Lots of heated male voices. I ran up the steps that led to the back hall and my bedroom.

Once there, I closed the door and started pulling out gear.

Back to being a boy again. Black leggings and Goth tunic from home. Leather arm bands. My black leather fanny pack with the important stuff. Boots. A sweet little knife to pack into a secret place.

Logan had been teaching me how to use a knife and I was getting good. I felt bad about Logan. He would pull a 'Thane' when he found I was gone.

I didn't bother packing a dress. There would be something at Huel to wear.

It would be good to be back at Huel. Gramps would be so happy to see me.

I started to hum one of those silly songs that Row sings.

Blacky was excited to see me in the stables. I saddled her, and made it look like I was going for a quick afternoon ride.

"Going to give her exercise?" Alfred poked his head around the doorway.

I smiled up at his kindly weathered face.

"Yup. Back before dinner."

"Mind the burdock at this time of year." He went back to his work.

I swung up onto Blackie and coaxed her out to the meadow beyond, where I knew Loki would be waiting for me.

It would be good to have his company on the long trip back to Huel. Damned good, as it turned out.

PART 3: Rowena in the Enemy War Camp

Chapter 23

Lars must have risen early the next morning. When I awoke, Jory was doing guard duty over me.

"He's sparring with Sven," Jory said. "The man is a tyrant for physical fitness."

I gestured for Jory to turn around, then reached for my extremely crumpled dress. Apparently, we'd been sleeping on top of it all night.

I sat up, slipped it on and tightened the bodice.

"He gave you that necklace." Jory shook his head in wonder. "It is supremely valuable."

My hand went to my neck. "He insisted. Jory, is this wise?"

Jory shrugged. "I've never seen him this way before. He has never bothered much with women."

He paused. "Rowena, will you stay?"

I wasn't sure what to say. "Do I have a choice?"

"For now, no. I concede that." He gave a smile, then it disappeared. "I was thinking after. I don't know how to put this."

I stayed silent. I knew what he was asking, even if he didn't.

"Lars is my brother in every sense but lineage, although our mothers are related. I am awed by this passion you most obviously share. It is glorious to watch. But I worry that he will be wounded in ways much worse than battle."

Jory's eyes bore into me.

What could I say? I wanted to be honest.

"He is a good man, Rowena. The best. He would provide for you well. And he loves children. Watch him with Sven."

I had to smile. Jory was a good PR man. He said all the right things.

"You are a good friend to him, Jory. I long to put your mind at rest, yet I want to be honest too."

He waited, watching me.

I frowned and decided to talk freely about what I *did* know.

"This is my home, Jory. Castle Huel is my home. If Lars is victorious in defeating my cousin Cedric, then I go with Huel. Either way, I go with Huel. Do you get what I mean? My grandfather needs me. I have responsibilities here. I won't leave my home and the people who depend on me unless I am forced to. I have a duty to them."

This was so strange. I was seeing my choices clearly now, and it made things obvious to me.

"So if Lars is victorious…"

"Then I stay with him."

Jory nodded. He accepted my attachment to Huel as right and natural. I took a moment to regard him more closely.

In a movie, I would have called him a classic Viking. He was a different build from Lars, shorter and stockier, with legs like tree trunks. But his hair was Viking red, and he had those odd high cheekbones, like Lars. His eyes were a light hazel.

At first, I though him really scary looking. But I liked the man. There was something simple and natural about him.

"Sit down, Jory, please. Don't stand on ceremony." I gestured to the chair by the bed.

He grinned and plunked himself down. I smiled back at him, humored by his lack of grace.

"Tell me more about Lars. What does he do when he's not at war?"

Jory's brow wrinkled.

"What do you mean? He's the Stallari, the commander of all our fighting men. The king relies on him completely for strategy."

"Oh. So he's a career military leader. My father was an officer in the American military for many years." *Air force*, I thought to myself. That wouldn't mean anything to the men here, of course.

Jory brightened. "Lars will be pleased to hear that. Was he a good warrior?"

I grimaced at the term 'warrior.' "He's still alive."

Jory nodded. "Then he was good."

I gave some thought to that. Dad learned to fly during his duty in Viet Nam. After that, he stayed on in the military for a while, before marrying Mom and becoming a commercial pilot.

I wondered what he would think of Lars?

But I still couldn't let the questions go. I needed to know more about this northern man.

"What does Lars do for hobbies? I'm thinking, for fun."

"Ah. He likes to build things. You should ask to see his drawings, they are masterful. He admires your castles here greatly, and is always trying to figure out how to duplicate your designs. Movement of water within a dwelling is his current passion."

So an architect, in a primitive way. Or maybe an engineer. Lars must be good with geometry and numbers.

I still didn't know if he could read.

"And what about you, Jory? Do you have a family?"

Jory seemed pleased that I would ask about him.

"Two children. My wife is dead."

I nodded sympathetically. It was a common story. Fifty percent of women died in childbirth before 1920. I tried not to think about my own chances.

"And what do you do?"

"Me? I'm a simple man. I come from a family of purveyors."

I thought about that. "Merchants?"

He waved a heavily-muscled arm. "The wagons you see carrying supplies at the back of our camps, I organize these."

He seemed proud. As well he should be.

"That is a very important job," I said. "More wars have been lost to insufficient supply chains than anything else, I've been told." Dad was always spouting military history. Little did he know I would be experiencing it in person.

Jory got excited. "Exactly! So many people don't understand that. You can't feed an army on enemy blood."

I guess I must have started, because his face blanched.

"Forgive me, m'lady. That was coarse."

I sighed. "I just can't get used to the fact that the enemy blood you talk of is that of my family and people."

My words had made him uncomfortable. He hung his head. "I know this must be difficult for you."

"*Hell*, is more like it."

I rose from the bed and walked to the window. Cumulus clouds were moving in today, creating shadows on the earth. I looked off in the distance toward the west.

What about Thane? How did I feel being away from Sargonia?

The answer came swiftly.

I felt *free*.

This appalled me.

Why was it so important that I be free to live at Huel? Yes, there was the magic I could learn there. That was a big draw. But it was more than that.

I belonged at Huel, and I would never be able to explain this to Thane.

Jory had been watching me carefully. He seemed to sense I was thinking of another kingdom, but he got the man wrong.

"You would not return to the Earl of Norland?"

My eyes dropped. I fingered the necklace.

"I won't, although for everyone's sake maybe I should." I was thoughtful. "Gareth won't believe that I am choosing to stay with Lars of my own choice. He wouldn't care anyway. That will mean more war. Don't believe this temporary truce, Jory. Gareth feels betrayed and will wait for his chance. He will try to kill Lars, I am sure of it."

My hands balled into fists. "I want it to stop. For the sake of my own people, I need war to end. How do I make it stop?"

Jory smiled. "I think you have just answered my question, Rowena. And I thank you."

Poop. Did I just signal my choice without even thinking?

I did. *Gareth won't believe that I am choosing to stay with Lars of my own choice.* I said that.

Although it may not matter, because I probably won't have a choice.

For there was one thing of which I was certain: only one leader would survive the coming war. And there was absolutely nothing I could do about it.

We met the others for luncheon in the back room. Lars, Soren, Sven and Jory, my new surrogate family. I didn't know whether to smile or grimace.

But it was a pleasant scene. Lars and Soren were comfortably engaged in guy talk as they ate. It pleased me to see Soren fitting in so well. Probably best not to examine why that was important to me.

It was a simple repast again. Roasted fowl and mutton, buns, cheese and ale. I skipped the ale because of the baby but scarfed down everything else in sight, especially the fowl. Jory matched me with gusto.

"It's nice to see a woman enjoy her food," he said.

"These days, I'm so hungry, I need a snack between bites."

He chuckled and shook his head.

Sven sat beside me, lost in reverie. Occasionally, his eyes would stray my way, and then look down if he was caught.

"Penny for your thoughts," I asked him playfully, between bites.

"I don't understand?"

Jory got it. "She's asking what you're thinking, young warrior."

Sven blushed.

"Out with it, man. Unless it is too crude for the lady, of course."

"Oh no," Sven hurried to explain. "I was just thinking about my mother. Your hair reminds me of her."

A hush fell over my companions. Lars and Soren stopped eating to listen.

I felt a need to be kind to this young lad so far from home.

"Is she a redhead?" I asked.

"No, she's blond like me," Sven said. "But her hair is long, like yours. May I touch it?"

It was such a shy request, from a young fellow missing his mother. I was moved.

"Of course," I said quickly, before Lars could reprimand.

His right hand reached out to stroke my hair. Then—tentatively—both hands lifted the weight of it.

"Yours is softer than hers," he said, running the strands through his fingers. The awe in his voice was clear.

"I probably wash it more often." In fact, I had washed it the morning of my arrival in the camp, thank goodness. There didn't seem to be a way I could do it here.

"She used to let me brush her hair," Sven murmured. He seemed in a trance.

"None of that," Lars said, with a smile. "Get your own young woman, lad."

Sven withdrew his hands immediately. No doubt he was accustomed to taking orders from his older cousin.

"Don't be like that," I scolded Lars. "Sven is missing home, is all."

Lars watched me, his face relaxing into thoughtfulness. He seemed to like my defending Sven.

I turned back to the boy, and smiled. "Tell me about your family. Do you have any sisters?"

He brightened. "One. Inga. She's named after my aunt, Lars's mother. She's five."

"And a hellion." Jory laughed. "Makes the lads do her will, she does."

"I should like to meet her." I had a weakness for spunky little girls.

"You shall," Lars said, lazily lifting a goblet. "She'll adore you. Don't you think so, Sven?"

Maybe, I thought, but would his mother adore me?

Good gad, why was I even thinking that?

Chapter 24

In early afternoon it was time for the council of war meeting.

I stood outside the fortress next to Lars watching the Norse lords ride up. I stared at the riders, trying to recall which of them I had been introduced to before, and if I could remember their names. A few smiled in recognition when they saw me, but most of them gazed at me with hard eyes.

Soren came up beside me. "A grim lot, don't you think? We need to liven them up."

Maybe it was the company. Maybe I was just feeling a little restless and wicked due to my enforced confinement here.

These horses were 'acquired', I knew. The Vikings didn't bring work animals with them on their sea voyages. So these horses had been captured during raids across the east.

I did a little equine mind probing. As expected, they weren't all pleased with their new masters. I reached out to them, putting a little idea in their heads.

Who knows how far my gift with animals would go? I'd never really tested it here.

There was a delay of a few moments. Then *bingo*! The first horse reared back and dumped his rider. Then a second horse reared and Gustav went flying. The horse and rider left standing upright in between them looked bewildered.

Two more horses threw their riders. Then another.

"Odin's balls, what's happening?"

The entire yard erupted in total mayhem as more beasts bucked and men leaped to control them, yelling and swearing.

I turned away, giggling.

Soren whipped his head over to me. His blue eyes were piercing. "You did that."

I clapped my hand to my mouth.

Gustav was cursing up a storm. Lars had moved forward to grab the horse to keep it from trampling him.

"Well, well. Little witch has a sense of humor." Soren lowered his voice, and put his arm around my shoulder. "Best stay turned away, as that man won't appreciate an audience."

I couldn't stop giggling. Soren guided me into the hall.

"You, my dear, are dangerous," he said. "Already I am enjoying this."

"I've never tried to do that before. Usually, I just call them and they come."

"Animals?" Soren raised an eyebrow.

"Of course, what I mostly do is calm them. I'm an animal healer, you see. It's a good gift, to be able to calm a wounded animal before you touch him."

Soren swung down on a bench. "Have you tried this gift with humans?"

I shook my head. "It only works with men who are part animal. Sargon was that." I shivered.

"This Sargon is dead. And you are glad of it."

I nodded. "He was the king. Remember I mentioned that Thane was King of Land's End now. Sargon was his elder brother."

"Ah," said Soren. "And you were his queen. All is starting to make sense."

Soren thought for a few moments.

"Who killed him?

"My cousin Cedric, the Earl of Huel."

Soren smiled. "And we ride to meet Cedric in battle the day after tomorrow. What fun."

"Not for me, it isn't." I said dryly.

"Well no. You are my brother's captive. We attack your land and troops. Bad luck for you. But I shall keep you safe."

I looked up at him, and the strangest feeling came over me. "You know, Soren, in some ways you are rather like a mischievous older brother to me."

"I seem like that?" He looked surprised and his eyes sparkled at me. "Then I must be doing something wrong."

Twenty men had gathered in the great hall. I caught bits of conversation as they filed in to take their places. An older, grizzly man hit his hand to his head.

"How many times do I have to tell them? Pillage and burn. Pillage and burn. Not the other way around."

Hearty laughter exploded around him. I had to check my smile.

I sat in the corner, away from the men, as Lars conducted business. Soren stood beside me, leaning against the wall with his big arms crossed.

It was odd, the relationship we had. Whenever he was nearby, he sought me out and stood right beside me, just like a twin brother would. I got the feeling that my being the source of his release was a far more emotional and powerful bond than he let on.

The other men sat on benches at the rectory tables. They spread out, no more than two to a table, on either side. Weapons clattered as they dragged on the floor. They were in full armor, minus helmets. Definitely a show of power and rank.

It was a strange assembly of men. Most had blond or light brown hair, quite long. Very few had grey hair. I expect they didn't live long enough to acquire it.

Evidence of inbreeding was everywhere, in height, and facial features.

No introductions were made. Everyone seemed to know each other and who I was.

These were very scary men. They were all armed to the teeth. I had to remind myself that not only was Land's End a primitive world, but the men who survived to become leaders were the toughest of the tough.

Eyes tracked me almost constantly. I actually felt myself leaning toward Soren to assuage my unease.

In a strange way, he took this in his stride, my reliance on him. Nothing and no one scared him, of course.

He was well-accepted in the group. These men recognized him as Soren, the fearless leader who had led the troops to conquer the lands east of us. Soren acted the part well. He was inherently violent by nature, and he easily absorbed my lessons to put him in the know. No one suspected the truth, I was sure.

The men spoke in their native tongue of troop movements. I tried to tune it out, so I wouldn't react and blow my cover. No one knew I could understand them, not even Soren.

But at one time, about half an hour into the meeting, I heard something that I couldn't ignore.

I knew that voice. My head shot up.

"What do you intend to do with the woman?"

Soren was across the room in a flash. His hand was on Gustav's neck, closing hard.

"She is a *queen*. You will treat her as such, you insect, even though she is our captive."

Gustav was red in the face, gasping. In seconds, he would be dead.

"Soren, release him! Please." I dashed over and placed my hand on his bare arm.

Soren whipped around. He raised his hand and swept it around the room. Everyone froze into statues except the two of us.

"You touched me," he whispered.

I withdrew my hand, but before I could move it ten inches away, he had grabbed it and pulled the inside of my wrist to his mouth.

"You're scaring me," I said. I couldn't tear my eyes away from his.

"You smell delicious. I want to taste you." His tongue swirled along the inside of my arm. I tried to back away but it was impossible.

Soren pulled me closer and grabbed the back of my head with his other hand. His mouth came down on mine.

I wanted to scream. I couldn't breathe—it was Cedric, but it wasn't Cedric. A volcano of desire shot from his mind into my body, through his mouth, through the hands that held my back and head. I was falling into a dark pit of lust—

"Oh, that was fun. You are an infant witch, a sweet untouched thing. I shall take you under my wing and teach you, shall I?"

My vision came back. I was sitting on the floor with my legs out front and my hands behind me, supporting me. The laces of my bodice were loose, one shoulder had dropped down, but otherwise, I was fully dressed, thank God.

What had happened?

Soren waved his arm. The men came back to life.

Gustav had his hands to his throat.

Lars roared when he saw me on the floor. No one seemed to realize that they had lost some seconds of time.

"Steady on, Brother. She is pure and undamaged." Soren lifted me without touching me. I don't know how he did that.

I hastened to tighten my bodice.

"Shall we return to the question? What shall we do with Rowena?"

I fought hard to control my shaking body. Soren had spoken in English and was looking right at me, appraising.

I cleared my throat and remembered to reply in English. "If you will give me a tent and table, I will set up a MASH unit."

"A what?" Even Soren was puzzled.

"A mobile army surgical hospital. I'm a healer. I can treat your wounded." I nodded in satisfaction. This was a good thing to offer. It would show that I was not just a pretty face (or ample bosom,) so to speak.

I had an honorable profession. And I could be professional, and put aside my horror of this invasion to treat whomever needed my help, regardless of for which side they fought.

Jory was translating into their language for the others. To my dismay, laughter started. Then it grew from guffaws into a roar among the men.

I looked to Lars, bewildered.

He was gazing at me in surprise. Then his mouth turned up in amusement. He folded his arms across his chest and shook his head.

"Rowena, we have no wounded. If you fall, you are killed."

"Tis so," Jory added, nodding. "It is a kindness, if they are badly wounded. As well, we cannot afford to have an enemy surprise us by rising up from the ground behind us. So we finish them off."

I stared at him, absolutely horrified.

"But...but that's not totally true. I've seen injuries in this camp. I can help some of you with less fatal injuries."

Soren sounded amused. "Such a kind female."

"But I can!" I insisted. "I know how to set bones and bandage wounds. I can sew a gash so that you will hardly see a scar later."

Without thinking, my eyes settled on Gustav. He stared back, with a look so cold it frightened me. I quickly looked away.

"I can protect her," Soren said in a lazy voice.

"I need you at the front with me, Soren."

Soren smiled. His handsome face lit up. "Oh, I would not miss that. I know of another way. Leave it. I will tell you later."

I waited until Lars had moved away to talk to one of his allies. Then I turned to Soren.

"Soren, promise me something. If Lars dies, and Gustav tries to take me, kill me first."

Soren snorted. "That insect will not touch you. I shall see to it."

When Soren suggested I leave the room, I did not argue. The talk had changed to battle strategy. When it really came down to it, I could not bear to hear the plans for killing my own people.

When I got back to the back bedroom, I checked out the other dress Lars had managed to scrounge for me. It was cream linen and seemed big enough and even clean. I took off my good dress to preserve it and whipped this one over my head. It would do. Then I lay down on the bed to rest.

Chapter 25

A short time later, there was a knock at the back door. Word had gotten around about my being a healer, apparently. The sweet young lad who had called me beautiful earlier stood on the step. He spoke shyly.

"M'lady, can you help? My friend is in pain."

I didn't hesitate. I rose from the bed and grabbed my fanny pack. It didn't even occur to me to be afraid. That is what being a healer means, whether a medical doctor, a paramedic, a nurse, or an animal vet. You forget about being in danger. All your focus is on the creature that needs your help.

"What is your name?" I asked the young lad.

"Tyr," he said. "Would you follow me please?"

He led me along the back of the fortress, where two grizzly men stood supporting another between them. The wounded fellow was younger and looked faint from pain.

"What is it?" I asked them.

"It hurts to walk on, m'lady," said the one supported.

I swung my pack to the ground. "Is there a wound?"

He shook his blond head.

"Here," I instructed the two holding him up. "Let him support his own weight, but stand ready should he start to fall. I'm going to feel along his leg and up his thigh."

"Don't be frightened," I said to the man in pain. "This will only take a moment."

I already thought I knew the cause of his pain. But I'd check for a break first.

When I finished, I stood up and went behind him. "I'm going to ask you to bend over. I want to watch what happens. Here, let me help you."

A small crowd was watching us now. After a moment, I bade him to straighten up.

"You've dislocated your hip," I said, pointing. "The ball-joint of your thigh fits into your hip, and it has slipped out of place."

"Can you do something?" Tyr's voice held fear. "This is my brother."

I nodded.

"Let's get him on the ground. What is your name?"

"Axel." His blue eyes watched me all the while.

"Axel, I won't kid you. This is going to hurt. But I will be as quick as I can about it. And you should feel much better in just one minute."

I signalled to the other men. "Hold his shoulders down firmly. I'm going to pull really hard on the leg to reset the joint."

I got down on my knees, and took the leg in my hands.

"Axel, in a few seconds I'm going to pull your leg really hard. I don't want you to tense up, so I won't tell you when. You can count with me, if you like."

I started counting. One, two, three, four, five, six.

On six, I jerked his leg with all my might.

Axel cried out. I fell back on my butt.

And then…

Someone gave me a hand up. I stumbled a bit on my skirt, which of course, ripped at the waist.

"How do you feel?" I asked Axel.

"Sore," he said, with surprise. "But the shooting pain is gone."

"Stand him up," I ordered the other men.

When Axel stood up, he was all smiles. I beckoned him to walk forward toward me. He did so gingerly.

"Magic," he said, with wonder in his eyes.

I smiled and shook my head.

"Not magic. Medicine."

The men were jubilant. Hands slapped on backs, others were called over to see the miracle.

As for me? I felt wonderful! For once, I had done something positive in this land.

This is what I was here for. I knew it now. I could help the people in Land's End by being a healer.

Tyr came up beside me. "You are an angel," he whispered.

Others were nodding their heads at me, not sure what the protocol was for expressing their thanks. I had made some fans today, for sure. Hopefully, these men would come to my aid if needed in the future.

There was a commotion off to the right. A stout man pushed forward.

"M'lady, my friend bleeds. Will you come?" He pointed to a distant camp.

Word had indeed gotten around.

I hesitated, a little nervous about moving so far away from the fortress.

I turned to Tyr. "Will you come with me? I should not travel far without a man to protect me."

Tyr nodded. He looked pleased to be chosen, as I thought he might.

But I wasn't alone. A whole troop of originals followed along behind us, passing the word as they went.

In front, the stout man moved swiftly, pushing his way through to make a path for us. After a few minutes, we came to a small fire. A young man lay on the ground, panting hard. He had sustained a nasty gash on his left thigh above the knee.

"It opened again, m'lady. It won't stop bleeding." The older man sounded grim.

I dropped to the ground beside the lad. "Boil me some water. I need to clean the wound before I sew it."

No one moved. I looked up.

"There is no water, m'lady. We have ale."

Bugger. This is something I didn't know. Would there be enough alcohol in their ale to kill germs? Probably not.

"Do you have anything stronger?" I asked.

They did. Big surprise. Someone handed me a small jug. I tested the contents first, to judge the strength.

I choked. "Holy hell! This stuff would knock out a rhino. Give him a good slug of that first," I instructed.

While they did that, I rummaged around in my fanny pack. I had good sewing thread and a strong, sharp needle. This would hurt, but the men here were no strangers to pain.

Mainly, I was worried about not having a proper bandage. The little ones I carried would do nothing for a wound this size.

I looked around the campsite. The twenty or so men who milled around us had been wearing their clothes for days. I could tell by the ripe smell—don't ask. There didn't appear to be anything I could use.

I sighed. The new gown I was wearing had two layers, a sheer outer layer and a solid under. Both layers had already ripped from the waist. I figured the slip layer would be cleaner and more resilient.

I stood up.

"Tyr, can I have your knife?"

He looked puzzled, but did not hesitate to unsheathe it and hand it to me.

"Can you explain to them that I have to make bandages? I don't want the men to think I'm doing this for their entertainment."

While he talked to the folks about us, I took the knife and slit the bottom of my slip across at the knees. Then I ripped along the slit line, so the piece came free.

There was a mighty hush. Yup, it was the hush to end all hushes. I deliberately didn't look at faces.

I dropped to the ground then. "Hand me the alcohol," I said. First, I cleaned the wound as best I could. The poor fellow was already gritting his teeth. Then I dipped my needle in the alcohol, and threaded it with silk.

"Be brave. This will hurt," I told the wounded man. He didn't look more than sixteen.

I started to sew. I worked as quickly as possible. Human skin is easier to sew than horse hide, so I was well prepared to perform the task.

The poor lad was sweating hard when I finished and knotted the thread.

All around us were talking now.

"Give him more of that brew," I suggested. "He's earned it. Brave lad."

I cut the piece of underskirt along the seam line, and folded it to make a large bandage, which I wrapped around his thigh. I had a few safety pins, but really what I needed was another layer of skirt to tie it firm.

Well rat poop. Here's hoping this wouldn't cause a riot.

I used the outer layer of my skirt this time, slitting it at the knees as before, and ripping it into two ties. There were several gasps. Then silence.

"Help me with this, Tyr. I want to tie this firmly above the wound." I showed him where to hold it, then I drew the two ends together into a knot.

You had to get the pressure just right. Too loose and the tie would slip off. Too tight, and you could cut off circulation. So intent was I on the job, that I didn't hear the shuffling and chatter from the men around us. Voices got louder, and I simply worked faster.

"Rowena, what in the name of Thor are you doing?"

I pushed the hair out of my eyes and looked up. The men had parted. Lars glared down at me."

"I'm bandaging this man's wound." I said, glancing back at my work. "Tyr, hold this tight."

"Come now," Lars ordered. He grabbed my arm.

"I'll just be a minute—"

"What the devil have you done to your skirt?" He sounded aghast.

"I needed bandages."

Men's voices continued to rumble.

"That is enough," Lars said. He pulled me upright and then hoisted me over his shoulder.

"Eeep! Tyr, just tie that one snug. Bring him back to me tomorrow—Ouch!" It was no fun being bent double over someone's big brawny shoulder. Especially when they were kind of angry and stomping hard.

Lots of noise accompanied our departure. I could see Jory behind us, and I sort of waved at him. He grinned and shook his head.

I hated to think how much of my backside was showing.

Lars carried me across the camp, each step pounding the ground. I tried to ignore the startled cries of the men and pointing fingers. He didn't stop until we were through the back door of the bedroom.

I was flung on the bed like a sack of potatoes.

"Ouch," I said again. My head hit the mattress with a thump.

"Jory, leave us."

Jory hesitated. He seemed to be weighing whether Lars had control of himself. Finally, he turned and left through the door.

Lars strode across the room and went right to the window. His whole body was still from holding in anger.

"I guess this is the part where I'm supposed to say I'm sorry." I tried to be cheerful.

He snorted.

"But they asked me to help, Lars. This healing those in need, it's what I do. And I didn't go by myself. I had Tyr with me. See? I can be sensible."

"Who?"

Oops. I had made a mistake. Guess Lars didn't know Tyr. But really, why would he? Lars was a prince. Tyr was a…I don't know what.

"Do not…" His voice was hoarse. "Do not go around the camp without me or one of my trusted men. Promise me you will not do this again." His voice cracked on the last word. I couldn't judge the emotion, but it sounded strong.

I gulped. "I promise."

His fist opened and he started striking the sill with the palm of his hand. One, two, three, four…

"What is it?" I was immediately on alert.

He glared at me. "I have a war raging within me. When I look at you as you are now, with your skirt ripped to your thighs, knowing you have been that way before my men, my blood fires instantly, and I am consumed with violence to ravish you."

I sucked in air. What a confession.

"At the same time, I wish to hold you tenderly and kill any man who even thinks to do you the same violence."

I shivered.

"I did not think these two feelings could reside within me at once."

I looked down at the floor.

"Do not fear, Rowena. I am keeping the beast in control."

I chose my words carefully. "As long as I know the beast loves me, it may not be totally unwelcome at times."

He snorted. "Do not say that. Never say that. You cannot know."

Soren sauntered in the room.

"Jory said you were back. Is the wench intact?"

I flinched. "Soren, don't be crude. I was helping some of the wounded men, that's all."

"So I heard. I also hear that men are wounding each other right now so that you will tear up your skirts for them."

I blushed hard.

Soren turned to Lars.

"As we discussed, 'tis a simple thing I do, Brother. With your permission, of course." His voice was subtly mocking.

"You have it." Lars sounded grim. "Do it now."

Soren turned to me and smiled. He came forward to stand right in front of me. Then he silently mouthed some words, raised his hand before my head and swept it down in one movement.

I felt a blaze of heat, like an oven door had been suddenly opened.

"There," he said with satisfaction. "Only males of our bloodline can touch her without burning, until I undo the spell."

Lars grunted.

I backed away in horror, as the full extent of this hit me. No males could touch me, but Lars and Soren? And maybe Sven? I did not know about Jory—did he say he was a cousin?

That meant Gareth could not. Or Thane. Oh Lord, I understood now why Lars had agreed to this. Who needed a chastity belt? This was the ultimate protection.

But already I could see a problem.

"But my grandfather! Soren, please. I must be able to tend to my grandfather."

Soren sighed. "What say you, brother? Her bloodline as well? Her direct bloodline. The Huels I mean."

Lars nodded.

Soren repeated the spell. "But none other. She is ours."

"But I can help others still, can't I? This spell only makes it so if others touch me, they are hurt, right?"

Soren raised an eyebrow. "You are thinking as a healer?"

"Yes. I want to be able to help the wounded among your men. They may not all be Gredanes."

Oh please, please, I begged silently.

Soren looked to Lars.

"Make it so," Lars said. He didn't hesitate, I'll grant him that.

Soren cocked his handsome head. "Warn them not to touch you."

I was instantly relieved.

"There's one more thing." I was not sure I should say what I was thinking.

"Yes, sweet witch?" Soren watched me.

"If Lars should die..." I thought the words.

"If he dies, the spell will be released. But he won't die. You should trust me."

I shivered. It occurred to me that I had not spoken out loud.

Neither had Soren.

He had read my thoughts, and I had read his.

I started. He was watching me, smiling.

"Brother, you should go back to the council. They are waiting. I will speak with our lady for a moment and then leave her to Sven and join you."

Lars came over to me and put his hands on my shoulders. "I know you must be angry with me. But this episode today has shown me that I must act. If I could think of another way to keep you safe..."

I stayed frustrated. "You said I would be free if I stayed with you. Did you lie?"

Lars stepped back, as if slapped. "I did not mean to. Rowena, I love you. I will release you, when this war is over, and the danger has passed. I give you my word."

I sighed. "Yes, but did you think of this. Do you really think Soren will release me?"

He pulled me to him, in a gentle hug. "He is my brother, little bird, even if he has adopted dark ways. He will not betray me."

He bent down to kiss me lightly on the mouth. Then he turned and left.

That was the problem, of course. This Soren wasn't his brother.

I sat down on the bed. "*Will* you release me?"

Soren shrugged. "I haven't decided."

I sighed. "Thank you for not lying to me, at least."

"You are the strangest woman." He shook his head. "You accept each event as it happens without wasting a moment to rue it."

"Soren, I have spent years as a scholar. I've been trained to accept facts and not waste time wishing for what isn't and what cannot be. I suspect you have never met a woman like me, is all."

"Not in the many hundred years of my existence." He sounded amused. "No one before has had the courage to weaken the barrier between earth and the underworld. I delight in you, sweet witch."

I held my head in my hands and groaned. "Why do I think that one little time shift is going to cost me for the rest of my life?"

He flung his body down beside me on the bed. "Think of the adventures we will have. You, me and my Warlord brother." He laughed.

"Soren, I care about Lars. Please don't hurt him."

He snorted. "I have no intention of harming my big brother. I like belonging to people again, having a family. I've missed companionship. You two suit me. Big Brother is very violent. And you..." he smiled. "You are perfection."

Oh Lordy. Soren was lonely. Now I was worried about how lonely.

"You don't expect to share me...oh hell." I gulped. "Soren, I can't be with both of you...in that way."

He grabbed my hand and kissed the palm.

"You will learn to trust me, beautiful woman."

"Yup, and that wasn't an answer," I said dryly. I snatched back my hand.

He laughed again. "See? Always with you I have fun."

I was focussed on a technicality. "So this action just proved that you won't burn by touching me. What really does this mean, Soren? What exactly will happen if a man puts his hands on me?"

He laced his hands behind his head. "I suspect it will be like touching hot embers. Poor men. For some will try, even knowing this. Especially if you go out wearing that dress."

Oh poop.

"Turn around," I ordered. "I need to change."

"Infant, I can see you without your clothes at any time. Would you like me to demonstrate?"

I swatted at him with my hand. He laughed and handed me the green dress.

Chapter 26

I suggested to Soren that he walk among the troops without me. He needed to show himself to the men and learn what his recent exploits had been on the battlefield, so as not to blow his cover.

He had a good laugh over that.

"See how well you take care of me? Just like a devoted wife."

"Let's make it a devoted sister for today, okay?" I scolded.

But he agreed it was a clever idea.

After he left, I took another vitamin pill and washed it down with tepid water. *I'm trying, baby-dearest. Trying to be a good mom-to-be.* Then I lay down to rest.

When I woke up, Lars was talking to Sven by the door. He chuckled once, and ruffled the young lad's hair with his right hand. Sven grinned in response.

When Lars turned to see me watching him, his eyes lit up. Then, just as quickly, the smile left his face.

"What is it? Tell me."

Lars approached the bed. "I need to talk serious matters with you for a moment, and I dread this. I do not wish to cause you grief. Can you be brave for me?"

I nodded.

"I will not be able to prevent looting, Rowena. The men expect something for their efforts, and as you know, there are no women—I am sorry. I know that shocks you. What is there of yours that I absolutely must protect?"

I swallowed hard. "The tower bedroom. My clothes are there, and I don't have many. You will want the room for your own, Lars. There are windows on all sides and you can see in almost every direction."

He nodded. "Any treasures?"

I shook my head, and fingered the necklace. "This is enough."

His face softened.

I thought about the book of spells in the cellar. Cedric had spelled it so it couldn't be removed. I was hoping no one would discover that room before I could get down there.

But there was something more important than material things.

"If you would spare my grandfather, I would be forever grateful. He is very old and ill. Bedridden."

"I will try."

I thought about Grandfather. If he were awake, he would try to rise with his sword and fight the first man through the door. How could I stop him?

It would not matter if the cause had no hope at all. Grandfather would go down with a sword in his hand, the old earl defending Huel, no matter what.

Somehow, I had to keep him prostrate when the castle was stormed.

Oh Lordy. I couldn't believe it. Here I was already calmly discussing my home being sacked.

Lars shifted on the chair and continued.

"You have male relatives. I cannot guarantee their safety after capture. I will try, but...most likely they will die on the battlefield. I expect they will not allow themselves to be taken."

I thought about that. Cedric would never give up, never. He was of the 'return *with* your shield or *on* it' school. Jon...I expect he was the same. But I really worried about Richard.

"Tell me their names, in any case. If I can spare them, I will."

"Jon and Richard. Richard is so very young—like Sven." I felt sick, thinking of Richard. "And then, of course, Cedric. But I know that's not who you mean."

He didn't need to say it. The battle with Cedric would be to the death.

"You talk as though there is no doubt you will win this, Lars."

He shrugged. "I have never lost a battle, little bird. And I am well prepared this time, like never before."

Prepared to slaughter my people, I thought grimly. What a strange position we both were in.

I thought of another thing.

"Lars, there are more of your men who need medical help. Would you allow them to come to the back door of this room here, so I could treat them within steps of the fortress? I would be safe with one of your guards, and I'd be within yelling distance."

His face twisted. "It is so important to you, to be able to help them?"

"It is what I do," I said simply.

He sighed. I could see he was deep in thought. Probably, he recognized this was some sort of test for him. Would he be able to abide my being independent in this way?

Finally he said, "Then you shall. I will send some men to assist you. But mark you, keep your apparel intact, Rowena. Make bandages of something else."

And so that's the way I spent the rest of the day until the sun set.

Sven was my constant companion. He made an eager assistant.

Word got around about my impromptu MASH unit at the back of the fortress. Almost immediately there was a lineup.

Gashes, which had been previously covered up as a sign of weakness, appeared from nowhere.

Rashes were commonplace, also sunburn. I expect the sun was hotter here than the northern men were accustomed to.

Someone even brought me a horse with a cut to mend, I was pleased to see. Nice that they cared for their newly acquired animals.

Sven managed the lineup like a sergeant major. Some patients were turned away before I could see them, no doubt sporting ailments in places it wouldn't be seemly for me to view. I didn't know the prevalence of STDs in this world, nor did I have the wherewithal to treat such things, sadly.

Sven also helped me with makeshift surgery. At one time, when he was holding a wound so I could sew it closed, he said, "Could you teach me to be a healer?"

I glanced up. "Of course. I'd be delighted to. It's what I do in my homeland, Sven. I teach the art to my students."

He nodded in satisfaction.

How gratifying. I could hardly wait to tell Kendra. She would be excited to meet a guy in Land's End who was interested in her field of study.

Damn. I wanted her here. But I wanted her safe, even more.

We did a good afternoon of work on these poor men. I was feeling pretty chipper. Nothing like feeling useful.

"What are you singing?" Sven asked at one point.

"Was I doing that? I don't even notice anymore." It was true. I often hummed or sang while working. Kendra was always teasing me about it.

"It was pretty. What is it?"

I had to think. Oh for goodness sake, I'd been singing a cowboy song. *'Buttons and Bows.'*

I started to sing it quietly, with the words this time.

Within moments, we had a crowd around us. So I switched to singing it in their language—dang, that language spell was handy.

Before you knew it, all sorts of male voices were humming along to 'Don't bury me on this prairie, take me where the concrete grows...'

You really haven't lived until you've heard a bunch of harsh Viking warrior voices singing a Bob Hope cowboy song in the middle of Land's End.

I went through it twice to let the others join in, and when I was done, there were all sorts of happy comments.

"Can you sing something sweet?" one of the grizzliest men asked.

I smiled. It always surprised me when the most rugged of men asked for a feminine song. I guessed they were missing their women at home.

I tried to think of a song that would be sweet and also tuneful, easy to follow. I decided on a waltz that my dad used to sing to my mom.

And so I began.

"Sometimes in the mornin' when shadows are deep. I lie here beside you just watching you sleep. And sometimes I whisper what I'm thinking of. My cup runneth over with love..."

I sang all three verses in English. Then I sang them again in their language.

When I stopped, all was quiet. No one clapped or cheered. It was rather disconcerting. A few looked sad and filled with longing. But didn't they like it?

Then I realized we had gathered an audience from the other direction. The lords from the council meeting had come outside to check out the commotion. Jory, Soren, Eric, Karl, Gustav, Ejnar, Henning, all of them.

Lars stood staring at me.

My face went totally red. I had sung the lyrics in their language.

As he came forward, I could see strong emotion on his face.

He reached for my hand and brought it to his lips.

"Beautiful, little bird," he whispered.

He straightened up. It looked like he was going to say something else, and then thought the better of it.

He turned to go back to the meeting. The others followed suit, all except Gustav, who continued to stare at me.

I looked away quickly. Hopefully, the men would accept this as modesty, and not the unbridled fear I felt whenever he was near.

To my dismay, he appeared at my side. "You have a voice like an angel," he said smoothly.

I stammered, "Thank you." *Go away, please.*

"Would you look at my hand. It troubles me."

I almost quaked when he took off his glove.

But what could I do? I couldn't make a scene.

He held his hand forward, waiting.

I looked at it closely, trying not to touch him, and could see the problem immediately. His hand had white dry patches on it over the knuckles.

"Turn it over, please."

He did so. The palm was equally afflicted. I knew instantly what he was worried about—leprosy—and hastened to reassure him.

"I think this is psoriasis," I said. "Not serious, and not contagious, but it is uncomfortable. My father has this ailment, and it looks just like this, so I can be pretty sure of my diagnosis. I can try to make an ointment to ease the discomfort, if you will be patient and wait until after the battle."

He took back his hand and replaced the glove. "No need." He stared at me again, face totally devoid of emotion, and nodded once. I could imagine the relief he must be feeling. He stood there for so long, I was compelled to look down. He probably took that as modesty, but I didn't care. I just had to break eye contact.

Then he walked away.

Sven came to my side holding a goblet of fresh water. I took it gratefully. My thoughts had been grim.

"Sven, will you do me a great service?"

"Of course," he said, smiling shyly.

"When we get to Castle Huel, my younger cousin Kendra may be waiting for me. She is very dear to me, and a Huel—next in line, after Richard."

I took a deep breath. "Don't let the men touch her. I beg you. Believe me, you will be rewarded."

He looked very solemn. He raised his right fist to his chest and said, "On my life. I have some rank here. Fear not for her."

I breathed again. "Her name is Kendra. Do you know who I mean?"

He nodded. "The doe-eyed girl."

I started.

"Oh. They have a name for her." I was amused. "Do they have one for me as well?"

Sven blushed red. He shook his head violently and turned away.

Chapter 27

Late that night, when we were undressing for bed in the back bedroom, I asked Lars the same question.

He laughed and told me.

This time, I blushed.

"But that's—"

"Crude?" he said. "But apt."

He grabbed me and threw me playfully on the bed.

"You're doing it right now."

He leaned forward on all fours and bit me on the lower lip. I couldn't pull away. He waited until I stilled, and then released his hold on me and lifted his head.

His eyes were about eight inches from mine. They looked steely.

"But first. Tell me how you know our language."

Uh oh. Damn, he was sharp. He had not missed that. I'd better tell the truth.

"I know all languages. Cedric spelled me."

Lars put all his weight on me to pin me down.

"So you have understood our battle talk and plans from the start."

I nodded.

He cursed. "I am a fool. A besotted fool. I wonder how many of the others have figured it out."

I kind of hoped they hadn't, if this reaction was typical.

"You tricked me. It was very cleverly done. And now you shall pay for this." There was a wicked glint in his eye.

"Tonight I have a mind to take the queen," he said. "Not a playful wench, but a full-blood Saxon queen, and I am going to make her scream for mercy."

"Not full-blood Saxon, actually, only on my mother's—"

"Shut up," he ordered. "Enjoy your fate." He kissed me lightly, to assure me that this was only in play.

But it didn't seem like play. I was no fool. It seemed like a Viking Warlord desperate to assert his dominance over the woman who outranked him in this land, and had fooled him with her language skills. A woman who would soon have to beg for mercy in other ways as her troops were decimated and her castle lay open for pillaging.

But I could never play the victim. Whatever came tomorrow, I vowed he would remember tonight for the rest of his life.

Lars began his assault with me moaning for him, begging for him. But in the end, I had him on his back, with me on top, riding him *not* to sweet victory, but to the lusty gates of hell.

There was nothing sweet about me that night. His eyes burned into mine as I stoked the fire that rendered him rock hard. My hair flew like a wild wind about us. I didn't check my voice.

He struggled to take command. I gripped his chest with my nails to control him. He grimaced and took the pain.

He wanted a Saxon queen. I gave him one who could ride like the Valkyries.

In the last moment, I lost control, and he rolled me to my back. I surrendered willingly then, and he finished me off with Viking forged steel until I cried out his name, clutching his shoulders.

After, when his arms were around me and his panting had subsided, I heard him speak softly.

"I do not care about this Saxon kingdom any longer. I just want their queen."

Many things went down that night.

The first was the most dramatic.

I fell thoroughly and irrevocably in love.

Lars fell asleep before I did. I watched him for a long while, marvelling that once, not very long ago, we had not known each other. How could that be?

This man controlled my life and future. Yet even then, he respected my profession and my need to work at it.

He had captured my heart.

He was the most powerful man in more than one land.

He was the only man I wanted now.

I watched him breathe. His chest moved slowly up and down. His face was relaxed.

I studied that face. He was not handsome like his younger brother, it was true. This was a man's face, coarse and rugged with steep planes, like the mountains of the far north. His facial hair was streaked with grey.

I studied his nose, which was large and sharply made. His eyes were closed, but I knew them to be light grey when they danced, and more steely when he was angry.

White-blond hair grew back from his forehead. It was receding slightly.

This was the face that would haunt me for the rest of my life.

I knew that he loved me. I had come to it later, but in my heart I knew also that I loved him just as deeply.

He stirred. For a moment, his eyes opened and he gazed at me, in a dream-like state.

I smiled. "Go back to sleep, my love."

He relaxed at the sound of my voice and closed his eyes.

The second thing was most mysterious.

It was deep into night and I sensed that Lars had left the bed.

Low voices came from just outside the doorway, speaking in that guttural tongue.

"I still don't ken how you will manage it."

"Spread the word. Oh, and another thing. Let it be known that if one of your men touches the queen, he will be drawn, quartered, and burned. I will do it myself."

"Yes, but—"

"I reward my friends well, Magnus. But to those who defy me, I am ruthless. You know this."

A late arriving leader with his troops, receiving instructions, I surmised. Other voices joined in. I tried not to listen.

They weren't long. I feigned sleep when Lars returned to bed.

The third thing was most disturbing.

It was a very dark night. The two moons of Land's End were hidden behind clouds. Something wished me awake.

Lars was snoring softly at my side, curled up in the other direction.

I lay on my back. The sheet had pulled away from me. I felt something warm embrace me, but there was nothing there that I could see.

Was I awake, or was it a dream? The warmth traveled up my legs to my hips, and then higher, until it covered me completely in a sweet blanket.

I purred.

Like an electric blanket suddenly switched on, the heat increased. It—I don't know how to describe this, but it filled me everywhere…my mouth, between my legs. It seeped in to every bit of me. A wind licked my ear. I moaned.

When I opened my eyes, I could see that a dark grey mist enveloped me. At first I was frightened, but then sweet wisps played with my mind, calming my beating heart.

I closed my eyes and fell back into the dream. Invisible hands caressed my breasts…the wind licked my nipples. I relaxed as the mist moved over me, within me, softly pulsing, pulsing, riding me like a mystical man, and then I felt a shudder.

The warmth remained. I fell back to sleep and slept soundly.

Chapter 28

When I awoke in the morning, the sun was high. Lars had gone and Soren was sitting on the chair, both legs resting on the bed, watching me. He smiled slowly.

And then I knew.

What's worse, Soren knew I knew. For a few seconds, I panicked. Almost immediately, my mind filled with warm, calming wisps. Then gently, when my heart returned to a normal beat, they dissipated.

He didn't leave me time to be embarrassed.

With one hand, he held out my green gown. "Get dressed quickly," he said. "I sense a crisis. The drums are beating."

I didn't bother with false modesty. I moved to the side of the bed and donned the gown quickly, drawing the laces to tie them.

Soren raised an eyebrow when I strapped on the daggers Lars had given me.

Before I could complete the task, Sven was at the door.

"He wants her."

Soren nodded.

I slipped into my soft shoes and looked around for a mirror.

"How's my hair?" I asked Soren.

He raised his hand. A warm wind blew at me. Every hair fell into place.

"Perfect," he said. "Come."

I followed him out the empty great hall to the fortress steps.

Soren moved forward to stand with Lars. I stayed back with Sven on the raised porch where I could better see over heads.

The air rippled with the sound of drumming. It started far away, and then became louder with each second. I shivered. It was a terrifying sound.

"What is that drumming?" I asked Sven.

"The men in the distance are beating on their shields. They do that before battle, or when they are welcoming back others."

The drumming grew louder, closer. Then the men around us started beating their shields. I put my hands over my ears in a futile attempt to block the volume.

Sven pointed. I could see riders in the distance. All along the southern pathway, crowds of men parted to let them pass, then closed in behind them. A wave of bodies followed the riders toward us.

As they drew close, there was a roar of welcome from men all along the path. With a flourish, horses pounded into the courtyard toward us.

Two young men vaulted from their mounts. By their armor, I could tell that they were high born. They looked weary but triumphant.

Lars strode forward to greet them. He used a special arm grip as a welcome, one I hadn't seen him do before.

"What is it?" I whispered to Sven. We stayed on the steps.

"Nial has sent riders back from the southern battlefield. They're reporting to Lars."

He strained to see.

The cheers got louder. Lars was given something green and gold, splattered with bloodstains.

Our colors.

I felt instantly sick.

"What does it mean?" I asked Sven. My heart was beating wildly.

"They've taken something from a Lord who has fallen."

Lars was about twenty feet away. He turned to me. His eyes were hard.

He threw the colors on the ground. His left arm held a heavy shield. It was well worn from battle, scored in a dozen places. One edge of it had been sheared off. He raised it upright, facing me, so that I could see the insignia.

"Who is it, Rowena?"

My heart was in my throat. It was our house coat of arms. But something had been added and painted red. I knew that Celtic scroll.

"Jon." My voice was hoarse. "He added the red so his men could see him in the field."

"Is he second?" Lars demanded.

"I'm second," I said foolishly, like it mattered who was older. "Jon is after me."

But not anymore.

"He died bravely," Lars said with gravitas.

The wail started deep in my lungs and gained strength with each inch it traveled. It ripped out of my throat and across the field, above all the other voices, as far as the heavens.

"Sven, catch her." Lars's voice.

Strong arms caught me before I hit the ground. Then Lars was there, pulling me against his chest. "This is the worst it will be, my love. Hold on."

Voices rippled through the crowd from the men who had come from the south. They didn't know of my capture here.

"The Dark Lord's cousin."

"Lars has captured their queen!"

"The second is dead."

More cheers and roars of triumph.

"I hate you," I whispered into his chest.

"I know. But we have an audience. Weep like a woman or get angry like a queen. How do you want them to view you?"

I pushed back from his chest with all my might. "I hate you!" I yelled. And I struck his face hard.

He laughed and caught both my wrists. "You can hate me in bed tonight."

He said it too loudly, so I knew he was acting. The men who heard roared in delight. I could hear the words repeated from man to man through the crowd, along with 'wildcat.'

Wildcat Queen. So much better than weak woman.

Lars was damned good at strategy.

I struggled against my locked wrists. His left hand held both of mine easily, like I was a mere child. His right hand grabbed my hair and pulled my head back so he could control me while he kissed me.

I couldn't fight at all. The crowd went wild.

"Well played," he whispered to me after the kiss. And then louder, "Soren, take her for me."

But I wasn't playing.

Soren grabbed my wrists and I fought him, too. He twisted me around until I was facing out with my back against his chest and my arms trapped by his own.

The thunder started then. Dark clouds moved in from all directions, swirling, turning the sky an angry grey.

Men cried out, startled and fearful.

Thor boomed overhead, huge earth-shaking roars of violence so startling that the entire sky seemed to be a battlefield.

"How are you doing that?" Soren asked in awe.

"I'm not," I said, watching the clouds collide. "Cedric is. He felt my grief."

Soren hissed. "Your cousin Cedric is one of us?"

One of you, I said. But I didn't say it out loud. I didn't need to. Soren heard me.

He laughed. "This day just gets better and better."

Lars tried to yell over the celestial crashes. It was almost as if the heavens had conspired to drown him out.

But not the heavens, I knew. The very opposite. I shivered.

At last the rumbles subsided and became distant.

Lars was barking orders to his men. They would attack tomorrow at dawn.

Dawn! And Grandfather was alone at the castle!

"Let me go, Soren." I broke from his arms and ran to Lars. He caught me with one arm.

"Lars, let me ride to Huel. I should be there now, with Grandfather, when they bring him news of Jon."

Lars turned and frowned. "No. Too dangerous."

I put my hands on his chest and pleaded. "Would I really be better off here? I know you plan to keep me with the wagons at the back, but is that really safe? If I were at Huel, I would watch for you from the tower and come to the steps to meet you. I swear I would!"

He hesitated. "We'll talk later. My plan is to be first through the gates. But I cannot be sure that will happen."

The shouts around us grew louder. More warriors came forward with other battle trophies. Lars put me gently aside to address his commanders.

I turned away, not wanting to see more.

So this was war. My cousin Jon had been killed, and I was a prisoner in the enemy camp. This was real now. Only Cedric and Richard stood between Lars's great army and the fall of Huel.

What horrible irony.

I loved Lars.

I hated his mission.

These men—Jory, Sven, Lars, even young Tyr. They had been kind to me. I had come to care about them, and yet here they were about to destroy my home and family.

And Soren. He had vowed to protect me. Yet he seemed to *crave* the blood that would spill tomorrow.

How could I like such men?

Never had I been so confused.

All eyes were on the increasing pile of battle trophies. No one was watching me.

Or so I thought. I was wrong.

I melted back to the steps. Tears were starting, blurring my vision.

Grandfather was alone. He would be alone when these barbarians stormed the castle. Jon was dead. Richard—he would probably die, too. And then what would I tell Kendra?

Kendra! I needed to get to Kendra.

A huge hand slapped across my mouth and an arm wrapped around my waist. I shrieked, but my captor screamed louder. I could smell burning flesh. Soren's spell had worked.

The assailant let go of me and I fell forward on my hands and knees.

Another man cursed and took his place…Gustav. His gloved hands reached round my body and roughly lifted me off the ground. A second man held a sack.

"Lars!" I screamed.

This time, he heard. He and Soren swung around as one. Soren raised his hand to enact some form of magic, and as he did, the infant witch came alive.

I didn't think. I reacted on instinct. Magic swirled toward me. My hand covered the bracelet, the air around me blazed yellow, and I pitched into the sky.

Chapter 29

Apparently, my last cohesive thought had been of Kendra. That was why I didn't land at Castle Huel.

Instead, I fell into a river of freezing water.

"Shit!" I yelled, fighting to keep my head above water. The heavy skirt and my daggers were weighing me down.

I heard a splash.

"Row!" Kendra whooped. Arms eagerly reached about me.

"Get me out of here," I wailed.

We stumbled to the river's edge.

Kendra scrambled out first. I needed help. She grabbed my left arm below the shoulder and hauled me onto shore. I landed flat on my belly. Luckily, the grass provided a soft cushion.

"Holy hell, that's cold."

Loki leaped forward to lick my face.

"Good thing the air is warm," Kendra said happily, shaking herself like a dog. "It's really quite refreshing."

"Not so much, when you're drowning," I muttered. "Well, I won't have to wash my hair now…as long as I can get this duckweed out of it." I swiped at a long green seaweed-thing.

"Hey, is that a new dress?"

"And I haven't even wrecked it yet," I said drolly.

Kendra was dressed in 'Arizona Goth.' Black tunic, black tights, black boots, leather wrist bands, lots of silver chains, and a cool dagger on her belt. Disguised as a boy, no doubt. Good plan.

I dragged myself up into a sitting position. Loki landed on my lap and demanded scratches.

"Drat, you're heavy. I swear he's grown." I shoved him off, but continued to scratch behind his ears.

"He has," Kendra said enigmatically.

Loki rolled on his back, expecting tummy rubs. I obliged, while struggling to get my questions in some sort of priority order.

"Where the hell are we?"

"Somewhere between Castle Sargon and Huel. A little over half way, I think. I just stopped here for a drink of water."

Kendra was always a little short on detail.

"And why are we *here*?"

"Oh," she said, drawing her knees up to her chest. She wrapped her arms around the knees. "That nice messenger got through to me. I was on my way to Huel to meet you. But I lost my horse yesterday."

She lost her horse.

"How?"

Kendra sighed. "It saw a snake and bolted."

Okay, that was reasonable. "So they do have snakes here. Ick. And you stayed here overnight?"

"Not here exactly. Further back. Loki kept me warm."

Good old Loki. What a great guard pooch. He deserved all these tummy rubs and more.

"I tried Arizona first, but obviously you weren't there."

"You went through the wall?"

She nodded.

I could hardly believe it. Kendra hated going through the wall! And yet she had done it without me.

My heart quickened. "Did you talk to Dad?"

She shook her head. "Figured I shouldn't alert him. I phoned your cousin Janet. Told her I was just stopping by for an hour to pick up a few things at the drugstore and thought I would give her a call. She dropped everything to come and pick me up. I played it real cool and said you would contact her soon, when it was your turn to go through the portal."

"Smart thinking, Kendra." I nodded in satisfaction. No sense scaring everyone back home when they couldn't do a thing about it.

"Oh, and Val came with me."

"Val?"

"We showed him around. He decided to stay behind with Janet."

"*What*?"

"Only for a little while. I think they have a thing going on."

Val and Janet. What an incredibly cool thing. I shook my head in amazement.

"Loki came too, but in a smaller size. That's how I knew you hadn't stayed there. Loki sniffed you going back through the wall."

My head was spinning. "Okay, I give up. Perhaps you better take me through this from the start."

While we sat on the grassy bank in the warm sun, she told the tale of the last few days.

"*Medieval Man*?" I blurted at one point.

"Yeah. It was the cape," she said. "We had to get him away from the crowd real fast. He wanted to give autographs. In Latin."

I groaned, thinking of the photos that would go up on Facebook.

"Well, I'm glad he's with Janet. She'll watch out for him. The timing could have been better though."

"You mean, he won't be here to help us if things get bad."

I nodded. Not that I faulted Val. He didn't know what was about to take place in Land's End.

Nobody did, except Gareth. And who knew what he would actually do?

Then I brought her up to speed on my last few days. Well, almost up to speed. Not that it mattered. She picked up on the parts I left out.

"So. You like this Lars a lot."

I felt my heart rate pick up.

"Not sure I can explain this. But he understands me, that I need to be free. He's the same sort."

Loki curled up in the grass beside me with his head on my lap.

I felt Kendra staring at me.

"Be honest. Are you doing this to save Huel from burning, Row?"

"Yes, of course I am. And to protect Grandfather. But—" How could I explain this? I licked my lips. "It's not the sacrifice you think it is."

Now she smiled. "You're blushing!"

"Get outta town," I muttered.

"Must be some hot guy."

"He's older, very Nordic looking. You've seen him. He was Gareth's Viking friend."

"Not anymore, it sounds." Kendra was rocking back and forth, holding her knees.

"No." I paused. That was true. Gareth would happily take his head when they next met up. Some things, you just didn't forgive.

"I know this won't make sense to you, Ken. But in some strange way, things have come full circle. I don't know how to put this, but...I have found where I belong."

"You mean, with this guy?"

"I mean at Huel. And yes, with this man, if he should win this battle. You could almost say...the gods predicted it."

I told her about the time I first landed in Lars's bed. What Lars had said then about the gods, and how I had recently come to think that a Viking invasion might be a good thing for Land's End.

She whistled low. "So this invasion has been the plan from the start."

"There's been a lot of treachery you could say. Lars holds all the lands east of Huel now and his brother Nial is fighting Cedric in the south. They'll close in by tomorrow."

She took a moment to digest that.

"Is Richard with Cedric?"

I nodded. She would care about Richard, of course. And then I gave her the really bad news.

"Jon is dead. They brought me his shield." My voice broke while saying it.

She shivered then.

"That sucks. I'm so sorry, Row. Jon was a good guy." She paused. "We aren't going to win this, are we?"

I didn't hesitate. I shook my head. This was the good thing about Kendra. Now only was she uncommonly brave, but she was also a realist.

"Lars has the east and south. Gareth is holding the north, and he wants the Huel men dead after what they did to his cousins. I told you about that, right? Ivan, John, and Richard killed his cousins when they came after me, when I had been kidnapped."

She nodded grimly.

"I knew them slightly." My voice was solemn. "They liked to hear me sing. Two of them had bright red hair. It was so…unnecessary."

We sat in silence for a short time.

"That only leaves the west." I paused. "Will Thane come to our defense?"

"Thane isn't going to do anything," Kendra told me. She sounded bitter. "He's waiting to see who wins this."

"Damn." I felt disappointment clear to my toes.

Still, I wasn't surprised. Thane was a lot like Sargon. I remembered an earlier conflict, where Sargon pulled all the fighting men from Castle Huel to protect Sargonia. Grandfather had been spitting mad, being forced to leave our own home unprotected.

"Hamlet," I mumbled.

"That's just what I was thinking," Kendra said. "He's procrastinating."

"Even I can see that isn't smart. Lars will be even more powerful when he captures Huel." But I guess the others didn't yet know how strong Lars really was.

Actually, they didn't know there was a Lars yet. Funny how that had slipped my mind. It seemed unimaginable, when my own mind was so full of him.

"Then good thing this Lars guy wants *you* as well as the castle," Kendra said. "Did he give you that necklace?"

My hand flew to my neck. It was still there. "Yes."

"It rocks," she said simply.

We sat in silence for a moment.

"Row, are we staying here?"

I looked around, baffled. "Here? Why would we stay here?"

She smiled. "No, I mean in Land's End. For good."

Oh. That was something we hadn't discussed yet, not since the month we last traveled through the portal, whether our stay here would be permanent.

I sighed. "I think so. Would you believe, in the last three days, I've never even considered going back to Arizona? I kept bouncing back and forth between returning to Thane, escaping to Castle Huel and Grandfather, or staying with Lars for the course of the battle. I never considered the option of us leaving Land's End behind and going back through the portal."

"I guess that's an answer," Kendra said. "If it wasn't even on your list—"

"—then it couldn't have been something I would do. Let me think about it one last time."

Should we go back to Arizona? I should at least consider the arguments.

Dad was there. My baby might be safer there. At least it would be born in a hospital.

Yes, it might be safer for all of us.

But could I seriously think about separating this baby from its father now? Cedric had shown how much he cared for me, and he longed for this child. If we were a world apart, Cedric would never know his own child. That just seemed so cruel.

I couldn't do it.

Just as I knew I couldn't leave Grandfather and the people of Huel who depended on me here. I had a place in this world. As a healer, I could make a difference to so many. And as the consort of the man who ruled, be it Lars or Cedric, I could have some influence on how those people were treated.

It was my duty to stay in Land's End. Dad would understand. He knew the meaning of duty. I would find a way to visit him regularly, or bring him here.

"I'm needed here, Kendra. And we can do some good here," I said finally.

She nodded. "I feel the same way. So that's that."

There was no point in my saying that she could go back without me. Kendra was uncommonly loyal. She would get all huffy and take it as an insult. No, we would stay together through thick and thin.

"It's a funny thing," I mused. "Before coming to Land's End, I would have thought that if women were rare, they would be more valued, and thus have more power."

She cocked her head. "Explain.

I cleared my throat. "Instead, I've found that we are indeed valued, but if anything, we have less freedom because of it."

She nodded. "They aim to protect us. That means restricting our movements."

I snorted. "You can see how well that's worked. Ironic, isn't it?"

She got it. "Here we sit in the middle of nowhere—and nobody knows where we are."

It was strangely satisfying, and yet at the same time, chilling.

And now I had a question to ask.

"How did Thane react when he found out I was gone?"

Kendra stopped rocking. She looked me square in the eyes.

"I think he's accepted the fact that you won't be coming back. I had a long talk with him."

I gulped. "How did it go?"

She shrugged. "At first, he was really angry. But then I got him to see that you couldn't ever be caged. You just wouldn't be happy. And as he isn't prepared to leave his kingdom, ever."

One more important thing to get clear.

"Did he at least try to go through the portal to bring me back from Arizona?"

"No," she said slowly, as if testing my emotional state. "He said he couldn't be chasing after you all the time."

I felt the cold then. It was as if a chill wind had whipped down from the north. Well, that settled it. At least in my mind.

Cedric had followed me through the wall, without a thought for anything else, including his own safety. He would do it again, in a minute.

Lars…once this battle was over, he would come for me. I would stake my life on it. I'd already staked my heart.

"So just Val came with you?" I asked.

"He had a wonderful time."

I smiled bravely. "Good for Val. I wonder if Janet will come here for a visit?"

"That's what I'm predicting. But Val was pretty cool with Arizona. He loved the gadgets. Maybe he'll stay there for a while."

I smiled at the thought of them together. Loveable Janet, the fashion queen, with her own personal designer. Talk about a match made in heaven. I hoped Aunt Mellie would like her. It would be such wonderful company for her.

But a part of me was hurting.

"It's sad," I said, plucking little pieces of grass from the ground. "I never thought it would be like this."

"Don't be too hard on Thane. He's in a tricky position. He understands the bit about being responsible for your people and not wanting to leave Castle Huel. He feels the same about Sargonia."

The reality was, my family was at Huel. The father of my child was at Huel. I was second in line to the Huel dynasty. If Cedric were to die, I would inherit the castle and lands. Would I not want to return immediately to Huel?

Thane wouldn't allow that. He would expect me to stay with him. Even now, while Huel was in grave danger, he would insist upon it.

But I couldn't sit by and watch Huel burn without doing everything in my power to protect it, just like a man would.

"Thane needs a woman who will be happy being his wife and nothing more. He doesn't want someone who will go running off to help save her family home when it's threatened, like I'm doing now."

Kendra frowned. "All these men here are attracted to us because we're different. But I'm not so sure they actually *want* different in the long run."

"Some do." I gazed at the rolling river. It was almost a metaphor for what I was feeling. "Cedric does, believe it or not. He wants me to learn as much magic as possible and become as powerful as I can."

"That's cool. And Lars?"

"Lars appears to. He wants to use Huel as his home base. But he also wants me to travel by his side and see the world. He doesn't intend to leave me behind."

"Wow." Kendra was impressed. "But not Gareth."

"No," I said, sadly. "Gareth is like Thane. It's all about Norland. He wants me there with him."

"You know, if you look at this from a distance, all of you are pretty much alike. You, Thane, and Gareth are all totally fierce about wanting to defend your own homelands. Thing is, you're a woman."

"You got it."

Kendra rose to her feet. "Well, they'll just have to deal with it. Let's get going." She held a hand out to me.

No doubt about it. The rest of the world might be crumbling around me, but I had the best friend in the world.

Chapter 30

We had been walking along the main path to Huel for about an hour.

At this rate, we'd never get to Huel in time. I was just about to suggest we try something else, when Kendra started to grumble.

"I'm starving. I finished all the food I brought last night."

That gave me an idea.

"Let me try something." I stopped walking and concentrated.

What was that spell again? Damn, why didn't I write it down when I had the chance.

I chanted some words out loud.

Poof!

A bunny appeared on the path before us. It was light brown with a white tail and looked bewildered.

"It worked!" I clapped my hands and nearly jumped up and down.

"How did you do that?" Kendra exclaimed.

"I've been practicing with Cedric. He's showing me how to do all sorts of magic. Stuff I can do without the bracelet." This was cool. This was stupendous. I couldn't wait to tell Cedric that I did this all by myself.

"Awesome. But you aren't really suggesting we eat that, are you?"

The bunny faced us and wiggled its nose. It hopped toward us.

Loki growled.

Gulp. No way could I kill and roast a rabbit with my own hands. Unfortunately, I didn't know the spells for that, either.

"How hungry are you?" I asked.

"Not *that* hungry."

Lucky for that. Before we could move a muscle, the darn thing had turned tail and disappeared—quick as a bunny—into the forest.

Loki took off after it, in a wild chase.

"Oh dear. That wasn't part of the plan."

"Here, bunny, bunny!" called Kendra.

Not a leaf moved in the forest.

"Anybunny there?" I said, giggling.

Kendra gave me a dirty look. "What do we do about Loki?"

I shrugged. "He'll find us when he's ready."

I hated to think what could happen before he was ready. Oh well. I hated even more to think about what was going to happen tomorrow.

"Let's get going," Kendra said. "The sooner we get to Huel, the quicker we get fed."

She grabbed my arm and coaxed me forward.

I groaned. "Don't think I can walk all the way to Huel, Kendra. It's got to be at least another ten miles."

I was about to suggest something when a man stepped out from the forest.

He was big and mean-looking, and he held a round shield and an axe. I looked at the burly Viking guy and knew exactly what to do.

"Run!" I yelled.

I took off back toward the river like a crazed bat.

Kendra was yelling something. I turned around to make sure she was right behind me.

She wasn't. In fact, she hadn't left the path.

Her back was to me and the Viking guy was lying on *his* back on the ground. His shield was about six feet away. Kendra was holding the axe.

I ran back to her side.

"What did you do?" I asked, panting.

She shrugged. "There was only one of them, Row."

He obviously didn't know martial arts.

I poked his body with my foot.

"Is he dead?"

"I don't think so," she said. "Do you want him dead?"

I hesitated, then shook my head. "As long as he doesn't wake up before we get away from here."

"That's good. I killed a man once already." Her voice held an unusual tone.

"You did?" This was news to me.

"When I was with Henry riding to Sargonia. We were sort of cornered. I shot one as an example to the others."

I gulped. "Did it work?"

She nodded. "They vamoosed."

Hoo boy. I hoped we didn't encounter any more loners like this one. But have to say, I was feeling pretty safe with Kendra at my side.

"This is a cool axe," Kendra said, reaching down. "Can I keep it?"

I stared at her. "Do you need it?" It was a really big one, the type with a curved head.

She grinned. "Probably not. I was thinking as a souvenir."

What the hell. Keep the damn thing, I thought.

"As long as you don't start cutting notches into it," I told her.

She smiled wistfully. "Wish Richard and Logan could have seen that."

I rolled my eyes.

But it did make me worry about how far Lars's troops had extended. I assumed this fellow was with his brother's forces from the south. The battle must be getting closer.

"What was this guy doing this far west, do you think? Was he a deserter? Or maybe a scout."

I shook my head.

"Unlikely. Scouts don't attack people. They try to stay hidden. Probably this guy was an opportunist. He cut away from the main troops to see if he could get a head start on the pillaging."

"Nice." Kendra gave him an extra kick. He didn't move.

I couldn't help the nervous feeling that crept over me. "Look, I think we really need to get out of here. There may be more around."

"What are you suggesting we do?"

I hugged my arms to my chest. "I'm going to try to get us some transportation. Bunny style."

Now she was totally baffled.

"I'm thinking you might want to have that dagger handy. I'm not exactly sure this will work."

Her eyes went wide. "What are you going to do?"

"I was thinking a horse, but it would be better if we could avoid meeting any other travellers on this path here. I'll try to conjure up something with wings, like a pegasus. But I've had a little trouble with big animals, so we need to be careful. The mastodon was a mistake."

"*Mastodon?*"

"Way too much poop."

"*You conjured a mastodon?*"

"I messed up the spell."

"Didn't you run it through Spellchecker?"

I waved a hand at her.

"Just be ready."

I took in a big breath. Then I chanted the words the best I could remember, and waited.

Poof!

Something stood on the path in front of us. It was quite large and it had wings.

Not a unicorn…a *dragon*.

Oh! It was the cutest little dragon you ever saw! Okay, not so little. It stood at least six feet high and twelve feet long.

I did a quick check for gender. Definitely a female. She had big green eyes, huge folded wings and a dainty forked tail.

"Row, that's not a unicorn."

"I know! I must have messed up the spell again. Isn't she pretty?" I probed her mind a little.

Kendra whacked my arm with her hand.

"Unicorn…dragon. Not much difference there. Except one is a sweet little horsey, and the other a *fire-breathing beast that can char us to cinders.*"

"That's her name, by the way. Cinders."

Kendra's big brown eyes stared at me. "You named her already?"

"Oh no. That's her real name. I peeked into her mind."

She smacked her hand to her forehead.

"We can't keep it, Row. This thing could torch us."

"Oh, don't be a wienie, Kendra. This one is almost tame. See?"

I stepped forward to stroke its nose. It wiggled its tail and giggled out a fireball.

"Yikes!" The left side of my dress was dancing with little flames.

"Jesus Murphy," grumbled Kendra. She jumped forward and threw the contents of her canteen on my skirt.

We both looked down.

"You've wrecked it now," she said.

"Damn." The whole front hemline was singed with black. There was a new slit that rippled up past my left knee, like it had actually been designed that way.

"Good thing that dress was still damp from the river. Otherwise, it would have been toast. And you, too."

Cinders looked very sad. I went over and gave her a hug.

"So I guess we know why she was called Cinders."

"Yes, poor thing. Apparently she has a hiccup or burp problem. The other dragons tease her about it." I stroked her neck. "We just need to stay to the side of her."

Cinders started to purr. I let her feel the joy in my mind, and she giggled again.

Just a little fireball this time. It scorched the ground in front of her.

"Oops."

Kendra sighed. She threw up her hands. "So what's the plan?"

"We get on her back and ride her to Castle Huel."

Chapter 31

"We *what*?"

"She'll let us, Kendra. I already asked her."

Kendra smacked her head again. "You're kidding me."

"No, really. I think she's lonely. She hasn't got an owner because of the burping problem and she's dying to be claimed. All the other dragons her age have a home. It's really quite sad." I gave her another hug.

Kendra was pacing behind me. Mumbling and pacing. "We're going to *ride* her. Up in the *air*."

"Yes, but don't worry. She doesn't mind."

"That *wasn't* what I was worried about."

I decided to try it out. Just myself, for the test run. That was the plan. It got a bit hijacked.

Apparently, the bunny business in the forest had wound down.

I heard a low growl.

Loki appeared at my side, and he wasn't happy about the huge winged creature in front of him.

Cinders squealed. Okay, screeched like a banshee.

Loki barked in return and commenced stalking forward.

"Oh frig—Loki, come back here! Come—oh dammit."

Cinders freaked. A fireball left her mouth, heading right for the huge wolf.

Loki yelped. The flame caught his backside just as he turned, singing his poor furry tush. He took off into the woods. Seconds later, were heard a splash.

"At least he made it to the river," Kendra said. "Smart wolfie-poo."

"What did you call him?"

She explained.

I sighed. "Guess we better leave him here. I can't imagine he'll want to ride to the top of the castle on Cinders. Besides, he really shouldn't be anywhere the near the battlefield tomorrow. It wouldn't be safe."

Kendra nodded.

It wouldn't be safe for us either, but at least I could keep the animals clear of danger.

I sent a loving farewell message to Loki, pleading with him to stay away until I sent for him.

When I turned around, Kendra was stroking Cinders to calm her down. She was looking very sad indeed.

I was glad they seemed to be making friends. It was going to become important in the next few minutes.

"So I'm thinking it would be best if I tried riding Cinders first. I'll take her a short distance and then send her back for you."

Kendra went rigid. "You're kidding, right? Isn't this something we should do together?"

I moved up to Cinder's side. "Nothing to worry about, Ken. It will be like riding bareback."

"I've never ridden bareback," muttered Kendra. "Not even on a horse, for chrissake."

"Piece of cake," I said cheerfully. "You just use your knees."

I patted the young dragon and cooed to her. "Now lie down, Cinders. I'm going to climb on your back."

She flopped down on the ground.

"Good girl! I'll just put my leg over your back now. Ken, give me a hand."

Even with her lying down, it was a bit awkward. Her wings were in the way.

"Okay, this isn't working. Cinders, I'm going to start at your tail and climb up that way. Okay?"

She whapped her tail on the ground.

"I think that means 'yes'," I said to Kendra.

She looked doubtful. "Are you sure this is a good idea?"

"Well, the only other ride I know for sure how to conjure is a Mastodon."

"Okay, we'll try the dragon," she said quickly. "Watch the barbs."

I lifted my skirt and plunked my right leg over her tail, avoiding the barbs. Then I shimmied up her back until I was just behind her head. I gave her a good pat. Then I sat up awkwardly.

"There's no good place to put your legs," I said. "Her wings are in the way."

Kendra groaned. "This is a bad idea. I just know it."

I kept my knees bent.

"Okay, Cinders. Stand up."

She sprung and I bounced. "Yikes!" I wrapped my arms around her neck and held on.

Cinders was delighted. She started to prance around in a small circle.

"Cinders, stop!" She did. Abruptly. My chin whapped against her neck.

"Ouch!" I was also seriously out of breath.

Kendra was chortling. "If you could have seen yourself. Maybe we should call her Tigger."

I raised myself to sitting again and stroked Cinder's head. She purred. I shared some thoughts with her.

"Believe it or not, this is just what the poor thing has been wanting. A human companion to do things with. So I shouldn't have any trouble getting her to fly me places, as soon as we get the hang of it."

"Hang," Kendra muttered. "That's one way of putting it."

"Of course, it would be better if we had a saddle. Not sure how we could fasten it though, with these wings in the way. And some way of attaching reins, because I don't think she would tolerate a bridle."

"Are you kidding me? Her breath would burn the thing to ashes in a second."

"Oops. Forgot about that."

I patted Cinders again. "Well, baby? Want to take me up for a spin?"

I felt pressure against my knees as she raised both her wings.

"Holy hell, those wings are HUGE!" said Kendra, backing away.

"Aren't they amazing?" I was super excited. They were pretty formidable at rest. But when she unfolded her wings, they were triple the size you expected.

And then, more gracefully than I could have imagined, Cinders flapped them and lifted us into the sky.

"Don't go far!" yelled Kendra below us.

I was mesmerized. We soared up into blue sky. Birds scattered, and the deep green of earth became further and further away.

I laughed excitedly. She caught my mood and soared.

She wasn't a bit jerky while we were in the air. I was reminded of ducks. They always look so awkward walking on the ground, but they were magnificent flyers, fast and sleek.

So was my dragon friend. She circled the sky above Kendra, and then I was able to guide her in the direction toward Huel by pressing my right knee against her side.

She caught on quickly. This was far more fun than when Cedric had taken me into the air. With Cedric, I was always on guard and wary of his ultimate motive.

Cinders was happy just to have fun.

Can I begin to describe the elation of being up in the air with no metal cage around you? I imagine this is what the early pilots of bi-planes felt like, with their faces exposed to the glorious wind.

The earth is so amazingly beautiful when viewed from above. Lush green hills were segmented by winding blue rivers that continued into the horizon. I could see Castle Huel clearly in the distance, a grey square against the green.

After several minutes of blissful travel, I looked for a clearing below us and prompted her to land.

Good thing I hadn't eaten in a while. She circled several times on her descent, and then landed with a slight thump.

Pretty good for a first try. I was proud of her and let her feel it.

She wiggled in pleasure.

Of course, then she burped and scorched the grass in front of us. I hoped the embers would die down.

"Hold still," I said. "I'll just slide off your back."

I slid myself down her until I hit the barbed tail, and then pushed myself to stand and dismount.

"Good girl," I praised, careful to keep to the side of her. I patted her and gave her a hug. She was positively beaming with happiness.

"Okay, now we need to get Kendra. Cinders, I'll stay here. You go back there and pick her up."

This didn't go over well.

Cinders squawked. She squatted on the ground and lay her head down. Her big green eyes looked sorrowful.

"Oh dear. I think I understand. You don't want to leave me. Hmm..."

Poor dragon. She had finally found a mistress, and of course she didn't want to be separated. But this made things awkward. I couldn't leave Kendra behind. What to do? How much weight could Cinders carry?

"Okay, let's go back and see if we can bring Kendra, too. Do you think you're up to it?"

She sprang back up, eager to be active. I straddled her tail again, and shimmied up her back.

This time, I held on tight with my arms around her neck when she took off.

Was it smell that led her directly back to Kendra? She seemed to have an amazing sense of direction. Within minutes we were landing in the little clearing where Kendra stood waiting.

Cinders landed daintily. Kendra rushed forward from the forest edge.

"What happened?"

"We had a slight problem," I said, dismounting in that awkward tail-way. "Cinders didn't want to leave me."

Kendra groaned. "So what now?"

Dragons love to be petted. Cinders was purring under my ministrations.

"We ride her together."

Kendra gulped. "You're kidding. Tell me you're kidding."

I continued to stroke Cinders. "It shouldn't be difficult. You see two people riding one horse all the time in the movies. Cinders is at least as big as a horse. She should be able to do it."

I tried to let our dragon see what I was envisioning in my mind.

Meanwhile, funny sounds were coming from Kendra, who had commenced pacing.

"Ride a dragon bareback. I don't even like dragons. What the hell am I saying? There *are* no dragons. Dragons don't exist. I'm in a bad dream, that's all. This is a nightmare, and I didn't just almost kill a guy back there. Soon I'm going to wake up back at the townhouse in Scottsdale." Pace, pace, mutter, mutter.

There was more, but I tuned it out for Cinder's sake.

"Oh, don't be such a wienie, Ken. It's only a little dragon ride. You've been on scarier rides at the fair. What about rollercoasters? This isn't nearly as scary as a rollercoaster, I can assure you."

"I hate rollercoasters," she muttered.

"Cinders, lie down again. I need to get back on you."

Cinders dropped her belly to the ground.

"Good girl." I remounted her from the tail and shimmied up her back, giving her a nice pat at the end.

"Kendra, do just what I did. Put your leg over her tail and climb up behind me."

Kendra mumbled something unrepeatable. Good thing Cinders didn't understand 21st Century slang.

"Just do it," I scolded. "Don't be a baby."

That worked. Kendra marched over and swung her leg across the tail.

"Yuck. Feels slimy," she said.

"Nonsense. Her skin is soft. Wiggle your way up here and hold onto my waist."

Kendra did as told, wrapping both arms around my tummy.

"Okay, Cinders. Think you can take us both up into the sky?"

I probed her mind. She seemed to have no doubts.

"Anytime, sweetie. Let's go!"

Cinders took off, lifting into the air with grace. Our weight slowed her down, but didn't prevent her from sweeping up and up into the sky. She leveled off a little closer to the ground than before, but still high enough for safety.

Once again, I marveled at the stunning landscape that presented itself below.

We flew over flowing water, fields of lush green and burnished yellows…a splendor of life and color.

"Look, Ken. Isn't it beautiful?"

"Can't. My eyes are closed."

I laughed. The wind rippled through my hair. It felt wonderful.

"Row, I'm slipping!"

"No! Don't do that, Ken. Hold on to me tight."

I could feel her arms slipping. And I couldn't do anything about it because I had to hold on to Cinders for both of us.

"EEEEeeeee!"

"Kendra? HOLD ON!"

I turned my head as far as it would go without moving my arms.

Relief! Kendra was still there, but had slid down some. Her bum was against the barbs at the end of Cinders' tail. Cinders had helped by raising the end of her tail as much as she could. Kendra was holding on with all her might.

"Just stay like that, Ken! We don't have far."

Cinders, thank you, I whispered to her.

Nothing but happiness in that little brain.

A grey patch against the greenery came into view. Castle Huel.

I coaxed Cinders with my knees toward our destination.

"Row, help!"

My head whipped around.

Bugger!

All I could see were arms and legs wrapped around the end of Cinders' tail. Kendra's body had rotated right around so it hung down!

"Hold on there," I commanded. "Cinders, head right for the roof." I tried to show her in my mind.

She was a clever girlie, I'll give her that. No way did she intend to land in that courtyard where the men were working. Not too many men, mind you. There didn't seem to be many around. Most had accompanied Cedric south, of course.

But her instincts were good. She headed for the highest spot with enough room to land, which was the roof of the backmost tower. Perhaps it was instinctive? Did dragons normally roost in high places?

I guided her in and directed her to hover just for a moment before landing, so Kendra could drop off before being sat on.

"Let go with your legs and drop down," I yelled back to her.

Plop!

Some mild cursing.

In contrast, Cinders landed with perfect grace, about ten feet away. I gave her a hug and several pats.

"I am never doing that ever again. EVER," said Kendra, rising from the floor.

I slid off Cinders, and pushed myself upright. Cinders rubbed herself against me, nearly knocking me over.

"Whoa there, girl." I stroked her softly until she purred.

"Where are we?" Kendra asked.

"On top of the tower bedroom. The stairs down from here lead right to it."

"That's convenient," said Kendra. "So what do we do now?"

I wasn't looking forward to this. But it had to be faced.

I turned to meet her eyes. "We go find Grandfather and tell him what is happening."

Chapter 32

We found Grandfather in his bedroom, lying prostrate on the bed. His eyes were closed and his breathing was shallow.

"You don't have to be quiet, My Lady," said his man, Ronald. "He cannot hear you. I'm not able to wake him up."

I felt my heart contract.

"How long has he been like this?"

Ronald hesitated. "It's been on and off since yesterday. His eyes open but are unfocussed. He took some water two hours ago. But he doesn't seem to know where he is. He can't speak."

I felt his forehead. No fever. Oddly enough, he looked serene and at peace, which was the last thing I felt. I wanted to sob, but had to force myself to be brave.

"I fear this is another stroke, Ronald. I'm not sure that we can do anything but keep him comfortable. Time will take its course and tell us more."

Kendra shifted behind me. "I'm so sorry, Row."

I leaned forward and kissed Grandfather on the forehead. No response.

"You take care, Grandfather. Cedric is coming back soon," I whispered. "I'll be here to check in on you regularly."

Tears were starting in my eyes. I used one hand to brush them away, then straightened and turned to Ronald. "I have a few things to take care of. We'll be back soon to check on you both."

I motioned for Kendra to follow me out the room. I led her down the stairs and through the great hall to the back kitchen.

"It's bad, Ken. I honestly don't think he'll live through this." I wanted to cry like a baby. And then that set me off. *My baby.* Chances were, they would never know each other.

I vowed right then, that in the future, my son or daughter would come to know everything I could remember about my grandfather.

"Row, you need to clear your mind of this, in order to get through the next few hours."

I sighed. I was uncommonly weary from all that had happened so far today. "You're right, of course. Honestly, there's little we can do for him at this stage, other than keep him comfortable."

"Ronald will do that. We need to eat something," she said. "There may not be much chance after tonight."

Kendra was already doing a survey of edibles. A pot of stew hung in the fireplace, no doubt a meal prepared for the men still remaining. She filled two large bowls and brought them to the table. I pilfered the bread supply while gathering spoons, and also found butter and preserves.

I dug into the stew. Then I went back for seconds.

Kendra smiled wryly. "Does anything take away your appetite?"

I looked up, mouth full of bread and butter. I chomped and swallowed quickly.

"I had the flu once. It was terrible. I couldn't eat a thing for three hours."

She giggled and shook her head.

After three bowls of stew, I was stuffed. At least the baby would be properly nourished tonight. *Dearest baby...how can I best keep you safe over the next 24 hours?* Which reminded me—I should take a vitamin pill next time I was in the tower room.

Kendra patted her flat stomach. "That was a nice break."

I grimaced. "Just like The Bible says, there is a time and a place for all things."

That had been the time to feed. Now was the time to plan. And panic.

I rose from the harvest table, my mind a whirl.

What to do with Grandfather? What to do with the remaining men? Cinders could stay hidden on the roof for now. But how could I keep the others safe?

I paced. I fretted. Kendra watched me with dismay. I finally sent her to the top of the castle to check on Cinders.

When she was gone, I hurried up the stairs to talk to Ronald.

He was still sitting patiently by the bed. Grandfather had not moved.

I switched my eyes back to Ronald.

"Tell me truthfully. How many men remain?" I asked him.

He told me.

There was no way we could defend the castle with fewer than twenty men. And those remaining were frail or old, certainly not warriors.

It would be a slaughter. And for no purpose at all.

I made a solemn decision.

"Ronald, gather up all the remaining men. Tell them to start for Sargonia immediately. Take every remaining horse and cart to carry their personal belongings. My orders. Remind them that I am their queen."

Ronald nodded slowly.

"Tell them to ask King Thane for shelter. They are to tell the King that I request it."

Thane would do that for me, I knew. He would protect my people within his own fortress gates. What would he think of me remaining here and not seeking safety with him? I could hazard a guess.

It was no more grim than the realization that he wouldn't come for me.

Ronald hesitated.

"The Earl won't go."

"I know he won't," I said. "I'll keep him here with me." We talked as if Grandfather were conscious and able to be a part of this decision. Both of us knew we were kidding ourselves. But we also knew that if he woke up and discovered we had moved him from Huel, it would kill him.

Better he die here. Nix that. Essential that he die here, one way or another.

"I stay with him," Ronald said simply.

I measured the old retainer, assessing his determined brown eyes.

"Of course," I said. "We both will."

He shifted uncomfortably.

"'Twill not be safe for you. He would not want this."

"I don't give a fig for what he wants. I stay." My voice was firm. "I'm the Earl's granddaughter."

He stared at me. I held his eyes in a battle of wills. Finally, he nodded and smiled. "That you are, m'lady."

It was twilight now. The two moons punctured a dark blue sky. High up from the tower bedroom windows, Kendra and I watched the remaining men leave through the gates of Huel.

Soon it would be full night, but the moons would light the way fine enough. I knew they would not get lost. The road from here led all the way to Sargonia.

Three carts had been loaded. Bone-weary men and their meager belongings piled on the flatbeds. It was a ragtag group.

All the workable horses had been commanded for the cause. The stables were empty save for two elderly mares that were deemed unlikely to survive the journey.

But ducks and geese still moved in little groups about the courtyard. Their squawks were the only sounds now. I had asked that the farm animals be left behind. A hungry army coming through the gates would demand food. Either hungry army. Best that we not anger them by depleting the stores.

"What do we do now, Row?" Kendra said.

"Might as well try to get some sleep. We'll be up at dawn."

I watched the last cart as it rolled out of sight.

My heart felt heavy. We were truly alone now. The old earl, his retainer, Kendra, and me.

And a dragon.

Kendra must have read my mind. She shifted uneasily. "What do we do about Cinders?"

"I was thinking we could move our bedding up to the rooftop and sleep beside her."

She nodded. "Good idea." She paused. "When do you think things will start?"

Lars had told me they would strike at dawn. That meant he would have the troops in place before then. Probably, he would march them through the early hours of morning.

Lars! Oh my God, he was about to go into battle. He might not live through the next twelve hours.

I couldn't help it. The vomit was almost instantaneous. I fell to my knees, helpless to stop it.

"Row!" Kendra cried. "Are you morning-sick again?"

I wretched again. Tears welled in my eyes. "Have you got a tissue?" I asked weakly.

Kendra was on her knees beside me, tissue at hand. After I used it, she fussed over me like a mother bear. I let her help me rise to my feet.

"Are you sure you want to sleep on the roof?" she said.

"Well, I certainly don't want to sleep right here," I replied, trying to smile through the tears.

She gathered me in a sideways hug.

Cinders was delighted to see us on the roof. She pranced around, made three circles, and then lay down in a flop. Of course, she burped and the side of my skirt caught a small bit of flame. Kendra stamped it out with her Goth boots.

"Goddammit, Cinders! You're a freaking fireball."

Cinders scampered to her feet and turned her face to the wall, whimpering and cowering.

I sighed. "Kendra."

"I know, I know," she mumbled. "Sorry I yelled, Cinders."

I brought Cinders a bowl of water and stroked her side. She calmed down enough to lap the water. Then she retraced her steps around the imaginary circle on the rooftop and plunked down inside it.

I lay down beside her with blanket and pillow, and Kendra put her own bedding on the stone floor on the other side of me. We stayed like that for several minutes, each knowing the other was still awake.

"Row, are you scared?" Kendra asked, finally.

I waited before answering. Should I tell the truth? Would she believe it?

"Strangely, at this moment, I'm not," I said quietly. "For some reason, I strongly feel the fates have taken over. I am…resigned to it. Nothing you or I can do will make a difference at this point."

She sighed. "I'm not sure that makes me feel any better."

I shifted, trying to get comfortable on the cold stone floor. "Well, for me it makes a huge difference, just knowing that it's out of my hands."

The stars were twinkling overhead now, tiny rhinestones against charcoal velveteen. I wondered if Lars was watching them, too.

"I sort of get what you mean," she replied. "You've had a whack of responsibility on your back for so long. At least now, nobody can blame things on you."

I had to grin. "That's part of it, of course. It seems whatever decisions I make tend to backfire. I just wish…" My voice got serious. "I just wish I could know for sure how to keep you safe."

"Oh, don't worry about me," she said. "I can take care of myself."

"I should have made you go to Sargonia with the men," I murmured.

"Not a chance," she said confidently. "You couldn't manage it."

I smiled. "Well, sweetie, for what it's worth, I'm damned glad you're here."

Cinders let out a small snore. Luckily she was facing the other way and the flame went out when it hit the stone floor.

A night chorus of crickets kept us company.

Kendra rolled over. Within moments, she was asleep.

I took longer.

Chapter 33

We awoke to the sound of Cinders whining and pacing.

Morning light streaked above us. The sky was cobalt blue.

And already the ground was red.

We stood on the roof of the tower, overlooking the fields to the east.

I gazed through the merlons into the distance. From there, you could see the battle raging below. As it came closer, you could hear the clang of sword on sword and the yells and cries of men falling, wounded.

I looked to the south. Battle raged there as well, maybe a mile from the outer castle walls, and moving quickly. The battle line was like a living thing, surging back and forth. Beyond the fighting, bodies littered the ground.

Cinders had crouched beside the wall, pressing her body against the floor. Her eyes looked terrified. She seemed to instinctively know that danger was all around us. Perhaps she could smell death?

Way off in the distance, behind Cedric's line, was a group of archers lining the crest of a hill. My heart hammered in my chest. I knew what those six foot yew longbows could do. Their white fletched arrows would rain death on the Normans from a distance.

But there were too few of them. For every Norman who fell, another came forward to press the line.

"Is that blood?" Kendra shivered. Both of her hands were pressed against the stone wall.

I followed her gaze to the fields below. The red stain was everywhere. I swear you could smell iron from atop the tower.

I thought of the horror movies I had seen as a teen, those *Chucky* and *Halloween* films. How hokey they all seemed now. True horror didn't look anything like Hollywood. It emanated from the very trees that lined the hilltops here...trees black from the crows and ravens perched there, waiting to feast.

And then the wolves would come...

I dragged my eyes away.

Kendra moved closer to my side. I pointed to the east. "See there. Those riders are skirting the hill trying to flank the main battle line." It was too far away to see their armor, but I could tell they were Norman by the shape of their shields and lack of color tabards.

"What are they doing?" she asked.

"Coming from the other side around the battle. They'll ride around the north side of the walls to come in from the west gate. They're trying to avoid Cedric's troops to the south."

I watched, barely able to move, as little toy horses carried little tin soldiers in a race to the castle walls to the west.

They didn't make it. A flash of green caught my eye. Huel horsemen surged from the south, racing along the stone walls, cutting off the path. Horses and riders came together in a deadly dance of swords until I couldn't tell which riders were ours and which were the enemy.

The enemy—Lars and Sven, Jory and young Tyr. This was unbearable.

It was bloody hand to hand combat now, with no Hollywood music to cover the killing sounds. The clang of swords, the yells of men—the swing of axes met with horrific screams. Riderless horses ran from the melee. Kendra gasped and pointed. Another two riders fell. Their horses bolted. One slipped on the slick ground and lay there, motionless.

"What is that awful drumming?" Kendra cried.

I held both hands to my head to shut out the hellish noise. Cinders whimpered. It was coming close now, all too close.

Time to move. I needed to get my plan in gear.

"Kendra, follow me." I bolted to the staircase entrance and without looking back, sped down the stairs.

"Wait! Where are you going?" Her voice trailed after me.

Round and round I went on the stone stairs, until light shone from below. The passage door was open. I whipped into the room I had shared with Cedric. No time for stopping. Out the main door and down more stone steps to the second floor bedroom.

I was panting hard when I dashed through the opening. Ronald sat by Grandfather's side. Neither seemed to have moved since I had left them. They made a solemn tableau.

Kendra flew into the room.

"Ronald, we need to get you and Grandfather to the cellar. It's the safest place. Kendra, I need you there to guard him."

Kendra's eyes went wide.

"You're not going to meet them alone, Row. That's madness!"

I shook my head. This was the hard part. I tried to speak with confidence so she wouldn't panic. "I'll be okay. I need you there with Grandfather, in case I get held up." *In case I can't be first to the cellar. In case I don't live through the next twenty minutes...*

"I'm not going to let you go out there by yourself, Row."

I almost smiled. We had a Mexican standoff, just as I knew we would.

I made myself look at her. Her hand was clenched over the dagger at her belt. Her face was one big determined frown. She was ready for a fight, with me or anyone else.

She looked years older than her age. I expect I did, too.

It didn't matter. I willed myself to be calm and met her gaze.

"He'll come for me, Ken. I know he will." I knew it just as surely as I knew I had to be there.

He would come for me. He would come for me through hell.

But whether he would make it through the gates before everyone else, was the real question. I wasn't about to voice that out loud right now.

For now, my task was to ensure that Grandfather and Kendra remained as safe as I could manage.

"You're crazy," she was saying. "I have to be there. We always do these things together."

"Not this time." My voice was firm. I took a breath. "They don't know you, Ken. There are thousands of men out there, and they've never seen you before. It's too dangerous for you. I can't risk it. But they know *me*. They know I am their leader's woman, and believe me, it would be death for any of them to touch me."

Her eyes were wild. She started to protest.

I raised both my hands like stop signs.

"I need to know you're safe, sweetie. I can't do this otherwise. Do you understand?" My voice shook a bit.

She stared at me. Her mouth quivered.

I continued before she could object more. "You'll be okay in the cellar. I've got it all planned. I told Sven to look out for you. Sven is Lars's young cousin, and he'll be in the forward guard. He's a good man, honorable and strong. Very tall, blond, about your age. If something should happen to me—*and it won't*—Sven will find you and protect you with his life. He swore he would."

It was the best I could do. If only I could be sure that Sven would survive the battle. That was the real flaw with this plan.

Of course, there was another, even bigger flaw. But I refused to consider that Lars could die. *He couldn't die.*

"Even back there at the camp, when you were their prisoner, you thought of me," Kendra said in awe.

We stared at each other across the room.

"Of course I did. I love you. You're my sister."

She wasn't my sister. She wasn't even my cousin, really. But it was true all the same.

Some families are born. Others are made.

"Come help me move him now."

I didn't have to plead.

"Of course," she said.

Chapter 34

I stood alone on the steps of Castle Huel. It took every ounce of courage I had.

The drawbridge was down. I'd made that decision earlier. No point in putting up a futile resistance by raising it. The Vikings would only destroy it.

This way, with the drawbridge down, Lars would know that I awaited him.

My enemy and my lover.

I wore the green dress he would recognize from a distance, and the daggers around my hips. His daggers, the ones he had given me.

There was always a chance, of course, that it would not be him in the clutch of riders to reach us first. There wasn't much I could do about that. I had some magic I could use to delay things. And Soren had worked it so any man not a Gredane or Huel would burn if they tried to touch me. But if the riders were determined to kill me with arrows or swords, there wasn't much I could do.

I waited.

Horses thundered onto the drawbridge and stormed into the courtyard. I counted at least twenty.

One was a large white horse with beige mane. I started to breathe again.

Lars vaulted off it. He was in full armor, and on his head was a helmet that came down to cover his ears, but I would recognize him anywhere by the way he moved.

He threw his shield to the ground. It was scored in a dozen places. Then he wasted no time, but strode up the steps.

Blood, fresh and dried, covered his armor and arms.

There was a nasty gash below his left shoulder.

His eyes looked wild.

He grabbed me and crushed his mouth into mine. I was bent back, helpless in his arms. Call it pheromones or chemistry, what does it matter—his sweat was like a drug to me.

He lifted me without a word and carried me swiftly into the great hall.

I tried to talk but the words seemed caught in my throat.

He kicked a bench away with his leg and deposited me on the great oak table. His hands reached down and took hold of my bodice. He ripped it apart at the laces.

I gasped. He said one word in a low harsh voice. "Claiming."

I understood then. This had to be done fast and thoroughly, with witnesses at the door. It was the only thing that would keep me safe from the other battle-crazed warriors.

I didn't object. This was my man. He loved me. He had fought through hell to get to me. He wouldn't hurt me.

He unfastened his belt of weapons. They fell to the floor with a clatter. He unbuckled his helmet, removed it, and threw it on the table. His white-blond hair flew free.

He grabbed my legs and pulled them forward until my thighs straddled his hips. He raised my skirt just enough, so that I was covered from the view of others. With one shocking movement, he entered me.

I cried out. He fell over me, both hands on the table, eyes closed, in a groan. I could see he was exhausted. Then with a Herculean effort, he pushed up on his hands. The muscles on his upper arms bulged as he righted his torso. His grey eyes were open now and they fixed on mine. He pulled back and thrust into me.

I moaned like an animal as he gripped my thighs to push himself into me again and again. This would not take long. I could feel him grow rock hard and he thrust twice more, jerking my whole body. His eyes closed as he came.

He was not smiling.

He fell forward again, and I took the weight of his torso on me. He was panting hard, but then, in a mood so counter to the last, he kissed me gently on each breast. My arms automatically went to hold his shoulders.

"You're heavy," I murmured.

He pushed himself up, watching me all the while. His eyes were heavy with emotion. His mouth moved to say something, but no words came out.

He pulled my skirt down and motioned for me to roll over on my side. I did, pulling my legs up into a fetal position.

I saw then that the door was open but guarded. Jory and Sven stood there. Jory was frowning and Sven looked sick.

I was glad they were both alive.

"It is done," Lars said.

"We know that, man." Jory didn't sound pleased.

"It had to be done."

"You weren't easy on her."

Lars brushed one hand through his hair in a jerky movement. His gaze switched to me, and I saw that he was feeling remorse. The beast had surfaced.

"I could not be easy." His voice was low.

"Let me see that wound." I tried to push myself up but the effort seemed too much, and I got no further than one elbow. I rested my head on my hand.

Jory stared at me.

I had spoken in their language.

Lars retrieved his weapons from the floor. I heard the slap of a belt being fastened.

"Rowena, are you hurt?" Jory's voice. He didn't bother to speak English.

I paused to assess. "I don't think so. Faint." I lay back down on the table.

Jory came forward to check for himself. He said low to me, "He fought like a berserker to be the first one through to you. Forgive him for this."

I met his eyes briefly, then my medical training kicked in to assess. Jory was covered in small wounds and dried blood.

Jory's gaze shifted from me to Lars.

"You need to do one thing more," Jory said to his friend.

Lars nodded.

What now?

"Rowena, keep your eyes closed. He is just going to show you to the men. Some of them weren't at the camp," Jory said.

I trembled. This was so barbaric.

Lars pulled me gently to the edge of the table. He picked me up in his arms like a baby.

"Jory, will you cover her."

I felt hands pull at my bodice.

"That will have to do," he said quietly. "You made a mess of it."

Lars grunted.

"You don't have to do anything, Rowena. Put your face against his chest. "

I did so and closed my eyes. Battle sweat assaulted my nostrils, but it was *his* scent, and therefore a drug to me.

Lars carried me out through the corridor. I heard shuffling and murmurs.

Strong sunlight hit my closed eyes when we reached the big double doors. Cool air swept across my chest where the bodice didn't cover.

He stepped out.

A roar of cheers went up from the courtyard. A hundred voices or more joined in.

"Stay close, Jory, Sven," Lars ordered. "Be ready."

"Have no worries," Jory said. "They respect you. They saw you kill Gustav back at camp. It was a fair battle. You fought alongside them today. But we'd better get some drink into them. Ivan, check the cellars for kegs."

I stiffened. Kendra was in the cellar!

I opened my eyes, about to say I would show him the way, when a strong voice rang out loud and clear.

"Norman! Put her down and face me now, or be called a coward forever more."

Lars went rigid.

Cedric stood on the other end of the stone wall. With one unnatural leap he covered the fifty feet between us.

What happened next is recounted in legends.

Soren strode forward from the hall. "Let me do this for you, Brother. You guard our woman." Soren raised one arm. A bolt of blue lightning leapt from his hand to Cedric's chest.

I screamed.

Cedric's hand glowed green, deflecting it just in time, but even then, the force knocked him over.

"He's a demon," I yelled to Cedric in English.

"So am I." Cedric's voice echoed across the courtyard.

Chapter 35

I struggled to be let down. Lars let me stand but kept his arms wrapped tight around me, as he had done twice before when Cedric had been a threat.

All eyes were on the two men who took center stage in the courtyard now.

"Is this tossing about of bolts to your liking?" Soren said, his voice lazy and slightly mocking. "Or do you prefer something up close and personal?"

"Choose your weapon," Cedric replied. "Make it deadly."

"Always." A sword appeared in Soren's hand. The blade glowed neon blue, like his eyes.

A hush descended on the courtyard. I watched, as an almost identical sword flashed brilliant green in Cedric's hand.

The two combatants circled each other.

I could see them each so clearly. One head white-blond like stark moonlight, the other titian like the sun, but each so equally matched in body and strength they could be brothers.

Soren's face was gleeful with anticipation. "This will be fun."

Cedric's visage was grim.

Soren lunged. The swords flashed like light sabers, flashed again and crashed together.

Soren was the master at this. He thrust forward. Cedric blocked. Soren cut at Cedric's neck. He caught the blade on his own, directing it away, then brought his own sword around in a stroke designed to cut Soren in half.

The Norman flew back, then raised his sword in salute. His eyes glowed blue fire. "Now, let's dance."

They came together in a clash of light. It was happening so quickly I couldn't see them move anymore. Just flashes of green and blue light swirling, leaving trails of color in the air.

Then they were still. Both were breathing hard, but Cedric was dragging in great lungfuls of air. They gripped their weapons with both hands, waiting.

Soren attacked first. Cedric leapt from the ground to avoid a wicked slash, then kept rising. With a snarl, Soren followed him into the air. Now the battle moved above our heads. Men screamed in fear, watching Soren and Cedric slash at each other like raptors in flight.

I could hardly find enough air to breathe.

This much was clear—Soren was forcing Cedric back with every parry.

Hit, hit, clang, clang—like lightning caught in a tornado, spinning, the air crackled and colors ripped across the sky, leaving jade and cyan jet trails.

I caught my breath.

The blue blade came down on Cedric's arm.

He screamed and flew back to the wall.

I moaned in response to his pain. Lars had a death grip on me, holding me so I could not be taken from him or be compelled to leave his side.

Silence descended on the courtyard.

Soren laughed and descended to earth. "You are a worthy opponent. But playtime is over. Are you watching, infant witch? I will finish him now."

He spoke in a language only we three would understand.

The swords vanished.

A ball of fire left his hand with deadly precision.

Cedric matched it with his own. The fire combined and exploded with a brilliant flash between them.

Another volley. Cedric met it. Then another, and another.

My eyes bounced from one to the other. My heart was in a vice.

Soren sauntering about the courtyard, a man unrushed, clearly relishing each encounter.

Cedric was fighting for his life. With one hand he deflected fireballs. With the other…

Clouds moved in swiftly over the courtyard. Black, murderous clouds that I would evermore associate with Cedric. Thunder roared and an arrow of lightning pierced the air, striking the ground where Soren had been.

"Damn the gods," muttered Lars.

"No!" I cried. Where was Soren? Had Cedric managed to destroy him?

A deep chuckle rent the air.

"Find me, Saxon."

Three Sorens appeared then!

The men around me gasped. Lars's grip on me was almost painful.

Three Sorens, all the same, hands on hips, laughing at us all.

Which was the real one?

My eyes shot to Cedric. Lightning flew from the clouds in three directions.

Two of the Sorens disappeared, mere illusions.

The third shot up to the sky and landed...where? I could hear him, but not see him.

"Use your magic, Saxon." The voice was an echo.

Cedric's head whipped from side to side, as he sought to find his opponent.

Soren appeared in front of him, then vanished.

The bolt missed him completely.

He appeared to the left. Then the right.

Then center again, bolts missing him every time.

Then—

I appeared before Cedric. *I appeared before Cedric!*

Yet here I was, still locked in Lars's arms.

Heads whipped over to me on the steps, and back to the other me in the courtyard.

Cedric hesitated. It was enough.

A ball of flame shot from the left, just as the illusion of me vanished from in front of him.

Men cried out.

Cedric was down. His body was bloody and broken. *Because of me.*

He would never risk hurting me.

I wanted to do something, anything. What could I do?

"Rowena!" Cedric's voice ripped through the air. I screamed as his pain reached me, channeled through the bond we shared.

Soren held up his hand to blast once more. I lifted my arm, covered the blazing jewels with my hand and willed the fire ball to deflect.

It shot straight up to the sky.

My gaze switched to Cedric. He could not get up! His body lay inert.

And then...I saw the grey mist rise from his body as it did before.

"No!" I cried.

His voice, again, in my brain. "*I'm still here.*"

Soren roared. His body dropped like a stone. A dark grey mist remained in its place, swirling up above our heads.

The two clouds circled, like sparring animals. They twirled around each other in a deadly dance. They collided and spun, whipping around until I could not tell one from the other, the colors blending, coiling, and then—

I watched in horror as the earth opened and a gigantic vermillion flame shot up like a fire fountain from the underworld, soared into the sky for a moment, and then descended in a fury through the ground taking the grey mist with it.

I struggled free of Lars's arms and ran.

"Rowena, no!" he yelled.

The ground had closed. I reached the place where Cedric had fallen. Nothing.

I fell to my knees.

Both bodies were gone.

The rumble of men's voices was getting louder. I tuned them out.

Lars lifted me gently from the ground. I pulled back, not wanting to leave that spot where Cedric had disappeared.

So this was mourning. The whole sky had gone dark; the sun was gone. The rich colors of Land's End had melted into shades of grey, like a faded black and white silent movie.

Silence. I heard none of the voices around me.

He was gone. Cedric was truly gone. I would never see those mesmerizing eyes again, feel those powerful arms around me, grow faint from the channeling of his desire for me.

And yet…

Something fought through my despair.

He was not gone.

The bond had not broken. A tendril reached from far, far away, barely able to touch my mind, but it was there. I closed my eyes to better concentrate. A tender, soothing touch, like a lover's hand wiping away tears, seeking to quell my grief.

I breathed again. How could I explain the importance of this curious spell between us? It was more than just the death of my cousin. Magic was a part of me now. Without it, without the mage who celebrated and mentored my powers, I would lose a part of myself in some unfathomable way.

The tendril faded for a moment, then drew more strength and touched me again. Cedric was testing it, from wherever he was. He would be with me, in some form, some way. He had not left me completely.

I was standing now, stronger in that knowledge. I could face the defeat of our family and plan for the future.

Lars stood behind me, with his arms wrapped around me.

"He died with honor," Lars said quietly, with a warrior's approval. "He died a hero defending his land and lady. I will give him a hero's funeral. And my brother…"

He kissed the top of my head. "Soren will be in Valhalla, glorious in death, as a warrior should be."

I didn't correct him. Best that Lars think his brother in Valhalla. I knew they both were in a different place.

Talk buzzed through the courtyard. Lars held the castle. The fighting was over. The remaining Huel troops were retreating to Sargonia. One lord still lived.

Richard. I sighed with relief. My youngest cousin had survived. So many had died today, but Richard and Lars were still alive. I thanked the gods of their land and ours for sparing these men so dear to me.

As if acknowledging my prayers of thanks, the sun peeked out from behind the clouds. Within seconds, it beamed warmth upon us.

I let Lars guide me toward the castle steps. With one hand, I held my bodice closed as best I could.

"Let me see your wound," I said again. I tried to twist in his arms to examine it.

"Why is your skirt ripped and burned in the front?" he asked.

I looked down. I had forgotten about that, and something else he needed to know.

"Oh. About that. I should tell you there's a dragon on the roof."

Lars stopped.

"There's a dragon on the roof," he repeated.

"Don't let your men hurt it! She's my friend."

"A dragon." He started walking again.

"She's really nice. Her name is Cinders. I thought she could help protect the baby."

"Protect the baby." Lars was shaking his head, as if trying to get the thought out of his mind.

"Of course, she burned my skirt a bit, but that was an accident. Intestinal problems."

"She burned—"

"Oh my God, Kendra! She's in the sorcery cellar with Grandfather." I had to get to the basement.

"You have a sorcery cellar." Lars was smiling now.

"It's only a little one," I assured him.

"Life with you will never be boring, little bird."

"I'm here!" Kendra popped out of the hall, pulling Sven by the hand. "I couldn't wait down there any longer, so I snuck up the stairs and went looking for Sven."

Sven was smiling as if he had just won the lottery. Which, of course, in this world, he had.

"Come," Lars said. "It is time for us to start a new life in Land's End."

Chapter 36

Five months later…

"You can't come in, Lars," Inga told her son at the door for the seventh time.

I screamed again as the pain ripped through my abdomen.

Inga rushed over. She stroked my forehead and focused her beautiful grey eyes on me. "Rowena, be strong. You're nearly there. Tell me when the pain comes next. And we will push with you.

"Nearly," the midwife said. "Now!"

I growled like a cornered tiger through gritted teeth, held Kendra's hand in a death grip, and pushed with everything left in me. Then I roared in agony.

Lars stormed through the door.

The unbearable pain gave way to blessed soreness. Lars grabbed my hand.

I heard a tiny cry. Then it became louder, wailing, reaching right through my hazy brain.

"You have a girl," Inga said with pure delight in her voice. "A beautiful girl with hair the color of the sun. See her, Lars."

"Cut the cord like I showed you, Kendra," I murmured.

"We know what we're doing, dear one. You just enjoy your baby."

I felt a wet warm bundle being placed on my breast. My hands reached to hold her. Someone placed a sheet on top of both of us.

A wisp of magic reached forward into my mind, filling it with warmth and love. *Cedric.* I relaxed and let my joy mingle with his.

Wherever he was, he would come to know our daughter through my thoughts.

"The first baby girl born to our family since I was a bairn. My son, I am so happy!"

Lars reached down to kiss me. His eyes were radiant. "Well done, little bird."

"She's gorgeous, Row. Ten fingers and ten toes, I counted. What will you call her?" Kendra asked.

The daughter of the Dark Lord and the last hereditary witch of Land's End?

I looked down at my darling baby's tiny head and smiled. "Sabrina, of course."

~ * ~

If you enjoyed this book, please consider writing a short review and posting it on your favorite review site. Reviews are very helpful to other readers and are greatly appreciated by authors, especially me. When you post a review, drop me an email and let me know and I may feature part of it on my blog/site. Thank you. mcampbell50@cogeco.ca

About the Author

Billed as Canada's "Queen of Comedy" by the *Toronto Sun* (Jan. 5, 2014), Melodie Campbell achieved a personal best when *Library Digest* compared her to Janet Evanovich.

Melodie got her start writing comedy. In 1999, she opened the Canadian Humor Conference. She has over 200 publications, including 100 comedy credits, 40 short stories and 6 novels. She has won 9 awards for fiction, including the 2014 Derringer Award.

In addition to writing, Melodie has been a bank manager, hospital director, college instructor, association executive, and possibly the worst runway model ever. She lives in Oakville Ontario, where she is lamentably addicted to fast cars.

Melodie is the Executive Director of Crime Writers of Canada.

www.melodiecampbell.com

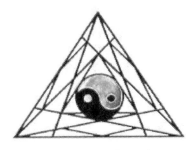

IMAJIN BOOKS
Quality fiction beyond your wildest dreams

For your next eBook or paperback purchase, please visit:

www.imajinbooks.com

www.twitter.com/imajinbooks

www.facebook.com/imajinbooks

Made in the USA
Charleston, SC
23 July 2014